Near-Life Experience

Emma G. Rose

IMPERATIVE Press

Hampden, ME

Emma G. Rose
Imperative Press Books
Hampden, Maine 04444
www.imperativepressbooks.com

Book Layout © 2017 BookDesignTemplates.com
Cover Art by Christine Gamache
Cover Design by AHD Design

Near-Life Experience/ Emma G. Rose -- 1st ed.
ISBN 978-1-7339079-2-7

To my mom who instigated this book.
And to the unknown first responder
who was there when we needed him most.

Near-Life Experience

Lightning Strike

The storm walked electric fingers up Eric's neck while he pulled supplies out of the back of the ambulance. "We're gonna have some weather," he told his partner, Susan, as though it wasn't obvious. Already, a lightning strike had hit a church on the other side of New Bedford, which was why they'd made it on scene before the fire trucks.

Standing in the grassy area next to the substation, they were exposed, but the lightning had plenty of other potential targets. Eric glanced at the power station, all metal, designed to conduct electricity, and at the cluster of tall pine trees close to the fence. Either of those things would make a better lightning rod than he would.

Susan grunted as she hefted the AED out of the bus. "Better stabilize the kid quick then," she said.

A boy ran up. He was maybe thirteen, dressed in a Day-Glo tracksuit and Nike high tops. His wide eyes alternated between fear and excitement. The electricity in the air raised the fuzz on his head, making it stand out like the fur of a startled cat.

"This way," he said.

All three flinched as lightning shocked the sky, followed almost instantly by a crash of thunder. The boy ran back toward the fence, where two other kids huddled together near the base of one of those big, lighting-rod trees. Their heads were tilted back, but they weren't watching the storm. Eric followed their gaze.

A boy hung upside down from the top of the fence, his stark white sneaker thrust into the air like a pennant of surrender. They hurried closer to see him more clearly. It looked like his pant leg was caught in the barbed wire put there to stop people from doing what he and his friends had apparently tried to do: climb over the top of the fence.

He must have gone first, gotten tangled, and spilled forward. Now he was dangling twenty feet above, clinging to the chain link. If he let go, his pants wouldn't hold long. Eric imagined him landing headfirst on the ground, his neck snapping. If he was lucky, he'd end up paralyzed.

By standing up close to the chain link, Eric could see the blood soaking the kid's pant leg. The barbed wire had bit him. Bit deep, if the amount of blood was any indication. The kid was crying, pale. He shouldn't be pale, not while hanging upside-down. The blood should have been rushing to his face. How much had he lost?

"What's his name?" Eric asked the huddled kids.

"Timmy."

The tree was an old pine. Easy to climb. And the branches rubbed right up against the fence. Without stopping to let fear creep in, Eric dropped his gear in the grass. He grabbed the tin snips and stuck them in his belt. They should be able to cut through barbed wire. Eric grabbed a branch.

"Eric, hold on." Susan snatched his shoulder. "The fire trucks'll be here any second."

Eric hesitated. Every hair on his body was standing at attention. The rain could start any second too, and then Timmy would be done for. He couldn't maintain his grip in a downpour.

"No time." Eric shook her off.

He heard Susan ordering the kids to back away, using the commanding voice every mom seemed to acquire around the time their child takes his first steps. She was looking out for their safety, of course, but also sparing them the sight of their friend's neck snapping like a twig if Eric failed.

Eric tried to move quickly while also testing every handhold before he put his weight on it. The tree seemed sturdy, but he didn't trust it.

He started talking while Timmy was still overhead. "Hang on, Timmy, we're gonna get you down. You just keep doing what you're doing. It'll all be—" Lightning, thunder.

Eric heard squeals from the kids below, but Timmy was silent. One more branch brought Eric level with his patient. Timmy's eyes were wide. Pupils dilated. He didn't seem to know Eric was there, although they were just a fence thickness apart.

"I'm almost there Timmy. You're doing great. Stay

with me buddy."

Eric paused, trying to assess. He couldn't hold Timmy up and cut the barbed wire at the same time. The kid was barely hanging on as it was, and without the wire wrapped around his legs, gravity would take its toll.

A noise reached Eric's ears, halfway between a whimper and a scream. Timmy was shivering, which twitched his leg and drove the metal deeper. The sound of sirens in the distance felt like a taunt. They were still too far away. But if Eric could just help Timmy hold on a little longer, he might have a chance.

One-handed, his other hand clinging to a branch, Eric pulled the tin snips from his belt and held them between his teeth. The cold taste of metal filled his mouth. As he unbuckled his belt and eased it out of the belt loops, his flashlight and multi-tool fell away, crashing through the branches. He could only hope the kids and Susan were back far enough. Coiling the belt up in one hand, he shifted his weight around until he was standing with his back to the tree trunk, his feet on two different, hopefully solid, branches.

He reached both arms toward the fence. It was about a foot out of reach. He leaned forward. Sweat dripped down his face. For a moment he was certain he'd fall, crashing like the flashlight through twenty feet of branches and pine needles to the hard ground below. Susan yelled at him. He ignored her. This was not a time to be distracted. Besides, he couldn't hear her clearly over the wind and the sirens anyway.

His hands closed around the chain links. Now he could reach Timmy.

The kid whimpered more loudly. Trying not to jostle him, Eric fed the belt through the chain link. Then he overbalanced himself even more to reach his arms as far as he could through the fence. Good thing Timmy was skinny. Eric managed to get the belt around the kid's waist.

He'd thought that he would be able to push back from that position, climb a little further up the tree, and cut the barbed wire. But stretched between fence and branch, he knew he couldn't move again without help. He was too off balance. Pressing his shoulder against the fence, he used both hands to tighten the belt around Timmy.

Lightning sizzled in Eric's ears just before the pain knocked him senseless.

~

Death arrived in the grass beside the power station seconds before Eric's body thudded to the ground. Death was a good judge of these things, and Eric was clearly within an inch of his life. The lightning strike had stopped his heart.

A woman wearing a paramedic's uniform identical to Eric's ran over, lugging a bulky machine. Death had seen them before. They were designed to restart a failed heart. Eric's soul hadn't yet appeared, so it might actually work.

While the machine charged, Death had time to reflect on the absurdity of human life. What were the odds that lightning would strike a tree at the very moment Eric was using it as a ladder to reach a kid stuck in the barbed wire along the top of a power station fence? Not high, he thought. But in the world of humans, the impossible happened every day.

Death watched the paramedic press paddles to Eric's chest. "Clear!" she shouted.

Eric's soul sat up. His body didn't.

Unable to see or feel the soul, she reached through it to try her machine again. Eric's soul scrambled away, stopping just before it went through the tree trunk.

"Shit. I'm not dead. Tell me I'm not dead."

Death would have answered but Eric wasn't listening.

"Did I at least save the kid?" Eric looked up to where another body was hanging from the fence. "Timmy! Hey, Timmy."

"He's not dead," Death said. "Yet."

Eric's eyes focused on Death. "Who are you? Don't just stand around watching. Help him."

"You're not dead yet, either."

"Thanks, but um." Eric waved his arm, which passed through several tree branches. "I couldn't do that when I was alive."

"You're having a near-Death experience." This should have been obvious considering he was standing right here, but humans took some time to get used to things. "Your body is not in good condition, but your friend may still be able to fix it."

"And if she does?"

This too seemed obvious. Death shrugged. "You won't be dead."

"Wait a minute. Are you—"

Before he could finish the sentence, Eric's soul had disappeared. The machine had worked.

~

Eric woke up in the hospital. He thought he must have crashed in an empty room between calls. His head was splitting. The steady beep of monitors, the squeak of nurses' shoes on tile, the clamor of hurried voices rattled in his skull. Had he left the door open? The buzz of a code shocked him wide awake. He tried to sit up...

...but he couldn't move, didn't want to move. The pain was everywhere. He was dying. That was his code buzzing, and he was dying right now. But no, pain means you're alive, right? In that case, Eric thought he must be intensely alive.

He turned his head as bodies flashed past—nurses, doctors, interns converged on the bed beside his. Someone pulled the curtain, but not far enough. He could see them working on a small form. He knew that face. The kid. Timmy.

They brought out the paddles. Eric wanted to scream at them, "No more shocks." He couldn't. His mouth was arid and his tongue was double-size.

"Clear!"

Timmy twitched. Amidst all that movement, Eric's eye settled on the point of stillness. Someone was standing beside the bed. Someone who looked exactly like Timmy. His twin? Why hadn't one of the nurses taken him away? He shouldn't have to see his brother like this.

Eric watched the twin pound his fist on Timmy's chest. The doctor somehow didn't notice. He put the paddles down again and they seemed to pass right through the twin's arm. That couldn't have happened. Eric tried blinking.

It took too long. When he opened his eyes again, the scene had changed. The doctors and nurses were still. Eric knew that look. The kid was dead. The doctor glanced up at the clock and murmured to a nurse.

The twin hung his head. For the first time, Eric noticed someone else who didn't belong in the scene, someone standing right behind the twin. A dark figure in a long coat. He seemed out of focus somehow. Eric couldn't get a good look at him. He tried blinking again, but this time completely failed to reopen his eyes.

~

Death arrived as Timmy's soul tried to pound life back into its own body.

"That won't help," Death said. He laid a hand on the soul's shoulder.

The soul spun to face him. "How do you—oh." The soul cocked its head. "You're Death."

Children always managed to spot the obvious more quickly than adults did.

"I am," Death said.

"We weren't going to steal anything. I just wanted to tag the place," the soul said. Death nodded as though he understood. Humans were always mangling their language, especially the young ones. Every generation seemed to invent new ways to make no sense. Death didn't even try to keep up anymore.

"That's not important now," Death said. "I need you to take my hand."

The soul scrunched his eyebrows. "Why?"

Death held back a sigh. It wasn't the kind of thing you wanted humans to know you did. "By shaking my hand you agree to take me as your guide on the journey to the afterlife."

"Wicked." The soul grasped Death's hand.

"Hey, there was a guy. He tried to save me. Did he—" the soul started to ask, but Death was already stepping, and the soul's voice was captured by the void.

~

Eric woke to the sound of his mother's voice. The golden halo around her head dazzled his bleary eyes. He wondered if he was awake or still dreaming. As his mother stepped away from the window, leaving her halo behind, Eric felt the pain come back and knew he was awake. His ribs, his head, his back, his chest, everything hurt. The smell of antiseptic and industrial cleaner told him he was still in the hospital.

He listened to his mother bullying a nurse, demanding to know when was the last time he'd had painkillers and how often had they checked on him. "Why have I been here thirty minutes and I haven't seen even a glimpse of scrubs until now?"

Her gaze fell on Eric and she ceased her assault on the nurse to strike a less defended target.

"Eric Dean Silva, what the hell did you think you were doing?"

He tried not to wince as he reached for the bed controls and sat himself up. It was hard to face a lioness lying down. "It's not as bad as it looks," Eric said.

"That's only because you don't have a mirror."

Eric shrugged and immediately regretted it. The motion set shock waves down his back.

"I'll be okay."

"You were struck by lightning."

"It was the ground that hurt me."

She looked up at him, eyes narrowed, lips pressed. Eric had succeeded in leaving her speechless. He thought he should probably write down the date. What was the date? Still October, right? Certainly still 1988.

He opened his mouth to ask how long he'd been out, but just then a doctor came into the room, stealing Mrs.

Silva's attention. Eric didn't recognize the doctor's face, which meant they weren't in the ER anymore. Eric had been in the ER though. He vaguely remembered waking up there. Seeing something. Something that didn't make any sense.

"Good afternoon, doctor. My son is awake, as you can see. And judging by his flippant tone, he's suffering a good deal of pain."

The doctor smiled like a man who was used to dealing with difficult people. "I imagine so." His gaze moved to Eric. "How are you feeling?"

"Like I was hit by a truck and the truck was on fire."

"He becomes a smart-ass when he's in pain," Mrs. Silva said over the doctor's shoulder.

Much as Eric loved her tact and discretion, he had to admit she was right. The pain seemed to intensify with every passing second. Eric closed his eyes for a moment. In the darkness, the memory came back more clearly. "The kid," he said.

When he opened his eyes nothing had changed. There were no ghosts in the room, time hadn't slipped forward. The doctor and his mother still stared down at him with worried expressions.

"Timmy died, didn't he?" Eric said.

"I'm going to order you some more painkillers—"

"Yes," Mrs. Silva interrupted. "And you could have died too. What were you thinking?"

"He was thinking about saving that kid." Eric twitched when his sister's voice entered the conversation. He hadn't even known she was in the room. She must have been sitting near the head of the bed, because her voice was close but he couldn't see her.

"But he didn't," Mrs. Silva said.

Eric managed to roll over enough to see Amelia in a chair pushed up against the wall. She was holding a copy of *Popular Mechanics* with a picture of a submarine on the cover. Amelia was always reading something. Although she was two years younger than Eric, he was prepared to admit she was about five thousand times smarter.

"Shouldn't you be in school?" Eric said.

"First of all, I'm not in school, I'm in college." Wellesley to be specific, early admission. "Second, it's Saturday. Third, I'm pretty sure 'my brother died today' is good for at least one absence."

"Oh, right," Eric said. The pain was cresting. He felt nauseated and hoped the doctor would come back soon.

~

A ringing phone startled Eric awake. He heard his mother's voice answer and was just about to let himself drift off again when she thrust the phone in his direction.

"It's that Andrew," she said and left the room. Even when Eric and Andy Templeton were in high school together, Mrs. Silva had never liked her son's friend. Eric had never worked out exactly why.

Eric took the phone and attempted some carefree swagger. "Hey Tempe, how's it hangin'?"

Tempe didn't buy it. "You got a death wish, Doc?"

"My will to live is as fit as ever. The rest of me…"

"I heard God kicked your ass."

"Close. My mom is here."

Andy chuckled. "Given the choice, I'd take the lightning."

"I think the nurses here would too."

"Any babes?" Andy asked.

"This isn't the movies, kid. I've got a nearsighted one with a mustache, a stick figure who's afraid to set foot in the room, and a man who washes my junk."

"So you're getting the sponge bath you always dreamed of."

"Not unless your sister is on her way." Talking to Andy was like playing ping-pong. He insulted, you volleyed back. Everyone got a good laugh. Eric actually felt almost normal for a second.

"I didn't tell you," Andy said. "My sister's getting married."

"Don't break my heart, it's the only part of me that still works."

"You're mouth still runs pretty good." Andy's laugh faded a bit as he said, "You must really be hurting."

Eric pretended not to hear that little edge of pity in his voice. Could it be that Andy Templeton was actually worried about him?

"Listen," Andy continued, "I've got some leave

coming up and I was thinking I might come up there—you know, when you're back on your feet."

"I'd love to see you, man, but I'm really okay."

"Damn well better be. I'm gonna need a wingman. Ladies love a man with scars."

"As long as you don't tell them I fell out of a tree."

"Dude, you were struck by lightning."

"Yeah, we'll tell them that."

"Alright. Keep your head down, Silva."

Eric reached to hang up the phone, but a hand plucked it away and set it in the cradle. Amelia again. Eric hadn't realized she was still there.

"You two are disgusting, you know that."

"You love us."

Amelia snorted. "I'm going down to the cafeteria. You want anything?"

"Are you kidding? I've eaten the cafeteria food here. I'll just starve, thanks."

She shook her head. "You're going to be okay, brother."

Eric's mind was drifting almost before she left the room. He remembered what he saw in the ER. He couldn't have been that doped up yet—not to be seeing things. Then again, he'd hardly been able to keep his eyes open and trauma could have unpredictable effects. He thought he should just forget it.

Except the kid was dead. He couldn't forget that.

CHAPTER TWO

Who You Gonna Call?

After four months of IV's, crappy hospital food, and physical therapy, Eric finally got the all clear to go back to work. At first, they made him hang around the station house, inventorying medical supplies and handling paperwork. When a few uneventful weeks had proven that he wasn't going to drop dead in the middle of a call, they finally let him out on the road again. It felt like coming home. Finally, he was back to doing the only thing he'd ever really wanted to do.

Everything would have been perfect if it weren't for the ghosts. He didn't see them all the time. It wasn't like he opened his bathroom door in the morning to find Beetlejuice sudsing up in his shower or anything. They only appeared when he was working on someone who was clinging to life by their fingernails. Every time he saw one, it made him feel like reality, or maybe his sanity, was slipping. He just wanted life to go back to normal.

At the very least, he'd like to know why this was happening to him. Maybe it was because he'd been dead for forty-five seconds. Maybe that had tuned his brain to the right frequency or something. He'd never heard of such a thing. Then again, most people who'd been resuscitated weren't in his line of work.

Which is why, on the drive in to his first night shift since the accident, Eric tried so hard to pretend that everything was completely and totally fine, normal, nothing to see here folks. When "Paradise City" came on the radio, he turned it up and jammed along. It had been in the Top Ten for months and he knew all the words. He told himself this was going to be a good shift. They'd get calls. They'd do the work. There would be no ghosts.

Eric pulled his '79 El Camino into the lot outside the station house. It had been his dad's car, which Eric's mother had kept for him even though Eric wasn't even old enough to drive when his dad died.

His dad had always been obsessively proud of the thing because it was the only car he'd ever owned outright. So Eric was careful to park near the back of the lot where it would be well illuminated when the street lights came on. It meant a slightly longer walk, but there was less chance the car would be dinged or vandalized. Not that this was a bad neighborhood, but it wasn't really a good one either.

The familiar scent of industrial antiseptic, rubber, and oil hit Eric as soon as he walked into the ambulance garage. Both buses were parked inside, waiting for their first call. As he walked by, Eric patted the side of his bus for luck. Hopefully, this was just a lull. The only thing worse than a night full of ghosts would be a night full of nothing to do. These days, if he wasn't busy or asleep, his mind tended to wander in unsettling directions.

His shift mates were already in the breakroom. Susan sat on the couch reading a magazine. There were always piles of them on the mismatched side tables. Guys pitched in for a few subscriptions. But others seemed to materialize years after their first printing, looking like they'd been used to insulate a house. No one seemed to know where those came from.

At the card table in the corner, Horton and Drew were playing some flavor of poker using assorted medical supplies as chips. From the look of Horton's betadine wipe stash, he was winning.

Drew grinned at Eric when he came through the door. Eric liked Drew for two reasons. First, he was the next newest guy on the squad after Eric, with just over a year in the field. Second, he was the same guy whether he was on a call or at a bar. Laid back, smiley, easy to talk to. Horton, on the other hand, could be a real pain in the ass.

"Hey, Flash, nice of you to join us," Horton said.

Flash. That's what passed for wit from Horton. Eric pouted. "Aww sorry, buddy, did you miss me?"

He made as if to ruffle Horton's hair, but Horton ducked away. Not that Eric had any intention of actually touching that grease trap.

Susan huffed. "It's almost like I'm at home with my

children," she said in a mutter just loud enough to carry to their side of the room.

Eric felt sheepish for a minute. Even though she was only about ten years older than him, Eric thought of Susan as a "real" adult. Somehow, she juggled this job and her home life, which included two kids, a husband, a dog, and if Eric remembered correctly, two guinea pigs. Meanwhile, Eric had managed to kill the cactus his sister had given him as a housewarming present when he'd moved into his apartment.

Eric sat down on the other side of the couch. He didn't want to annoy Susan, especially since he knew she'd been keeping an extra eye on him since the accident. On his first day back, she had clapped him on the shoulder and said, "You good?"

To which he'd made the only possible response under the circumstances. "Totally good."

Then she'd narrowed her eyes and stared at him, the way she stared at a scene when she was trying to figure out how to get an injured man out of a crushed car. Eric had forced himself not to squirm until she'd said, "Alright then."

After a couple of weeks with Eric back on the job and no incidents that she knew of, Susan had finally relaxed. She wasn't watching him quite as closely now and he wanted to keep it that way.

He sat down on the opposite side of the couch and tried to focus on a crossword puzzle. *Ten down: Went by, as time.*

When the alarm finally sounded, the noise startled Eric to his feet.

"Looks like you guys want this one." Horton smirked. "Go ahead. I'm winning anyway."

On his way out the door, Eric glanced over Horton's shoulder at his cards. He caught Drew's eye and gave him a thumbs up.

"All in," Drew said.

"You coming or playing?" Susan shouted from the doorway. Eric ran out to the garage after her.

The call was basic. Just a fender bender caused by poor visibility in the twilight hour. A Jeep turning at a stop sign clipped the front passenger side of an SUV. Everyone was out of their cars, walking around.

Cops were already talking to a woman in her early twenties who was standing next to the Jeep. Her hands were shaking and she was sobbing pretty hard, but she didn't look injured. Susan went off to check on her.

That left Eric with the SUV. The driver and her passenger were fine, but when you're standing there in an EMT uniform, someone is bound to think of something worth complaining about.

"My neck hurts," the passenger said.

It was probably a minor case of whiplash, or just the stress of the accident, but Eric checked her out anyway.

"You've got a nice smile," the passenger said. "It almost makes me wish I'd been hurt worse so I'd have to ride in the ambulance with you."

"If you were hurt worse, I wouldn't be smiling," Eric

said.

From there on out it was a busy night. Two more fenders, one guy fallen asleep at the wheel, and an OD with no sign of a ghost. Eric tried to tell himself that was because the whole ghost thing was behind him and not because the OD'd girl was already cold when the cops called it in.

By the time their sixth call of the night came through just after one a.m., Eric was feeling confident. It sounded like a basic crash, more severe than a fender bender, but nobody bleeding. He'd flawlessly handled every call so far, if he did say so himself, why would this one be any different?

~

Sixty miles away at Wellesley College, Eric's sister Amelia heard someone fumbling with the lock of her dorm room. It was the kind of sound that could make your heart jump into your throat when you heard it at one a.m., even if you knew it was your roommate stumbling home late from a party at a Boston University frat house.

Amelia was sitting on the bed, her legs crossed beneath her and a heavy textbook on her lap when Tammy stumbled into the room. Tammy held her high-heeled shoes looped over her fingers by the straps. Her hair was a wild cloud, and her lipstick had flaked away throughout the night until she was left with a ring of lip liner around her otherwise naked mouth.

"Are you seriously studying?" Tammy said.

"I was," Amelia said, closing the book.

"It's Friday."

Amelia glanced at the clock. "It's actually Saturday now."

"God, you are such a fun sponge," Tammy said. "I'm killing my buzz just talking to you."

Amelia shrugged. She didn't explain that she couldn't have slept even if she wanted to. Knowing her roommate would come crashing through the door at some undisclosed hour, or worse, worrying that she wouldn't, was enough to keep Amelia up all night. If she was going to be awake, she might as well be studying.

Tammy wove across the room and fell into bed.

"How did you get home?" Amelia asked.

"Don't worry, Mom," Tammy said. "We took the bus." Her heels thumped to the floor one after the other.

Amelia didn't push the issue. Tammy wasn't at college to learn, at least, not as far as Amelia could see. She was just there for the party. Amelia, on the other hand, had big plans and they started with a degree. Getting one required cracking a book every now and then. Amelia had no problem with that. She liked learning, even so early on Saturday morning that it was still Friday night.

"I filled your water bottle," Amelia said. "It's on your side table."

Her only thanks was a grunt. Amelia slid her textbook onto her own side table, then reached over and shut off the lamp. She lay back in the narrow dorm bed, thinking about how much easier life would be if other people were just a little bit more responsible.

In the darkness, the sound of the phone ringing was as sharp and sudden as a baseball through the window. Tammy groaned in one long complaining note.

It was up to Amelia to cross the room and snatch the phone from its cradle. "Hello?" she snapped, her voice low. It was Andy.

He'd called her a couple of times since Eric's accident. At first it was because Eric was too drugged up to answer. Then he started calling her claiming he couldn't reach Eric and wanted to make sure everything was okay. Amelia thought he might be looking for excuses to talk to her. She wasn't sure how she felt about that.

"Hey, Lia. How's it going?"

He was the only person in the world who called her Lia. She didn't know how she felt about that either.

"What's wrong?" Amelia went into the hallway. The phone cord would just stretch to let her sit in the doorway with the door mostly shut. If she kept her voice low, she wouldn't annoy Tammy or anyone else on the floor.

"Nothing, I was just...Oh shit. What time is it there?"

"After one a.m."

"Ah, I'm sorry. I didn't even think. We just got back from field training and I wanted to check in." Andy was stationed on a Marine base in California.

"Field training?"

"Yeah, you know, you go up into the mountains and

camp and stuff. It's supposed to be like practice for getting deployed."

"Are you getting deployed?" Amelia found herself clutching the phone cord. Clearly because she was tired and not at all because the idea of Andy in a war zone made her feel like she'd swallowed a hand grenade.

"No, not anytime soon. There's nowhere for us to go just yet. Listen, I'm sorry I woke you up. I tried calling Eric but he didn't answer."

Amelia leaned her head against the doorframe. She really was tired. "Maybe he's on night shift? Anyway, I wasn't sleeping. I was studying."

"In the middle of the night?"

She shrugged even though he couldn't see it. "I've got big plans."

Andy chuckled. "I know you do, Lia, but now you sound tired. You should go to bed."

"Hang on a second, it's after ten there. Why were you calling Eric at ten o'clock at night?"

Andy went quiet. Amelia could hear him breathing. "It's nothing. He just seemed kind of out of it the last time we talked. I told him I'd check in when I got back."

"He's different now, isn't he?" Amelia said. "Every time I'm around him, I feel like he wants to ask me something, but then he doesn't."

"Yeah, I know what you mean," Andy said.

Amelia yawned.

"Go to bed, Lia."

"Hush, you, I'm going."

Amelia went back to her room and crawled into bed. She lay in the dark listening to Tammy's drunken snoring. She tried to tell herself Eric would be fine. After all, the worst had already happened. If he could come back to life after getting struck by lightning and falling twenty feet, what couldn't he handle?

CHAPTER THREE

Uncertain Death

On the way to the highway fender bender, Eric was actually feeling chipper enough to attempt some small talk. "You know," he said, "if cars had autopilot, I bet we'd be out of a job."

Susan snorted. "Yeah and if penguins could fly they'd still look like tiny butlers."

"What?"

A police car was already on scene. Its headlights illuminated both the officer and a woman who was trying to talk and cry at the same time. Probably the rear-ender not the rear-endee, Eric decided. Nine times out of ten, the person at fault was the one who cried.

When Susan stopped, Eric climbed out, grabbed his gear and approached the rear-endee. The man was wearing dark slacks and a wide tie over a button-down shirt. Eric clocked him as a businessman. The type who worked really late. Usually not this late though. It was past the time when even that sort of guy should be home ignoring his family. Instead he was on the side of the road in the dark, red faced and rubbing his neck.

"Can you tell me what happened, sir?"

"Yeah, I was minding my own damn business when this bimbo smashes right into the back of my Seven Series."

"Are you hurt?"

"I'm pissed off is what I am. She better have insurance because that's a brand new car, just drove it off the lot last month."

Eric had his back to the road, so he didn't see what happened next. Susan had to tell him the details later. He heard it, though, loud and clear. A second police car had pulled up a couple of car lengths back to help block what little traffic there was. Its blue lights strobed across the business man's face, making him squint and angle away.

The officer had just climbed out of his cruiser when a Ford Bronco swerved toward the police car instead of away from it. The Bronco hit the officer, crushing him between the open cruiser door and the front end of the SUV. Metal screamed as the hinges tore free.

Eric turned at the sound. His heart pounded so hard that the shrieks of the woman from the first accident sounded muffled. The officer and the door slumped to the blacktop. Susan and Eric both reacted immediately, Susan running toward the ambulance to grab a backboard, Eric toward the officer to triage.

The officer was gasping and his breath gurgled in his

chest. Broken ribs, probably a punctured lung. Maybe a lot worse than that. Eric stabilized his head and started talking, trying to calm the officer. No such luck. The officer fought him, trying to stand. Some people had that response. They got hurt, and the fight-or-flight switch flipped to annihilate-anything-that-moves. Eric tried to hold him without causing any more damage.

Then Susan appeared with the backboard. As quickly as they could, they got him into the back of the bus. Eric climbed in beside him while Susan took the driver's seat. The officer had stopped struggling, which made Eric's life easier, but also seemed like a bad sign.

The ambulance had started moving before Eric noticed the ghost standing over the body. He felt his stomach tense. He'd been waiting all day for this, even though he'd told himself he wasn't.

It had to be the ghost of the police officer. They looked exactly alike except that the ghost was washed out and slightly transparent. Eric could see the monitor on the wall through its chest.

Working on the now-inert officer, Eric tried not to let the watching ghost distract him. This wasn't new. There was nothing to freak out about. Yes, he was seeing things, but he'd seen things before. Even if this was real, and Eric still thought it must be a hallucination, the ghosts had never hurt him. Mostly they just stood there looking sad or confused.

Eric had to stay focused. There was still time to save the officer. He'd managed to send a ghost back to its body once before. Based on his experience, all he had to do was stabilize the patient.

The ghost looked at Eric and then away. There was someone else in the ambulance with them. Eric couldn't see whoever it was clearly. Mostly it was a dark spot in the air and a sense of foreboding. The ghost felt it too, because he turned toward it and said, "So this is what? A near-death experience?"

He tilted his head, as if listening to a response.

Eric had never heard a ghost speak before. "Are you really there, or am I imagining things?" Eric asked.

The ghost ignored him.

"What?" Susan called from the front.

"Nothing, I've got it," Eric said, loudly enough for Susan to hear. Then he muttered to the ghost. "Hang in there. I'm doing what I can."

"So am I going to die or not?"

Eric looked away from the body just long enough to answer. "Don't worry. You're going to be okay."

The ghost finally looked at Eric. His expression was angry, still in fight mode. "How the hell do you know?"

Eric froze, shocked. No ghost had ever talked to him before.

~

Death was uncertain. Not uncertain about what he had seen. He knew exactly what he had seen. The human,

Eric, had talked to a soul. Worse, the soul had responded. A living human and a transitioning soul had conversed. Of that, he was sure. But he was uncertain what it meant, and he didn't like that feeling at all. Death was meant to be certain. Proverbially, he was one of only two things in the world that were.

Needing space to think, Death left the ambulance to stalk through the void between life and the hereafter. He still wore his humanoid form, not the skeleton and cloak of the old days, but a more corporeal rawboned man with pale skin and a conspicuous absence of hair and eyebrows. His long coat whipped in the screaming wind. It was always windy in the void. Windy and solitary. Its only inhabitants were lost souls and the things that hunted them. Neither bothered Death very often.

The police officer's near-death experience should have been a routine event. Death had just needed to appear, guard the soul for the brief moments that it was vulnerable outside the body before it was resuscitated, and then be on his way. He had done it for hundreds of years without incident. And now this.

No mere human should be able to see a soul in transit between the living world and the hereafter. The living human should have been oblivious to the soul standing next to him. That's how it was supposed to work. That's how it had always worked. Oh, there were ways for the living and the dead to communicate, but only through proper channels.

Death could think of only two possible explanations

for this unprecedented occurrence. Either human evolution had thrown up the wildest of wild cards, or something extra-human was meddling in the affairs of man. The last time that had happened, Prometheus had given them fire and look how that had turned out. In just a few millennia they'd managed to leave not only their caves, but their planet. They'd even plunged a flagpole into the moon.

It was bad enough that the council had given so many souls jobs in the hereafter. Imagine if living humans found a foothold there as well. They'd start running wires all over everything and beaming pictures through the air. The next thing he knew, the afterlife would be full of strip malls and disco halls.

Death sighed. There were places Death preferred not to go, places where he knew he was not welcome—delivery rooms, schools, daycare centers. If he was going to look into this, he'd have to go somewhere even worse: the records office.

Death stepped sideways out of the void and into the hereafter. Unlike humans, who had to walk the path laid out for them, Death could move freely through the worlds. A single step brought him to the door of the records office at the outer perimeter of The City. It was the only city in the afterlife, the place to which all human souls were drawn, and where their lives were recorded. It had grown since last he saw it.

This kind of thing made a personification long for the good old days when there was no city, just a single stone watchtower. Back then, the records had been kept in the mind of Sheshat, dressed in her leopard skin. When you sought a record she stared at you with eyes like the moon and recited from memory in a language the Egyptians would spend millennia trying to perfect.

That was until the humans started multiplying like bacteria and even the mind of a god groaned under the weight of their lives. Sheshat couldn't hold it all. She'd been relieved of her post some time during the fall of the Roman Empire.

The council had taken over. Pretty soon they were putting human souls to work. Now the afterlife was all plate glass and public works projects arranged by an incomprehensible organization called the Afterlife Beautification Commission.

Death walked through the door of the records office without opening it. Filing cabinets and manila folders stretched as far as the eye could see. The office theoretically contained a continuous record of every human life in process. When a life was complete it was bound and sent to the library for permanent storage. Death liked libraries. They were quiet and nobody cared who you were as long as you kept the books tidy. The records office could learn something from libraries.

Almost as soon as he stepped inside, a curly haired woman popped up between two filing cabinets and grinned in the face of Death.

"And how are you today, sir?"

"I don't see how that's relevant," Death said.

"Just making conversation, sir. No need to get huffy."

"Do you know who I am?" Death said. He was not "huffy." He was justifiably cross at the prospect of being greeted as though he were a guest in a cafe rather than the King of Terrors himself.

"Well, I seem to remember meeting you once before," the woman said. She winked at him. She actually winked at him. "Let me see...long black coat, no hair, no sense of humor. You're Death."

Death rolled his shoulders in his black leather trench coat. The last uniform change had been less than a generation ago. And he liked the coat. It had seemed right somehow—like a better sort of robe.

"Yes, well..." He resented the sense of humor comment. It just so happened he could be quite witty when he felt like it. He tried to think of a joke to tell the woman, but she'd already moved on to another topic. Humans were like that. No attention span.

"I bet you don't remember me, though. You must see a lot of humans in your line of work."

Determined not to let the woman have the upper hand, Death racked his memory. He did see a lot of humans, it was true, but he was a force of nature, not a god, and his memory was limitless.

"Bunny." He said. "Bernice 'Bunny' Williams. Age thirty-four. You died when you slipped on a toy car your son had left on the floor. You hit your head on a bookcase."

Bunny made a clicking sound with her tongue. "And

they say reading never hurt anyone."

Death grinned.

"I'll tell you a secret," Bunny said, leaning closer to Death and dropping her voice. "I sometimes pull Billy's file and check up on him. I'm not supposed to, but you know how mothers are."

Death chose not to point out that he never had a mother and, therefore, did not know how they were.

Bunny continued, "He's married and living in Bristol with his wife, Julia. They're thinking of adopting."

Death was getting tired of this. "I'm here for a record. Not gossip. The name is Eric Dean Silva."

Bunny nodded once. "I'm going to need to see your identification."

"For what reason? You know who I am. You just told me so."

"Still, it's regulations. I can't just give records away to anyone with a shaved head and no personality." Bunny crossed her arms and waited. She seemed to be purposefully antagonizing him.

The council had said, "All these dead humans roaming around, we might as well put them to work." Here was the result. Take away their fear of Death and humans start getting mouthy.

"Will this do?" Death said. He plucked his scythe from the empty air and felt satisfaction when Bunny's eyes widened. A seven-foot-tall farm implement with a blade as long as a man's arm will do that to some humans. Still, he missed the sword. Back in the days before everyone was a homestead farmer, Death had been allowed to carry a sword. It was called "Destroyer" in the old tongue. Now he didn't even carry the scythe all that often.

Not that he was complaining. At least the council wasn't making him reap souls with a clipboard.

Death let the scythe fade into the ether. Bunny reanimated. She bustled to a filing cabinet across the room.

"I've got more than one Eric Dean Silva. I'll need more details."

"Human, male, North America." She pulled two files from the drawer and laid them open on top of the cabinet. "Birth date?"

"Not my area of expertise," Death said.

Bunny rolled her eyes, but did it with her back mostly turned so Death knew he wasn't supposed to see it.

"Age?" she said.

"Old enough to know me, but not old enough to worry on the knowledge."

"Which means what exactly?"

"Twenty-one."

Bunny closed both files and stuck one back into the drawer. The other she handed to Death.

"This is probably the one you want. He lives in Dartmouth, Massachusetts. You can't leave the room with it."

Her bossiness grated his nerves. "Why not?"

"It's regulations. Files are not to leave this room until a life is complete."

"Nevertheless," Death said.

He stepped sideways into the void with Bunny's protests ringing in his ears.

Blissfully alone at last, Death sat on the ground and opened the file on his knees. The wind tugged at the papers. He snatched at them to keep them from blowing away. The last thing he wanted was to be faced with an angry Bunny if he returned with the pages out of order.

He plucked his scythe out of the air. It was the sharpest thing in the worlds and could cut a human soul from its body with a single stroke. Mere wind posed no challenge. He laid the scythe down in the silver dust. The wind retreated, leaving a pocket of still air where he could read in peace.

Death tried not to feel smug. Humanity might be a hopeless rabble, but the winds of fate knew who their antecedent was. Now to comb through Eric's life for clues about who or what had given him a power that could destroy the balance of the worlds.

CHAPTER FOUR

Life in Review

Eric let himself into his apartment. He looked around, no ghosts. Just a faded blue couch, a coffee table covered in unopened mail and moldering take-out containers, and a rickety TV stand he'd rescued from the curb two days after he'd moved in.

On the peninsula of countertop that separated the living room from the kitchen, the answering machine light blinked red. Eric pushed the playback button. Two messages.

The first was from Andy Templeton.

"Hey man, not to be a pain in the ass, but I'm putting in my leave today. If I don't hear from you I might just show up on your doorstep. Fair warning."

When Tempe had called him in the hospital and proposed a visit, Eric hadn't been in any frame of mind to make plans. Now it had been months and it sounded like Tempe was losing his patience. Eric rubbed the scar on his shoulder. He really should call Tempe. Now wasn't a good time though. It had been a busy night and Eric was tired. *I'll call him tomorrow.*

Eric wandered away from the machine and into the kitchen as the next message beeped on.

"Eric, it's your mother." She always announced herself this way. As though he couldn't recognize her voice after hearing it for the last twenty-one years. "I hope you haven't forgotten our family dinner tomorrow."

Eric groaned. He had forgotten. Or, more likely, his brain had dumped the knowledge out of self-defense. Eric opened the fridge. Inside, he found Coke, ketchup, and unidentified takeout he probably should have thrown away sometime last month.

His mother was still talking. "I expect a phone call to confirm your attendance. I won't have a repeat of Easter brunch."

Almost a year ago, Eric had been coming off the second night shift he'd ever done and had managed to sleep through the alarm that would have woken him up for Easter brunch. His mother had never let him forget it. She brought it up at least twice a month, as though he'd done it out of spite and not because he'd spent the night doing CPR on a guy whose organs sloshed in his chest cavity with every compression.

Eric sighed and closed the fridge. Then he walked over to the phone. What would his mother do if he just unplugged it? Probably call the police. Or break down the door herself. He imagined her in her pantsuit and perm, kicking through the door like on that new show, *COPS*.

That wasn't something to face on an empty stomach. Eric picked up the phone and called the pizza place.

Twenty minutes later, he woke to someone knocking. He sprang up from the couch. For a moment his sleep-filled brain expected to see his mother at the door with a squad of policemen. In reality it was just the pizza guy. No mom or cops in sight. He paid the kid, shut the door, and took the pizza back to the couch.

Someone was playing the bagpipes on TV. Eric didn't know why anyone would do that. It didn't seem like a thing that should be allowed to happen, but he kept watching anyway.

The next time Eric woke up, the pizza box was on the floor topside down. He didn't want to know what the pizza looked like. The television was still on, but now it was guys in suits talking about something. The news. Right. And the phone was ringing.

The clock on top of the television said it was three. Eric wondered who could possibly be calling at three in the morning. Then he realized it was light out. Not three in the morning. Three in the afternoon the day after a night shift. He fumbled for the phone, realizing too late that it was probably his mother and now that he'd picked up he basically had to talk to her or be labeled the worst, most disrespectful son in the known universe.

"Eric," his mother said. "So nice to know you're alive. What has been keeping you so busy that you couldn't find five minutes to call your mother in the past week?"

"Work," Eric mumbled. His mouth tasted like he hadn't brushed his teeth in a month. Come to think of it, when was the last time he brushed his teeth?

"Eric?"

He tried to refocus. "I was on night shift."

"And are you still on the night shift?"

"No, it's a rotation. We do one night shift every two weeks. Mine was last night." He desperately wanted a drink, but the phone cord was too short to reach the sink.

"Good, then you'll be joining us for family dinner this evening."

It was a command, not a request. Eric said, "Right."

"You'll be here at five. Dinner will be at six."

"Right."

Eric wondered, on a scale of one to ten, how dead would he be if he just went back to sleep until tomorrow morning.

"And Eric," his mother said in a voice like a sugar-coated knife blade, "I expect you to look presentable."

Nine-point-five, he decided.

~

Death read Eric's life with mounting concern. As far as he could make out, the trouble had started about five months ago, when Eric had been struck by lightning while trying to help a human child stuck at the top of a fence.

Death remembered that incident. He'd had a brief

conversation with Eric, who had taken the entire time to figure out that he was speaking to Death. Why did humans always struggle to realize who he was? Who did they expect, Bacchus? Alone in the rift, Death smiled to himself. There it was, proof that he was witty.

Reading through Eric's file was nothing to smile about, however. He found three troubling incidents after the lightning strike. Each time he'd been on the scene, ready to transport a soul or stand guard while it waited for resuscitation.

The first incident happened in the emergency room, immediately after Eric's accident. To be fair, it would have been almost impossible for Death to spot. He had been on the other side of the room with Timmy's soul while Eric drifted in and out of consciousness. Even Eric had thought that one was a hallucination.

The second one, though, that one was embarrassing because Death had noticed something was off but hadn't done anything about it. It was at the suicide of a seventeen-year-old boy. Eric had run into the room behind Susan and stopped just inside the doorway. He'd made eye contact with the boy's soul for just a moment before Susan called him away. Death had noticed Eric noticing the soul, he'd even told himself that he should look into what was going on here, later, when the work in front of him was done. But then he'd been busy and the incident had slipped his mind. It wasn't as though Death was in the habit of keeping track of living humans as well as the dying.

The last one was a heart attack. A man had collapsed in the middle of a 7-11 while stocking up on Twinkies and roller hot dogs. The clerk had the presence of mind to call nine-one-one. Death had arrived just a few seconds before Eric and Susan.

If Death had been paying attention, he might have noticed Eric watching the soul out of the corner of his eye while he worked on the man's body. But Death had been worried about more pressing matters. He knew there were soul eaters nearby. He could smell their rotten stench. At least one, maybe more. Already Death was splitting his attention between the anxious soul beside him and the defensive perimeter. There wasn't any of his mind left over to think about humans going about their work routines.

Death couldn't believe his own incompetence. Three times he'd stood by while a living human observed a transitioning soul, and he hadn't done anything to stop it.

Much as Death hated to admit it, it was time to inform the council about Eric's existence. He didn't actually expect them to have a solution, but they had to be told. If they found out about this and he hadn't already told them...well, then all hell would break loose. And when you were talking about the council governing the afterlife, there were so many visions of hell to choose from.

CHAPTER FIVE

Happy Families

As usual, the smell of Pine-Sol choked Eric as he walked through the front door of his mother's condo. She was a firm believer in the cleanliness is next to godliness theory. Every surface, from the fans to the baseboard, would pass a white glove test.

"Eric, is that you?" His mother stopped halfway down the stairs and looked at his khaki slacks and button down shirt. "Well, don't you look presentable."

"Gee, thanks mom. You look nice too." She was in a black skirt suit with cream piping and glossy nude heels. That's the kind of woman his mother was, the kind who wore high heels around the house.

"Your sister is in the kitchen, and Hector's run next door for ice."

Eric's jaw clenched. Of course Hector would be invited to what his mother insisted on calling family dinner. On the day she had moved in, Hector had wandered over from the adjoining condo to see what was going on. She'd invited him in for dinner and he never really left. Though he still technically lived next door, he ate most of his meals off her perfectly matched china plates. Eric didn't ask any questions beyond that. His mother's love life was not a topic he wanted to discuss, or even think about.

Eric hurried down the hall. In the kitchen, Amelia looked up from a textbook to twiddle her fingers at her brother. Eric waved back. They were not a hugging family.

Their mother shoved a pile of plates and napkins into Eric's hand. "I was hoping you'd get here early enough to help me set the table."

"I got here exactly when you told me to be here."

"Yes."

Another of his mother's charming quirks was the belief that fifteen minutes early was on time, and on time was late. Eric had once tried to explain that if people wanted you there fifteen minutes early they would have told you so, but apparently his logic was flawed.

His mother set to work folding napkins while Eric set the table with hard-learned precision.

"What are we having?"

"Meat loaf."

"You broke out the cloth napkins for meat loaf?"

"And why should meat loaf demand any less sophistication than steak?"

Eric didn't even try to answer that one. He heard the

front door open and a masculine gait approached down the hall. The man didn't even bother to knock anymore.

"Debra, are you here? I've got the ice. Is that Eric's car in the driveway?" As though Hector knew dozens of people who drove around in '79 El Caminos.

"In the kitchen," his mother called. Eric followed her in there, not because he particularly wanted to be in the same room as his mother's...friend, but because he knew she would just call him in like a dog if he didn't go of his own accord.

Amelia was still perched on a stool at the breakfast bar, reading. Nobody expected her to help set the table. As a college student, she had far more important responsibilities.

"Studying rocket surgery?" Eric asked.

"Close. Physics."

Hector closed the freezer with a thump and turned around. "They let girls study physics now? Imagine that."

Amelia rolled her eyes so hard Eric worried she'd fall off her stool.

"Hey there, champ," Hector said to Eric. "It's been a while since we've seen you around here. How are things?"

Eric tried not to take it personally. He'd heard Hector talk to waiters and mailmen and all kinds of other full-grown adults in the same way.

"Same sh-stuff, different day. Sit around, wait for the bell to ring. You know how it is."

Hector nodded like a bobble head on a mogul course,

even though Eric was certain the man did not know how it is. Hector was an accountant at one of the big old firms with an office downtown. He dealt with numbers all day, not people bleeding and dying and turning into ghosts, but he nodded anyway. His vanilla amiability set Eric's teeth on edge.

Eric's mother saved him from further small talk by thrusting a dish into his hands. "Here, take the meat loaf into the dining room."

She'd added some unidentifiable greenery for garnish. Eric sniffed it but couldn't tell what it was.

"And Amelia, dear, will you carry the asparagus?"

She shooed everyone through the door. Eric set down the meat loaf, trying not to show his distaste for it. Why anyone would grind up meat, shape it into a brick, and then eat it was beyond him.

The dinner conversation was exactly what he had expected. The smallest of small talk from Hector while Eric's mother tried to pretend that he was interesting. Eric's father had been a storyteller. He could hold a dinner party in thrall or set them laughing so hard they ended up under the table. Hector could barely string two sentences together without an "um" between them. Eric really didn't see what his mother saw in that man.

He snapped back to attention when his mother said his name.

"What?"

"Excuse me," his mother corrected, because he was apparently still eight years old. "I asked you how work is going. I had hoped that your accident would lead to some deeper reflection about what you want to do with your life."

Eric held back a sigh. This was an old argument. "I am doing what I want to do with my life. I want to be a paramedic."

"Your sister is going to college. She's going to be a, what was it, dear?"

"A molecular biologist," Amelia said without looking up from her plate. Eric wondered if she had a book open on her lap, or if she was just embarrassed that her mother was using her as a prop for this tired old argument.

"Yes," Eric said, "and I'm very proud of her, but I don't want to go to college."

"Think of what you could do. Instead of falling out of trees, you could be a doctor in a nice clean office with your diploma on the wall and Thursday afternoons free for golf."

"I don't golf."

She sighed as though he was the one being unreasonable. "That's not the point."

"What is your point, exactly?"

"My point is, your father and I worked hard to give you a better life than we had and you're throwing it away."

Eric felt his face flush. "Dad was never ashamed to be blue-collar. Never."

"Because he saw it as a means to an end."

"No, he loved his job."

Eric remembered that anytime he and his dad had gotten into an elevator he'd pat the wall of the car and say, "It's a big responsibility keeping these cars flying. You can't slack off when safety is at stake. Doesn't matter what kind of day you're having. You come to work and you do the job, and things keep on running smoothly up and down." That's what Eric was doing too, or at least, what he was trying to do. Just keep things running smoothly.

"You were a child, Eric." Mrs. Silva deployed her infuriatingly calm voice, the one she used when she'd picked a fight and now was trying to make you out to be the crazy one. "Don't pretend you knew him better than I did."

"I was fourteen. I knew him."

"I'm not going to argue about this," Mrs. Silva said.

Eric clenched his teeth so hard he felt it in his temples. This dinner could not be over fast enough.

~

After dinner, Eric offered to drive Amelia to the train station. She climbed into the passenger seat of the El Camino and ran a gentle hand over the dash.

"Remember when dad used to let us both squish into this seat so we could go get ice cream?"

Eric smiled. "Yeah." He braced his arm on Amelia's seat so he could look over his shoulder to back out of the driveway.

"I'm glad Mom let you keep the car," Amelia said.

"I bet she regrets it now, considering I'm such a disappointment."

Amelia sighed. "You know that's just her way of telling you she's worried about you."

Eric felt a little flush of guilt, but he buried it under a mound of indignation. There were ways to express concern that didn't involve questioning his every life choice.

"She doesn't have to worry about me."

Amelia turned in her seat so she could look at him. "Eric, it's not just Mom. Everyone is worried about you. I'm worried about you. Hector's worried about you. Even Andy is worried about you."

That caught Eric off guard. "When did you talk to Andy?"

"He called the other night." She said it like it was a normal thing for his best friend to call his little sister while she was at college.

"Why? Wait, why does he have your number?"

"I gave it to him, obviously." Amelia rolled her eyes. "How do you think he knew to call you in the hospital? Do you two have a psychic link or something?"

"But why did you have his number?"

"If it's any of your business, I wrote to him when he was in basic training." Her face flushed ever so slightly. Eric didn't like that one bit.

"It's encouraging to get letters from home when you're

away doing something new," Amelia added, like that explained everything.

Eric had to remind himself to keep his eyes on the road. His sister and his best friend had kept up a secret correspondence for years and nobody told him. Clearly they talked about him. He wondered what Amelia had told Tempe, and worse, what Tempe might have told Amelia.

"Listen, Amelia, Tem—Andy is a fun guy. But that's kind of all he is. He's around for a good time, but not really for a long time."

"Funny, I thought he was the one calling you and being ignored for the last three months. I guess I misunderstood." She took a deep breath. "Listen, the point is, you should call him."

"Right, thanks."

Amelia was quiet as they navigated between cars parked on both sides of a narrow street. When they were stopped at a red light, she said, "Is everything okay, Eric? You seem like there's always something on your mind lately."

If he hadn't been so surprised by the idea of Tempe and his sister having a...friendship he knew nothing about, he might not have said what he said next. He might have ended the conversation with a blithe comment like "you know me, always thinking about the job" or "just tired from night shift."

Instead he said, "Have you ever seen a ghost?"

Her eyebrows disappeared behind her bangs. "A

ghost? Like in *Ghostbusters*?"

They turned into the train station parking lot. "I was thinking about a more real-world example," Eric said.

"Well some of the girls at school think Beebe Hall is haunted."

"But you don't?"

"Eric, there is no scientific evidence that ghosts exist." She said it carefully, as though she expected him to start shouting like a street-corner preacher. "You haven't been seeing things, have you?"

Eric remembered to put the car in park. "No, of course not, no. I was just watching a show on TV the other day where these people were talking about their ghost encounters."

The look on her face clearly said he was full of shit, but she didn't press the issue. She just squeezed his arm. "Call Andy, okay?"

She climbed out of the car and turned back to grab her book. "And thanks for the ride."

"No problem," Eric said, even though he expected he might have just started one.

CHAPTER SIX

Death Seeks Council

Death surged to his feet, decisive, though not at all delighted by what would come next. He brushed his coat to remove the silver-black dust of the void, sighed hard enough to scatter the clouds, and stepped sideways into the foyer of the council room.

The space hadn't changed since Cecil, the receptionist, had taken his post some hundred plus years ago. It was maybe ten feet by six, with black and white tile floors and darkly finished wood paneling on all four walls. The doors to the council chamber were clad in the same wood, so you could hardly tell that they were there, especially in this light.

The candle-filled lanterns that were meant to illuminate the space only gave shape to the darkness. There was no telling how far away the ceiling was, or if one even existed. A single uncovered candle burned in a simple brass candlestick standing on the wooden slab of a desk that stood beside the chamber door.

Cecil looked up from his work and inspected Death over the top of his half-moon glasses. "Good day, Master Death." Cecil formed each word with precision. "You are not on the agenda."

Cecil had been human once, a long time ago. Death remembered reaping him. One minute he'd been quite contentedly copying a contract over onto a new sheet. The next, he was dead. An aneurysm apparently. Death had arrived to find the body slumped over a much smaller desk, the overturned inkpot dripping a dark pool on the rough wooden floor. His soul had tsked over the mess and tried to right the pot before he noticed his predicament.

It was rare that a human was offered a job in the afterlife immediately upon arrival, but Death had been unsurprised when Cecil was chosen to replace Anatolios, who'd finally decided to move on. There was something about Cecil, a sharp, single-minded focus coupled with an almost inhuman lack of imagination that made him perfect for the position.

He always seemed slightly piqued by the presence of Death. It wasn't the fear of a living human. It was more the irritation of a clerk who felt that other people were a distraction from his life's calling of perfecting the filing system.

Death could sympathize. He didn't particularly enjoy Cecil's company either.

"If I could stay off the agenda it could remain 'a good day' as you put it," Death said. "Alas, humanity is disrupting the order of worlds once again."

Cecil pushed back from his desk and stood in one economical movement. "And you have come to set things in order?" His expression said he found this unlikely. "I'll just interrupt their deliberations then."

Death let himself darken and flare taller, reminding Cecil exactly who he was being snide to. Cecil blinked just once, in a way that conveyed his utter lack of fear in the face of Death.

"May I tell them what this is regarding?"

Death shifted his grip on his scythe—upstart humans, getting into everything. They were like the old Roman gods, no sense of awe or propriety.

"A human with power above his station," Death said.

Cecil permitted the barest twitch of one eyebrow. "I see."

Death couldn't tell if his barb had caught, or if Cecil was merely aghast at the idea of anyone doing anything outside the bounds of propriety.

"A moment please," Cecil said.

He crossed to the huge oak door behind his desk, rapped, and opened it without pausing for an answer. Death watched him slip into the room. Cecil was unfailingly discreet. He returned a moment later with the same blank expression.

"The council will see you now."

Death bristled. They would see him now, would they? As though they were deigning to grant him an audience. He was older than any of them, older than Odin All-father, older than Innana of Sumer, older than the Spirit of the Beast. These oldest of the old gods had all, out of laziness, or carelessness, or perhaps even a sincere desire for peace in the worlds, stepped aside and let a council of their juniors govern.

Management of the afterlife fell on the council's shoulders. They ensured that records were kept, that public works projects were completed, that jobs were filled. They dealt with any little problem that might disrupt the smooth operation of the afterlife.

However, it was to Death that power over all living things had been granted. Soon he would remind the council of this, and Cecil and the damned records woman while he was at it, but for now the afterlife was running smoothly. So for the time being, Death shrugged, letting the façade of skin and cloth drip away to reveal his true form—the darkness within darkness.

Cecil didn't run screaming, but he did avert his eyes and attempt to look busy with his paperwork. If Death had still had a mouth in this form he would have grinned. The unflappable human machine could still be frightened. Perhaps there was hope for humanity yet.

~

Amelia didn't go directly back to the dorm when she got off the T. Tammy might be in the room, and Amelia didn't want to risk it. Her roommate was such a gossip, it was impossible to have a private conversation when she was on the same floor, never mind in the same room. So, Amelia stopped at the pay phone outside the dining hall and dug some quarters out of her purse.

Andy picked up on the second ring. The little jump of her heart surprised her. "Oh good, you're home," she said.

"If you can call a barracks room home. What's up, Lia?"

Amelia curled both hands around the phone set, pressing it close to her face. "I'm starting to worry about Eric."

"Did something else happen?"

"Else?"

"Aside from getting hit by lightning and falling twenty feet, I mean."

"Sort of?" Amelia described their conversation about ghosts, and Eric's less-than-believable cover story. "Do you think he's seeing things?"

Andy was quiet for just a moment too long.

Amelia filled the silence. "I didn't know what to say to him."

"I'm sure it's no big deal," Andy said. His voice was almost convincing. "He's been through a lot lately. Maybe he just had a weird dream or something."

"Yeah, maybe."

"I'll try calling him again."

"Thanks, Andy. I don't know what I'd do without you."

"Me neither," he said. She didn't ask him to clarify

exactly what he meant by that. She was pretty sure she already knew.

Again the silence stretched a little too long, and again, it was Amelia who finally broke it.

"Oh, and I told him we've been talking."

"Oh," Andy said, his voice perfectly neutral.

"Is that bad?"

"No, I really don't know why neither of us mentioned it sooner. It's not a big deal right? No need to make it a state secret or anything."

"Right," Amelia said. She suspected it might be a slightly bigger deal than he was making it sound, but now was not the time to get into it. Better to just let things lie for now.

"Don't worry. I'll be home soon and we'll get Eric sorted out."

Amelia swallowed back a little bubble of excitement. "You're coming home?" She didn't want him to think she was some self-centered little kid. Obviously he was checking in on Eric. It had nothing to do with her.

But then he told her his flight information and added, "I'll give you a call when I land. Maybe we can meet up before I head to Dartmouth."

"Sure," Amelia said. She heard someone shout "Templeton" in the background. Before she could ask what that was about, Andy said, "It's a date, then. I gotta go."

Amelia hung up the phone and drifted off in the direction of her dorm. For the first time since she was ten years old, she wished she had a female friend she could talk to. What exactly had Andy meant by "it's a date"?

~

Death stalked into the council chamber. He hardly recognized the place. Innana may have surrendered her claim of authority, but she hadn't given up redecorating the council chamber whenever the mood took her. She'd gone so avant-garde with this particular design that there was no chamber to be seen.

The long wooden council table stood at the top of a low rise in a grassy field dotted with tiny red flowers. They weren't any flower Death had ever seen on Earth, so either she'd gotten them from somewhere else, or she'd created them just for this installation. In the distance, the sun was setting, outlining each blossom and each council member in golden light.

Osiris was at the head of the table in his plumed headdress, his crook and flail crossed over his green chest as though he were sitting for a sculpture. To his right, spilling over either side of a high-back chair was Xolotl, twin brother of Quetzacoatl, the feathered serpent who had been worshiped in various incarnations by both the Aztecs and the Mayas.

Beside him was Yama, his perfectly groomed beard curling against the blue of his bare chest. With his four hands clasped across his belly, he looked ready to fall asleep. Yan Wang, ruler of the ten kings of China, and Izanami-no-Mikoto of Japan stared blankly at each other across the table.

Little Ereshkigal, sister of Inanna, sat next to Izanami, looking uncomfortable and out of her element. To Osiris' left, sat Lady Freyja of the Norsemen. She gave Death a welcoming nod, one professional to another.

Behind them all, and a bit to the left, stood Hermes at his own little desk. Despite a puckish disposition, he had faithfully kept the records for the deities since the heyday of ancient Greece. His eyes remained on his book as the door shut behind Death and disappeared into the air.

"Welcome, Lord Death," Osiris said. "To what do we owe the honor of your presence?"

That cooled Death's anger slightly. At least Osiris seemed to remember who was the greater spirit here. Death restrained his form into a rough humanoid shape wearing a hood and cowl of darkness.

"A strange event among the humans." What else would bring him here? He certainly didn't come for the company.

Xolotl's feathers rustled. "What have they done now? Another world war, I hope."

"I wouldn't come to you with such triviality. This is something stranger. A human man has developed the sight."

All eyes turned to him, giving him their full attention. Even Hermes looked up, his pen hovering above the page, his golden-brown eyes interested for once.

"You're certain?" Osiris said.

Death drew himself taller, ready to remind this whelp who he was speaking to. Before he could say anything, Osiris bowed his head again. "Forgive me, Lord Death. Of course you are certain. What exactly is the nature of this boy's power?"

"He sees the souls as they begin their journey into the afterlife."

Izanami-no-Mikoto folded her hands into her kimono. "What harm can he do? A human soul is fleeting, its journey ephemeral as the cherry blossom."

Insomuch as Death liked anyone, he liked Izanami. He liked her calm manner, her respectful tone, her gentleness. So he inclined his head to her.

"Perhaps that is so, Izanami-no-Mikoto San, but this is a human who works with the sick and dying, so although he sees briefly, he will see many. And what one sees one may someday hope to touch."

The corners of Izanami's mouth rose ever so slightly. Someone who was looking for such a thing might even call it a smile. Death had managed to be poetic. It was an aspect of his personality he rarely shared. Unfortunately, he had to break the spell by adding, "Already he has held a short conversation with a soul."

That caused some rustling around the table. The gods were not pleased.

"What is the source of his power?" Yan Wang asked.

"That is not yet clear," Death said, unwilling to say he didn't know in so many words.

"You don't know," Yan Wang said.

"And neither do you," Yama pointed out.

Osiris pounded his crook on the tabletop, halting the inevitable bickering before it had properly begun. "An argument solves nothing. We must discuss what should be done."

Xolotl waved a hand, making his feathers flutter. "Kill the human."

"What would that accomplish?" Izanami said. "We must discover the root of the plant. It is not enough to remove the blossom."

"It is not our job to destroy humans," Ereshkigal said.

"Our job is to keep the peace," Xolotl said. "This will do that."

Lady Freyja sat back in her chair. "No wonder your civilization died. With such strategic thinking it is a miracle they lived long enough to be conquered."

Yama chuckled into his beard. Ereshkigal blushed. Death hadn't known deities could do that. Across the table, Xolotl stirred, making a sound like the wind in the void as his feathers whispered against each other. "And where are your worshipers now you—"

Death was losing his patience. He had literally one hundred and eight other places to be right now. Although technically, he was in all of them, being in this one irked him. "If you're going to sit there arguing like Olympians," he said, "I'll just—"

The room erupted. Even Ereshkigal was speaking now. Comparing a deity to the petty, self-absorbed, and above all human-like gods of Ancient Rome was the surest way to wound her pride. Which was exactly why Death had done it. He was rather pleased that it had worked so well.

Osiris stood, slamming his crook and flail down on the table. The sun sank lower in the sky and the golden shadows fell away, slumping the table into the flat gray of near-twilight.

"Enough," Osiris said. "There is a problem before us and we will address it with the dignity befitting this council."

He turned his predatory eye on each of them in turn. They receded under his gaze. When he was satisfied that he'd cowed, or at least temporarily silenced, all of them, he sat down. His flail and crook returned to their ceremonial position on his chest.

"Now, Lord Death, please tell us what you have learned of this human man."

For once, the council members listened quietly as Death recounted what he had seen and read. In the corner, Hermes scribbled down his every word, preserving it for eternity.

As soon as Death finished, the gods began to speculate.

"The lightning could mean Zeus." Ereshkigal folded and unfolded her wings as she spoke. Her eyes remained demurely on the table.

"Then we have nothing to worry about," Yama said. "A stylish toga will distract him before he does any harm. What about Thor?"

Lady Freyja leaned back in her chair. "Thor hasn't left Asgard in many cycles. It's more likely that fool Loki."

"Or Anansi," Xolotl said. "It did happen in America."

Death needed to take charge of this situation. These deities never could see beyond their own politics.

"It could be the human did this all on his own," Death said. "Their minds are complex. They're always learning. Look what they've done to their world in the last two hundred years."

One by one the members of the council turned their heads to stare at him. The setting sun cast long shadows, darkening their somber faces. "A chilling thought," Izanami said.

"Clearly we are in need of information," Osiris said. "All in favor of sending Death on a fact-finding mission to observe the human and report back?"

Everyone said, "Aye." Except for Hermes who was only a scribe and didn't get a vote, and Death, who said, "I don't believe that's in my job description."

"The journey from life to afterlife is clearly your domain, and this human is intruding on it. I can think of no better psychopomp for the job," Lady Freyja said.

"You have auditors, don't you?"

"The humans are multiplying every second," Osiris answered. "We can't spare an auditor to focus on just one."

"Choose a lesser psychopomp. Perhaps a member of this very council." Death regretted the words as soon as he uttered them. It would do nothing but enrage them.

Besides, he already knew why no member of the council could take on this task. They didn't trust each other. Any one of them could be jockeying for more power in the afterlife.

"It won't be a hardship for you," Osiris said. "This human can only get into trouble when he's near the newly dead—where you will already be. We ask only that you remain aware of his movements."

"And you are technically infinite," Izanami said.

"But, I—"

"The council has voted. If the scribe will read back the vote?"

"Seven in favor, none opposed," Hermes read in a flat tone.

"Fine," Death said. "Fine."

Death left the council, grinding his teeth loudly enough to be heard by every psychic on earth. The most finely tuned went to bed with a migraine, while the less sensitive snapped at their clients and wondered if they were developing tinnitus. He was angrier than he had been in centuries, which is why he was about to make a mistake.

CHAPTER SEVEN

Sightings

The police called for help with a homeless guy, belligerent and bleeding under an overpass. As Eric and Susan approached, Eric tried to assess the situation. The officers were using one of their cars as a barricade. They hadn't drawn their guns yet, but they also weren't approaching the patient.

Eric could see why. Ten feet away, the homeless man stood half shrouded in the shadow of the overpass. He had a bushy beard, layers of mismatched clothes, and a personal weather system of grime. Blood flowed over his eyes and around his nose. When he opened his mouth, blood seeped through his teeth. Eric couldn't tell where any of it was coming from.

For the moment, the man was on his feet, but his balance was unsteady. He wove back and forth, in and out of shadow. Either he had some sort of head injury, or he was on drugs. Possibly both. There were some new drugs coming out that could seriously unhinge you if you weren't careful. This guy didn't look like the careful type. Sooner or later he was going to fall.

One of the cops spoke to him, loudly and firmly, from behind the safety of the police car. The guy mumbled in response. He wiped his arm across his face, smearing the blood and mixing it with the God-knew-what on his jacket. Now Eric could see that the blood came from a gash on his head. The stuff on his hands was just from trying to clear his eyes enough to see.

Eric had seen his fair share of blood, and mostly it didn't bother him. He was like a trash collector who had gotten used to the stench of spoiled fish and half-liquefied vegetables. But it was a question of volume. There was still something unsettling about this much blood pouring out of a human body.

Blood belonged on the inside. Seeing it escape set off all kinds of instinctual alarm bells. It was like approaching your front door and realizing it was ajar. The stomach tightens and the mind starts running in circles. Training doesn't get rid of that reaction entirely, it just helps lock those feelings away so you can do something useful.

Right now, Eric wasn't sure how to be useful. The guy didn't seem to have a weapon but wasn't exactly predictable either. Approaching him could make things worse.

Moving slowly to avoid startling anyone, Eric and

Susan sidled up to the police car. "What's the plan?" Susan asked.

"The plan is to sit right here and make sure he doesn't hurt anybody between now and when he passes out," the cop said.

"What about himself?" Susan said. "He clearly needs medical attention."

Susan had a soft spot for addicts. The rumor around the station house was that she had an older brother who had gone to Vietnam and come back with a heroin addiction. Eric never asked her about it, and she never said anything, so he wasn't sure if it was true. It was just one of those mysterious stories that floated around the station house. Nobody knew where they came from and it was impossible to tell which, if any, were real. Whether the rumor was true or not, Susan was right. The guy needed help.

"We should try talking to him," Eric said.

"I've been trying," the cop said. He didn't even flick his eyes away from the swaying man. "You want to take a turn, be my guest."

Eric rose from his half-crouch behind the car with no plan. As soon as he moved, the man's eyes fixated on him. They tracked him as he stepped around the cruiser.

Susan hissed his name. Eric ignored her.

The guy was staring in Eric's direction. Eric tried not to lock eyes with him, in case that came across as threatening. He was still swaying a little, but less like a drunk and more like a tree swaying in a soft breeze. His feet stayed planted while his shoulders drifted side-to-side.

All eyes were on Eric. His throat was suddenly dry. He opened his mouth to speak, not at all sure what he was going to say.

The guy raised his bloody hand to point directly at Eric. As directly as he could, at least. He was still swaying, so his aim was transient, but his intent was clear.

"You!" He said it as though he knew Eric. He didn't. At least, Eric didn't know him. "What do you see? What-do-you-see? Whatdoyousee?"

He staggered a step forward, arm still outstretched. Eric could feel the tension of the watching officers ratchet up another notch. He swore he heard the click of guns being readied to fire.

"He's watching you." There was an edge of giggle in the guy's voice. Somehow, that was more unnerving than the blood and the pointing finger combined.

"He's right behind you."

Eric refused to turn. Susan was behind him. He knew that. He knew she had his back, just like she always did. There was absolutely nothing to be afraid of, unless you counted the bloody, raving addict and the cops with guns.

Eric took a breath to steady himself. This man was his patient. Eric would not fail him.

"We're here to help you," Eric said. "Will you let us help you?"

"Help me, help you, help me, help you." He tilted his head side-to-side as he said it, but out of sync with the swaying of his shoulders. Watching him made Eric feel like he was trying to stand on the T without holding on to anything.

He had to get closer. He touched the hood of the cruiser with his fingertips, steadying himself. Then he took a cautious step forward. Susan's fingers brushed his sleeve just before he stepped out of her reach.

"You're bleeding." He didn't know what else to say. What words would make the man trust him enough to let Eric take him in? Eric touched his own forehead, mirroring the source of the blood.

The pointing finger dropped and he raised his other hand to touch his forehead. It came away bloody. He stared at the blood for a moment. Then his wail broke the tense silence. It was like he hadn't known he was hurt until Eric pointed it out. Now he howled like a wounded child. The sound was high and piercing.

"It's okay," Eric said, even though the guy wasn't listening. "I'm going to help you."

Eric approached him slowly, one foot in front of the other.

"Get back here you idiot," the cop hissed.

Suddenly, the man collapsed, pitching forward. Eric lunged the last few steps and caught him before his head hit the pavement. As Eric lowered him gently to the ground, his hand scrabbled at Eric's arm, leaving bloody finger marks. His eyes rolled up in his head.

"Beware the messenger." The words were almost a sigh, and Eric wasn't really sure he heard them. Maybe he was imagining things. He felt for a pulse. It was there, but thready.

"A little help," Eric shouted.

Susan and the cops rushed over. The cops still had their guns drawn.

"He's out," Eric said. "You can lose the guns."

They holstered them slowly. Then they begin to sweep the scene, looking for drug paraphernalia, or maybe the rock that bashed the guy's head in.

After they'd deposited the guy safely into the hands of the ER docs, Susan drove them silently back to the station house. She had mom face, that tight-lipped hardness that says you're about to get chewed out for something you should have known better than to do in the first place. She pulled the bus into the garage.

"I've got a seven-year-old at home that listens better than you do," Susan said. "If I tell you to go clean up, will you at least do that?"

Before the accident, Eric would have gotten all hot under the collar and argued with her about how you have to trust your instincts and do what needs to be done and blah, blah, blah. But Eric had died four months ago, and although that hadn't given him any kind of window into his life's purpose, it sure did change some things.

Eric hung his head. "Sorry, Susan."

She blinked a few times and walked away. After she was gone, Eric stood there for a minute, just breathing. The garage was quiet with the other bus out on a call. Eric looked down at himself. There was blood on his sleeves, and on his hands, and smeared across the front of his shirt.

CHAPTER EIGHT

Runnin' Down a Dream

If the council thought they could order Death about, they had another think coming. Yes, he would investigate this matter, but he would do it in his own way. He would not go trailing after this human like a fool hunting a snipe. The first order of business, as it appeared to him, was to fill the gaps in what he already knew about Eric.

The biography file he'd taken from Bunny was limited in one respect: it could only record the conscious experience of the human. That meant there was a solid third of Eric's life that Death hadn't yet seen: his dreams.

In truth, Death thought, as he contemplated how to get a message to his brother, he probably should have gone to see Morpheus before involving the council at all. It might have saved everyone, most importantly him, a lot of trouble.

Morpheus' kingdom was far larger and more impressive than reality could ever be. All humans were his subjects from birth, and spent a generous portion of their lives under his eye. They lived such brief lives and yet, in order to function at even the lowest level, they were obliged to spend one third of that time asleep. Those who were fortunate enough to die of old age often spent their last moments, or sometimes their last years, firmly entrenched in his world.

Getting to Morpheus could be a challenge. Morpheus and the Dreamscape were entirely outside the authority of the council. Even Death himself couldn't cross into it uninvited.

Still, their two zones of influence sometimes overlapped. Humans died for many reasons: sickness, old age, failing organs, accidents, and of course, stupidity. Fortunately for Death, a small but useful number of them died in their sleep. In those places and at those times, Death was able to step briefly into the Dreamscape. From there, he could pass a message to Morpheus. But to accomplish this, Death would need a human.

It didn't take long for Death to find a young man with an undiagnosed heart condition that was about to be discovered too late. Death stepped sideways into a bedroom. The room was dark, lit only by moonlight through sheer curtains. For a moment, Death stood at the bedside, looking down at the sleeping man and the young woman beside him. Then he stepped into the young man's dream.

Death hated dreams on principle. They were unpredictable and nonsensical. Worse, the basic laws of nature and power didn't apply, which is to say, he was more or less powerless within them. The only consolation was that in a dream no one looked twice at a humanoid form carrying a scythe.

The human, Blaine Robbins, was dreaming of a party. He was inside a house that was overfull of people, but in the nature of dreams, most of the people in the crowd didn't have faces and their clothes were merely blurs of color placed near enough to fool the eye on a quick glance.

Blaine was in a hallway at the front of the house. Between him and the front door was an almost solid wall of people. Above him, a flight of stairs stretched up into the darkness. The stairs seemed to bother him for some reason. He kept looking up at them as though expecting something horrible to descend. Summoned by his fear, a flock of bats swooped across the room and disappeared up the stairwell. No one seemed to notice except the dreamer, who glanced around fearfully.

Time flowed differently in dreams, but even so, Death had only a moment before he'd need to step forward and declare himself. Darkness was creeping down the stairway and peaking in around the door frames. He needed to find one of Morpheus' people quickly. The Oneiroi were masters of illusion. At least one roamed in every dream to set the course and see that it was followed. They could take on any form the dream needed, which could make finding them a challenge.

Death searched the crowd for someone who looked

real. There, a woman in blue. He could see the individual strands of her hair. Her dress swished with each step in an almost natural manner. She was also beautiful, a perfected image of whoever it was she represented for the human. Oneiroi saw the images of the heart and used them. She had to be an entity and not a set piece.

Death strode through the fake people, who dissolved into gossamer at his touch. When he reached the woman, he grabbed her by the arm and thrust his face close to hers.

"I seek an audience with Lord Morpheus."

The Oneiroi stared at him, wide-eyed. Death wore his archetypal form—black cloak, skeleton frame, scythe— but the people of Dream worked too closely with illusions to be fooled by them. Standing this close to Death, she no doubt saw his true form, the darkness within darkness. It was enough to terrify even an immortal being. She nodded sharply.

Death released her and approached the dreamer. Most of the crudely drawn partygoers had vanished. Blaine, nearly alone, fell to his knees. All around him, the scenery began to deteriorate. Boards fell out of the floor. Windows dissolved like spun sugar in a rainstorm. Wind whipped through the house and tugged at Death's robe.

Casting his eyes about in fear, Blaine saw Death. "This is a dream," Blaine said. "It must be."

"It was," Death answered. "The dream is dying, and so are you."

"But I'm only twenty-three," the human said.

"That is not relevant," Death said. "Take my hand."

Blaine struggled to his feet. Beneath him, the floor was beginning to crack. He pushed past Death and saw the dream woman. Reaching out for her he cried, "Christina!"

Instead of answering, she began to melt like a candle. Globs of blonde and flesh-colored dream dripped down her face and spattered on the floor.

Blaine shouted and drew back in horror. "What's going on? Why is this happening?"

"An abnormal heart rhythm," Death said. "Caused by a thickening of the cardiac muscle."

He might as well have stayed silent. Blaine wasn't listening. Around them, the house had completely disappeared, except for the few cracking floorboards directly underfoot. The rest was dark and void. The dream woman, the one called Christina, had melted away, leaving a small winged troll in her place. Even with an Oneiroi present, the illusion would collapse without a human mind to draw from, as it was collapsing now.

Blaine turned away from the thing that had been Christina. "I want to wake up now. Please, I want to wake up."

He grabbed Death's cloak and clung like a child. "I want to wake up."

That was another reason Death hated dreams. Humans accepted his presence more easily, but they assumed that he was part of the dreaming. It could be difficult to convince them of the urgency of what was happening.

"I can take you home," Death said.

"Yes, please, yes," Blaine said. That was close enough for Death. He wrapped his arm around the human and stepped. Now he just had to hope Morpheus would answer his message.

CHAPTER NINE

The Ultimate Question

Eric normally didn't go to bars. But Drew had invited him out a couple of times since the accident, and he felt bad turning him down all the time.

Sitting on a bar stool, watching the other medics rack up pool balls, Eric realized he was actually enjoying himself. It was relaxing to be surrounded by people without being forced to interact with them. A couple of guys wandered over to the jukebox and pretty soon the first lines of "Going, Going, Gone" filled the bar.

Drew walked over and pulled out a stool. He didn't really sit on it, just sort of leaned his body against it in a super casual way that Eric wouldn't have been able to pull off in a million years.

"Hey, man. You alright?" Drew asked.

Eric set his beer down on the bar and rubbed the condensation onto his pants.

"Fine, yeah. Tired I guess." Which was true. He was

tired a lot lately.

Drew nodded. "What's it like being back? Does it suck?"

Something exciting happened in the game and the guys all started talking at once. Drew glanced over at the pool table and then back at Eric. He looked at Eric the way he would look at a stunned accident victim, ready to hear whatever Eric had to say.

"It doesn't suck," Eric said. "Being in the hospital sucked. Being trapped at home sucked. Being back is good. Really good."

"It's kind of your life, isn't it? The job?"

Eric sipped his beer, more for something to do than out of thirst. *That's why alcohol exists,* he thought, *so you have something to do with your hands while you talk to people.*

"It doesn't leave much room for anything else," Eric said.

Drew finally sat down on the stool with his back to the bar. He leaned on his elbows, his beer in one hand.

"I don't know," he said. "Sue has a family. A couple of the guys have kids and stuff."

"Yeah, I don't think that's in the cards for me," Eric said.

Drew's eyes narrowed a bit, like he was decoding this. "That's real. I get it. Some guys are just married to the work."

Silence stretched between them until Horton sauntered over and thrust a pool cue at Drew. "You're up, Ace."

Drew snatched the cue out of Horton's hand. "You lost?" He seemed surprised.

"Nah, it was a tie," Horton said. He tapped his fingers on the bar to catch the attention of the old guy who worked the tap.

"What do you mean it was a tie?" Drew said. "This is eight-ball, not tic-tac-toe."

"Yeah, but we both suck at it," Horton said. "So we quit four balls in. That's a tie."

Drew shook his head. "You're an idiot."

The bartender creaked over.

"Two pints of Sam's and a shot of your cheapest whisky," Horton said. So far, he'd barely glanced in Eric's direction. Which was just fine with Eric. He didn't really feel like making small talk with the brainless.

"That stuff will peel paint," Drew said.

"Yeah, I'm on a quest to see if I can burn right through my stomach lining," Horton said. "It's a great way to lose that extra weight."

He slapped his completely flat stomach as though it was a beer gut. Eric rolled his eyes. He knew for a fact that Horton didn't work out. He was just built that way. Eric, meanwhile, had to work to keep trim. Which reminded him, he hadn't been to the gym since he finished physical therapy. That should probably change soon.

"Like what you see, Flash?" Horton said.

Eric realized he'd just sat there staring at Horton for the last minute. He scrambled for a witty remark, but

Drew saved him before he could think of one.

"Come on, Silva. I'm gonna kick your ass at eight-ball."

"Sure," Eric said.

Horton smirked. "Trash talk, man. Work on it."

Drew led the way over to the pool table. Eric was relieved that Horton didn't follow them. Drew racked the balls then motioned for Eric to break. He did so, clumsily.

"Not bad," Drew said.

"Not great."

"Can I ask you something?" Drew started playing the table. "And you can totally tell me to go to hell if you want."

Eric shrugged. He didn't know where this was going, but he also couldn't imagine a situation where he needed to shut Drew down that forcefully.

"What did it feel like? Getting hit by lightning? I mean, it must've hurt, obviously. But besides that? Was it like licking the world's biggest nine volt?"

On one hand, it was a really stupid question. Clearly it didn't tickle. But on the other hand, he could see where Drew was coming from. Eric had basically been to hell and back. Who wouldn't be curious? He should probably be surprised that no one had asked before, not even Andy, who he still hadn't called. Come to think of it, that could be why he hadn't asked.

"It felt like getting backhanded by God," Eric said. "One second I was there in the tree, and there was this kid. This boy Timmy. And then I was on the ground."

As he said it, he remembered the pain. And he remembered something else. He'd talked to someone. Not Susan. Was it a firefighter? Another EMT? He'd been dressed in black, Eric remembered that at least, so he must have been a firefighter.

"I was dead for forty-five seconds or so. And then Susan shocked me and I was back for a second, but I don't really remember anything until the hospital."

And at the hospital he'd seen…a hallucination of course. He couldn't have seen anything real. It was just pain and stress and drugs.

"I died," Eric said. It felt more real when he said it out loud. He had died. As in last will and testament, call the next of kin, six feet under, Elvis has left the building. Not living. Inanimate. Mind stopped, breath stopped, heart stopped, dead.

"I fucking died."

The music had stopped and Eric realized he was talking too loudly. Everyone stared at him. He felt himself blushing, and that was worse than being struck by lightning. At least then he hadn't looked like an absolute pansy.

"Sorry," he said. "Sorry."

Horton slid a shot into Eric's hand. He wasn't sure what it was, but he drank it. It burned from his tongue to his stomach. His eyes watered—from the alcohol, of course.

"I'm sorry," he said again. "Fucking-A, what the hell was that? Furniture polish?"

Horton broke the ice by laughing. Somebody punched a button on the jukebox. Eric didn't recognize the song right away, but Drew did.

He said, "You guys are assholes, you know that?" But he chuckled.

Then Eric recognized the intro. It was "Lightning Strikes" by Aerosmith. Eric had to laugh or cry here, and there was no way he'd cry with Horton standing right there laughing his ass off.

CHAPTER TEN

Death and Dream

Death was everywhere and for all people. So while he was still in the dream of Blaine Robbins, he was also in a nursing home with Florence Edmund. The eighty-four-year-old woman was about to slip away in the night surrounded by machines that beeped and breathed.

In the old days, friends and family would have gathered around the dying woman, never leaving her unattended. Someone would have slept in her room at night and sat with her through the day. It showed a scandalous lack of respect both for the elderly, and for Death himself, that they had left her alone.

Of course, he'd heard the expression, "You come into this world alone and you'll go out of it the same way." Like many human expressions, it was patently false. No human had ever come into the world alone. At the very least, they had their mother in attendance. When they went out again, they had Death, the last and most stalwart companion.

Death approached Florence's bedside slowly. Her eyes were closed, the blanket pulled up around her chin. She appeared to be asleep, but Death knew she would die in this world, not in the Dreaming. He waited.

He'd been standing there for the space of an old lady's breath when her eyes fluttered open. She turned her head against the pillow.

"Why hello, dear," she said, smiling. "It's late for a visit, isn't it?"

"I'm sorry to disturb you, ma'am," Death said. "This business cannot wait."

"Oh, I never handle business," the old woman said, her voice dreamy as though she were only half awake, or drugged perhaps. That happened more and more these days as well.

"My husband always handles the business. I can't do sums you know. Never could, and what with my poor eyesight now…" She faded out but smiled in a befuddled way.

"Perhaps you'd like to come for a walk with me," Death said. She'd figure out who he was soon. They always did.

"I'm not much good at walking these days either," the old woman said, but she sat up anyway.

Death reached out his hand to help her to her feet. She managed to get her legs over the side of the bed and then leaned on Death to help her stand.

"So many visitors today," she said.

Death's ears perked up to hear that. "Who else visited you today?" he asked.

"I had the most wonderful dream," the woman said apparently changing the subject. "I was a girl again, dancing with Laurence Metzer at the spring formal. They played all my favorite songs. Laurence gave me a flower, but he said it was for you."

She raised one arthritis-ravaged hand, clutching the stem of a poppy. Death was certain the flower hadn't been there a moment ago. She'd plucked it out of the dreaming without even knowing she was doing it. It was unspeakably red. Its perfume filled the air as soon as Death's eyes fell upon it, as though it only had a scent when observed. Morpheus always had been a showman.

Death took the flower and extended his hand to Florence. "May I have this dance?"

~

The phone was ringing when Eric let himself into his apartment. It seemed like his phone never stopped ringing. He thought about letting the answering machine get it. He was tired, and he needed a shower.

Then again, there was something about letting a phone ring unanswered that made his eye twitch. He snatched up the phone just before the answering machine picked up. It was Tempe.

"Dude, you're alive," Tempe said.

"Yeah, why wouldn't I be?"

Eric's voice sounded sharper than he'd meant it to. The emotional roller coaster at the bar had put him on edge.

"I keep calling and you keep not answering. So either you're dead or you got a new girlfriend."

"Not me, but I heard a rumor you've been chatting up my sister."

"Chatting up? Dude, she's worried about you. She thinks you're seeing shit."

Eric sighed but didn't press the issue. He didn't want to put too much thought into the whole Andy-Amelia thing.

"I saw some shit this week, let me tell you." Eric told him about the bloody homeless guy and his raving. In the retelling, it became almost funny. That was the danger of talking to Tempe. He never seemed to take anything seriously. That made it hard for you to do so either. Which is why, great friend that he was, Eric didn't feel like he could confide in Andy about what was actually going on.

"Sounds like you need some time off," Andy said.

"I just spent four months out of work."

"Strapped to a hospital bed and drinking your meals through an IV is not time off," Andy said. "I'm talking about the kind of time off where if someone straps you to a bed, there's a fifth of Jack and some fuzzy handcuffs in the mix."

"Uh, I'm not sure that would help."

"Listen, I already put in my leave chit. I'm coming home in a week. Either you're making time to hang out with me or I'm faking my own death to get a ride in your ambulance."

Eric couldn't help but chuckle at that. "I'll find the time."

"Damn right."

~

After escorting Florence to the hereafter, Death used the poppy as a passkey to step sideways into the Dreamscape. He arrived just outside the door to Morpheus' workshop. It was the perfect archetype of a barn as any human might imagine it, a huge gambrel-roofed structure painted in gleaming red with white trim. Only the location, under a violet sky in the center of the endless fields of Dream, marked it as something unusual.

Oneiroi, in their true winged-troll form, were working the fields. They picked the raw dreamstuff like cotton and gathered it into shallow baskets for delivery to Morpheus. Somehow, out of this raw material, Morpheus formed the dreams of every human as well as the occasional dog, horse, or thoughtful reptile.

Death, never a creative sort, hadn't ever put much thought into exactly how this happened, or where the seeds to grow these plants came from, or why they needed to be harvested and couldn't simply be plucked out of nothing. He continued not wondering about it as he used his scythe like a knocker to announce his presence. Morpheus had invited him, so he should be expected. The door swung open unaided. When Death stepped inside, the door shut itself.

An eon had passed since Death had last set foot inside his brother's workshop. Nothing much had changed. It was still a large, airy room with high ceilings and mounds of dreamstuff heaped in every corner. Skylights let in more light than the murky purple sky of the Dreaming should have been able to offer. Death walked across the room, careful not to disturb any of the piles. Morpheus could get acerbic about such things.

Morpheus sat in the middle of the room on a huge, round, blue cushion. His legs were crossed under him in a half-lotus position. Between his twelve fingers, he wove strands of the dreaming. As Death watched, he drew a handful of dreamstuff from the pile on his left. Then, moving his fingers in a motion that managed to seem both languid and intensely controlled, he formed complex shapes out of the raw material. The result seemed to be a kind of orange chinchilla with oversized bat wings. Death couldn't tell if it was supposed to be scary or cute. Perhaps both.

Death stopped in front of the cushion. "Thank you for seeing me Lord Morpheus," he said. "I know you must be very busy."

"Well met, Lord Death." Morpheus looked up. At least, he raised his head. His right eye, the green one, looked at Death standing over him. His left eye, the blue one, looked beyond Death at the world only he could see, the dream world.

"You also have much to do," Morpheus said. "What brings you into the Dreaming?"

The subtext was: what are you doing here and how do I get you to leave again? Death and Morpheus were brothers, and they got along as well as brothers who were also mental constructs could, but they both tended to keep to their own sphere of influence.

"A question, Morpheus, about a human."

Morpheus finished the chinchilla and tossed it over his shoulder. It flapped its wings and swooped overhead before disappearing with a pop.

"You've never taken much interest in them I understand," Morpheus said. Judgement tinged his voice. He fancied himself a great lover and protector of humans, while Death merely transported them from one place to another. Morpheus pulled more strands from the pile and began weaving something new.

"And believe me, I would much rather not take any interest in this one, but there has been a development."

It was difficult not to watch Morpheus' hands. Between the extra fingers and the way they moved, swift as flowing water but with such concentrated purpose, looking away seemed impossible. He was fashioning a house with huge teeth and a psychedelic rainbow paint job.

"What sort of development?"

"I've found a human that can see and speak to the dead as they cross from life into the hereafter," Death said.

Morpheus set the house down. It grew rapidly, until it was the size of an average human dwelling. Then it stood on hundreds of little spider legs Death hadn't known it possessed, ran across the room and disappeared.

"An interesting development, to be sure," Morpheus said. "And I imagine it's causing some puzzlement amidst the council. But I don't see the connection to me and my realm."

Death remembered what he disliked about Morpheus. First, the affectation of the many-fingered hands and two-tone eyes were a low-grade source of irritation, especially when you knew that Morpheus had as much control of his form as any personification. Back in the days of the Ancient Greeks, he'd actually been known for his ability to mimic humans.

Second, after long exposure to him, the compulsive need to create senseless and ephemeral objects could become tiresome. Although it was hard to find too much fault with that. It was more or less his job, and a personification's job was his everything. At the moment he seemed to be crafting some sort of cross-eyed gorgon.

The third thing, the thing that really got to Death, was the fact that Morpheus used words like "realm" with no regard for the fact that they made him sound like a character from one of those fairy tales humans told their children.

"There may be no connection," Death said. "But I've

been observing the human. The only time I can't see him is in the Dreaming, and I've noticed that he sleeps a good deal more than seems necessary."

Morpheus added a second gorgon to the first, creating a chain of them, each one with a different, but equally stupid expression. When he let them go, they ran directly at Death.

"A common occurrence," Morpheus said.

Annoyed, Death swung his scythe out of the empty air and cleaved the line of gorgons in two. They wailed and smashed into each other, then popped out of existence.

Morpheus ignored the carnage. "Does he have reason to be depressed lately? The conscious state of a human can have a profound effect on the quality of his sleep as well as his memory."

"It's possible that's all it is," Death said. "He was struck by lightning and nearly came under my care. Since then he's seen what human minds were not meant to see."

"The human mind is a complicated thing," Morpheus said. "It comes to me in the Dreaming and receives what I create for it, but the dreams don't go unchanged. In some ways we are co-creators. The mind is constantly prodding and pressing, changing the Dreaming into something new."

He wove a cloud of monarch butterflies which became of flock of starlings, which rained down as carp. They exploded at Death's feet, their orange and silver scales peppering his robe before disappearing in a chorus of tiny pops.

"There is only one way to be certain. I must see what he dreams." Death realized he'd framed it as a command and added, "If possible, Lord Morpheus."

For the barest flicker of a moment, both of Morpheus' eyes focused on Death. Was he angry or just thinking? It was impossible to tell. Then the blue one drifted away, back into the Dreaming.

"I believe that can be done," he said at last. "But first, a riddle: Tell me Lord Death, what is the square root of an acorn?"

"Roots are not square," Death snapped.

Morpheus coaxed a sapling from the nearest pile of dreamstuff. He caught it by a protruding leaf and drew upward. The sapling grew explosively, upward and outward. Its growth engulfed Morpheus, blocking him completely from sight. Acorns fell like clattering rain, bursting into nothingness when they hit the ground. The leaves puffed upward in a flurry, and then the trunk of the tree split and fell apart in several directions. Death stepped smartly out of the way.

The shards of tree trunk disappeared. Morpheus was still seated on his cushion as though the theatrical interlude had never happened. *Irritating*, Death thought.

"You have, dear brother, a most remarkable absence of imagination," Morpheus said, his tone flat. "It is a wonder you can exist at all."

Morpheus opened his hand and revealed an acorn in the hollow of his palm. "Let us see what the human has been dreaming shall we?"

He surged to his feet, the movement more like a wave cresting than like a man rising. Most anthropomorphic beings took on at least some of the characteristics of the creatures they impersonated. The Dream Lord didn't seem to care about such things, or even be aware of them, at least not in his own realm. Get him close to a human though, and Death knew he'd go native in a heartbeat. He wouldn't be able to help it. Maybe that's why he professed to like humans so much but still kept such a healthy distance from them.

Morpheus didn't even bother to walk, but drifted a few inches above the ground. Death snorted. *Very irritating.* He stalked after Morpheus through an open door that hadn't been there a moment earlier.

Outside, they passed by a group of Oneiroi hauling the dreamstuff in their wooden carts. Death wondered, not for the first time, why the Oneiroi were so ugly. They were only three feet tall or so, with arms as long as their bodies and grins that split their faces into hemispheres. They wore no clothes, but were covered in a patchy fuzz. What Death first took for tattered cloaks turned out to be their wings, like bat wings, folded tight against their backs. Perhaps the inspiration for the winged chinchilla.

"Come," Morpheus said.

He led Death around the side of his workshop to a glass greenhouse. It was a typical hyper-real structure. From the outside it seemed small and quaint. Moisture fogged the walls, leaving Death with an impression of lush greenery that he couldn't confirm. Morpheus opened the door and revealed a space much bigger on the inside. It was full of rainforest.

Heavy, humid air insinuated itself around them. It was a detail Death himself never would have bothered with, but Morpheus would rather be caught naked than with an illusion half executed. He went in for the full sensory experience.

Morpheus led them into the forest. Within a few steps they were surrounded by greenery. As they walked, the plants shied away from Death, but reached out to Morpheus like supplicants greeting a prophet. Their branches and leaves swayed toward him as far as they were able. He let them brush his arms and face and shoulders, but did not return their affections.

When they reached a raised flower bed, barren of growth, Morpheus stopped.

"Here we are," he said.

He pushed the seed into the earth and stood back. Almost instantly, a tree sprouted and began to grow. Death watched it with interest. The growth of this one was slower and more natural looking than the one he had just witnessed. Branches begot branches, and leaves sprouted along twigs that grew and spread. Death imagined, and he did have an imagination thank you very much, that if you took a picture of a tree every day for a hundred years, in the end the flip-book you would make would be something like this.

As the growth slowed, Morpheus cocked his head to one side. He receded toward the ground, his feet touching the hard-packed dirt floor for the first time. "Interesting," he said.

"What is interesting?" Death asked.

It just looked like a fairly ugly tree to him. Why couldn't Morpheus just keep records in books like every other personification? If he cut down this whole forest he could have a truly impressive library.

"A human life sprouts from a seed and grows on the trunk of its childhood," Morpheus said. "As the child grows into adulthood he becomes more complex, and so do his dreams. Every twig, every leaf on this tree represents a dream remembered or forgotten. But see here?"

He pointed to a void spot near the crown of the tree. It wasn't much to look at, just a wider than expected space between two branches, an expanse of smooth bark where leaves and twigs would have seemed more at home.

"Someone has meddled with the Dreaming." His voice was sharp. Morpheus' nearly human form disintegrated, leaving a winged demon in its place. Death hadn't seen him this upset since humans invented LSD and started traipsing along the edge of Dream.

"Who would do such a thing?" Morpheus demanded.

Death shrugged. It hadn't been an issue of concern for Morpheus until his "realm," as he called it, was the one at risk. Death didn't feel inclined to sympathy.

"That is what I'm trying to discover," Death said.

Morpheus spun, wings flaring, eyes flashing red. The trees cowered away from him as far as their roots would allow.

"You've spoken to the council?"

"I've brought it to their attention, yes," Death said. "But I'm handling this personally. You can't see what the human has been dreaming?"

"I cannot. There's nothing to see. Someone has cut away his dreams. And when I find the culprit I will build him a nightmare that he will not escape without your intervention. I will castrate his brothers before his eyes and cut off the hands of his sisters. I'll burn his home with his children in it and set him just too far away to rescue them, but close enough to hear them scream. I'll—"

Death interrupted him. "We've concluded it must be a deity."

Morpheus settled a little. The red faded from his eyes, leaving green and blue behind. "You thought it was me."

Death did him the courtesy of not lying. "I thought perhaps you might be involved. I've been watching the human. He only escapes my notice in the Dreaming."

"The Dreaming is mine and I would not harm it," Morpheus said. "I would gain nothing by it." Mostly calmed, for the moment, he settled back into his nearly human shape.

"Of course," Death said. "Though I had hoped you would have an answer for me. I'd like to put this matter to rest quickly."

"Is it possible he did it on his own?" Morpheus said. "Humans are creative creatures. Perhaps they've finally learned to see what's really there."

"I presented the same idea to the council. They thought it unlikely. After watching this human I tend to agree. He seems baffled by his ability."

Morpheus cast one last annoyed look at the tree, and then turned his back on it. "He must know something."

"We keep records of the lives of every human as they live them," Death said. "I've been reading his life, his very thoughts. He doesn't seem to know anything. He thinks he's going insane."

"Is it possible he's deceiving you in some way? As I've said, the human mind is a complicated thing. You should bring him before the council and allow them to question him."

"An extreme response," Death said. "And what would it accomplish?"

"Humans have layers. So much of what they think and do is influenced by subconscious thoughts, thoughts they don't even know they have. They don't understand their dreams. They don't understand their feelings. If you bring the human before the council, their questioning may uncover answers he doesn't know he has," Morpheus said.

"Some members of the council suggested just killing him," Death said.

"That would certainly solve the problem," Morpheus said. "At least in the short term."

"I'd like to avoid that outcome if possible," Death said.

"Really? How interesting." Morpheus cocked one

eyebrow. "I would appreciate it if you'd keep me informed, Lord Death."

"And you as well, Lord Morpheus."

They bowed to each other and Death stepped sideways out of the dreaming. He didn't know exactly what his next move would be, but it was past time the problem of Eric Silva was put to rest.

CHAPTER ELEVEN

The Final Straw

A kid, the call was for a goddamn kid. Ryan Forrest, age eight. Calls with kids were rarely good and an accident like this...there was no good outcome when a kid calls to say he shot his little brother. In the bus on the way over, Eric tried to focus on keeping him stomach down. His mouth tasted like acid. He found himself trying to remember when he'd last brushed his teeth. Again. It was a dumb thing to worry about right then, but better than picturing a kid bleeding out.

An image of Timmy flashed through his mind. Eric pushed it away. He couldn't think about Timmy, couldn't think about his face upside down and somehow still pale.

By the time the bus turned into a driveway, Eric was almost relieved. He could stop worrying about what might happen and just handle the job in front of him. Almost before Susan put the bus in park, Eric was out the door and grabbing gear.

The front door of the house gaped like an open mouth. Eric ran inside. No frantic parents, no bleeding kids. He shouted, but no one answered. The back door was wide open too. Eric sprinted to the backyard.

On the way through, he glimpsed a living room with toys strewn across the floor, a kitchen with plastic lunch dishes still on the table, and then he was under a gray sky. A little boy was in the grass, bleeding. His brother stood next to him, sobbing.

Eric dropped to his knees, talking to both kids at the same time, not even sure what he was saying. Blood everywhere, on the grass, on his hands, on the kid. The little, little kid. The bullet had ripped through him and his blood was abandoning ship. Every cell for itself.

Eric was doing what he could but it wasn't enough. He saw the boy's ghost next to him. It was standing on the other side of the body, looking down at its own face. Confused. Terrified.

Eric looked up at the ghost. Met his eyes. The ghost saw Eric and, in that moment, Eric could almost read its thoughts. Here was an adult, an adult in a uniform. That means he's here to help. That's what parents tell kids. "If you're ever in trouble and we're not around, find an adult in a uniform." The trust was instant and complete. Eric had to help this kid. There had to be something he could do.

Suddenly, he knew exactly what that was, as though it came to him in a dream that he'd only just remembered.

~

Death arrived in the backyard, his mind still full of what he'd learned from Morpheus. Eric was already there and Death watched as he worked to save little Ryan Forrest. He wouldn't succeed. Death could see that the boy had already lost too much blood, but that didn't stop Eric from trying. Death stayed well out of the way, not wanting to get between the two of them just yet. He wanted to see if they would speak to each other.

Suddenly, Eric stopped working. He stared at Ryan's soul with a dreamy expression on his face. If Death had realized quickly enough what was happening, he might have been able to stop it, but he wasn't good at predicting human behavior.

Reaching over Ryan's body, Eric held out his hand to the ghost.

"Take my hand," Eric said.

Death lunged for them, arm outstretched ready to pull Ryan away. But it was too late. Eric's hand closed around the soul's. He had cheated Death.

The world went dark around Death. A cold wind gusted through the yard, setting the trees quivering. He wanted to strike Eric down then and there.

Death did not kill. It was one of his most basic rules, a way of staying inside the lines, of checking his own power. Yet he envisioned tearing this audacious fool's soul from its body and dragging it kicking and screaming into the void.

He had just enough self-control to step out of the backyard and into the void before he did something that no one would survive to regret.

~

As Eric's hand closed over the ghost's, a cold wind lanced through the yard. The trees shivered. Even the grass trembled. The ghost felt it too. Eric saw his eyes widen.

There was a shadow behind Ryan. A shadow Eric hadn't noticed before, tall and dark and menacing. But the ghost was already squeezing Eric's fingers. Eric's hand closed. He felt a tingling sensation across his palm, like pins and needles.

"Stay here," Eric said. "I'm going to help you."

Susan stepped through the ghost, without noticing him at all. "What the hell are you doing, Eric? Get your head in the game."

Susan dropped to her knees, working on the kid with the gunshot wound. Behind her, in the doorway of the house, another little boy was bawling like he'd lost his best friend. He probably had, too. Ryan was fading fast.

Eric refocused and did what he could to help. It wasn't enough. And yet, somehow it was. The kid hung in there, comatose but breathing for no reason that Eric could see. He'd lost so much blood.

Eric loaded him into the bus. While he'd been focused on the kid, the police had arrived, along with a tired-looking DHS lady who bundled the brother into the car. Eric hoped they weren't going to arrest him, or charge him, or whatever. It was an accident. Eric was sure it was.

Even though Ryan was inexplicably stable, Eric didn't feel like he could relax. The ghost was still with him, standing next to his body, just watching slack-jawed and blank-eyed. Eric wondered what that meant. All the other ghosts he'd seen had been more animated. This one almost seemed like it was in shock. Could a ghost be in shock? How would you treat it? You couldn't exactly throw a blanket over it.

Eric swallowed back a giggle at the image that had just risen in his mind. This wasn't funny. It was so far from funny that it was in a different time zone, so the impulse to giggle meant Eric himself might be experiencing some level of shock. He took a few slow deep breaths.

~

For the rest of Eric's workday, the ghost followed him, hovering just behind Eric's left shoulder and about an inch off the ground. He stood at Eric's elbow while Eric checked a car accident victim. He stared blankly while Eric explained to a little girl why you can't call nine-one-one just because your mom won't let you have a second piece of cake, even if it was your birthday. Eric had to keep reminding himself not to look at the ghost too much, in case Susan noticed and misinterpreted. She'd kept a sharp eye on him since the incident in the backyard.

When they finally pulled into the station house for the last time, Susan grabbed Eric's arm to stop him from getting out of the bus. Eric froze. *Here it comes.*

"What the hell happened back there, Eric?"

She never called him Eric except when she was really pissed off. Usually he was just Silva or "hey, you." He wished he could explain, but "I was trying to comfort a ghost" probably wouldn't win him sanity points.

"Back when?" Eric asked, as though he didn't know.

"When you almost let a kid die while you stared at nothing. Do I need to take this to the chief?"

"No, no. I'm fine," Eric said. "I just thought I saw something. That's all."

She narrowed her eyes at him, as though by staring hard enough she could read the secrets locked up in his head. "No more screwing around, Silva. Are you okay or aren't you?"

"I am," Eric said, his eyes practically watering with the effort of not glancing toward the ghost as he lied.

When Susan left, Eric climbed out of the bus and went straight out to his car. The ghost followed behind him, drifting effortlessly through walls and doors and, once, a lamppost. When Eric climbed into the El Camino, the ghost stayed floating just outside the door. Would he leave it behind when he started driving? He pulled away slowly, watching in the side mirror. The ghost kept pace with him, floating just above the ground.

A horn sounded. Eric slammed on his brakes just before he rolled out of the parking lot and into traffic. *Eyes on the road.* He'd never forgive himself if he crashed his dad's El Camino. As he drove to the hospital, Ryan's soul kept pace next to the car. Once he reached thirty miles an hour between streetlights, but it didn't matter to the ghost. Eric wondered what would happen if he hit the highway.

Nobody seemed to notice anything strange when Eric walked into the ER followed by the soul of an eight-year-old boy. The nurses all went about their normal business. The patients slumped in vinyl chairs. Family members circled from the bathrooms to the drink machines to the chairs and back again. Stepping into all this, Eric in his uniform was nothing remarkable, mostly because nobody else could see the ghost trailing along behind.

The triage nurses all knew him. They knew all the first responders, if not by name, then by sight. Eric stopped the first nurse he saw. A redhead with glasses, her name was Jane, he thought. Or Janet.

"A kid came in with a gunshot wound earlier today. Do you know where he is?"

She remembered him, of course she did. It wasn't often they got an eight-year-old with a gunshot wound. Thank goodness.

"You brought him in? They moved him up to ICU about two hours ago."

"What's his status?"

"Apparently stable." She dropped her voice and angled her body to shield them from the nearby waiting area. "Nobody seems to know why. He should be dead with all the blood he's lost. What the hell did you do?"

"I have no idea," Eric said, honest for once.

Eric took the staff elevator up to the ICU. At the door marked "ICU, no unauthorized entry beyond this point" Eric paused. Technically, unauthorized means anyone who's not a doctor or an on-duty nurse. Visitors were supposed to be next of kin, and they had to sign in and out during specific visiting hours. He shouldn't really go in there without good reason. He looked back at the ghost. That felt like a damn good reason.

~

Ryan was in a room with six other beds. Two had people in them. The others were empty. Apparently it had been a slow day for tragedy. Walking up to the bed, Eric couldn't help but notice that the kid looked like a corpse. His dark hair was plastered to his bloodless skin. At his lips and fingertips, Eric noticed a tinge of blue. Not enough blood flow to oxygenate his extremities. Only the monitors and machines indicated that he was still alive.

Eric was standing there, looking down at the boy who should be dead, when something came through the wall. It didn't smash through, didn't break the wall or make a sound, it just sort of drifted in like a bee through an open window. Eric only spotted it out of the corner of his eye, a shimmer of movement. He turned to look. It was, it had to be, a ghost, but it was nothing like the ones he'd seen so far.

It didn't walk along the ground, but drifted three feet above the linoleum floor. Although, drifted wasn't the right word for something that seemed to be pulled forward by an invisible string in its chest.

Every other ghost had been slightly transparent, but still recognizably human. This thing looked like a demon that had decided to dress up as a human for Halloween. Eric stared at it, taking in every detail with the hyper-awareness of deep terror.

Its limbs flapped like gruesome pennants in an invisible wind. Each one had too many joints, all bending in the wrong direction. The long dark hair and the shredded remains of its clothes were plastered to its body or streaming away behind it.

That wasn't the worst part though. The worst part was its face. The jaw wasn't properly attached to the skull. It gaped open, impossibly wide, reminding Eric of a snake that had unhinged its jaw to eat something ten times the size of its head. The rest of the face was no better. The nose was a smashed blob, the skin along the cheekbones eroded away and shredded down to the chin.

Whatever had destroyed the face had done a number on the chest as well. Eric could see the sternum bone that should have been covered in skin, and the ribs curved against it. Enough flesh remained to tell Eric that this thing had once been a woman, or at least, was wearing a woman's skin. That thought was enough to trigger panic.

Eric reeled away. He stumbled against a heart monitor. It rocked and threatened to topple. Eric hardly noticed, he was scrambling toward the door. All he had to do was get around this bed and he'd be out in the hall, away from that thing. His heart pounded against the cage of his ribs like it was trying to escape without him. His breath was shallow and gasping. Panic attack, his brain diagnosed unhelpfully.

Eric knew better than to look back. The important thing now was to run, escape, but he had to know if that thing was closer to him. Had to know if he would feel its hands at his neck in the next moment. He glanced over his shoulder.

The apparition was paying Eric no attention. It had drifted close to Ryan's ghost, which was still in the spot next to the bed that held his body. Ryan hadn't even noticed the thing. All of his attention was on his body in the bed. But the specter was very clearly looking at the ghost of the boy. Its arms reached forward in slow motion, its wild joints aligning for one purpose, to snatch the child and...do what? Eric couldn't imagine, didn't want to imagine, but he knew it wouldn't be good.

He cursed to himself. Then, with every fiber of his being screaming at him not to do this, he went to rescue the ghost. The specter reached. Eric lunged. His arms closed around the ghost. Again that tingling sensation, this time shivering through his heart.

Bone fingertips brushed Eric's shoulder just before something thudded against his back, sending him crashing against the hospital bed and onto the floor with the ghost boy locked in his arms.

Eric tried to roll upright, but the bed was in his way. He squirmed around, determined to face the thing before it sucked the flesh from his bones.

Someone else stood between him and the beast. A tall, dark shadow. The shadow seemed to expand outward. Then there was a flash, and a feeling like all of the air had been sucked out of the room taking his attacker with it. In the sudden emptiness the shadow turned, grabbed Eric by the throat, and lifted.

CHAPTER TWELVE

In the Grip of Death

Death looked at Eric suspended in his hand and cursed in a language older than the gardens of Babylon. He knew that there was no point in being angry at the human. It was like being angry at a child. You could only get so mad that he'd taken the goldfish out of his bowl to play land explorer. The fish died, of course, but the child was hardly at fault. He didn't understand the consequences of his actions.

Death released his hold, allowing Eric to stand under his own power. Really, Death was most angry at himself. He had let this go on too long. He'd underestimated the scope of the problem. Now, due to his carelessness, this child's soul could have been forfeit. It was an untenable situation. Yet here Death was.

In extenuating circumstances, Death could take temporary custody of a human soul, as long as it was returned in short order. He used that ability sparingly. It was the kind of thing that could turn you into a careless Olympian, too much power with nothing to check it. So he kept to the rules, mostly, unless it was really very important. Like now for instance. Death swung his scythe.

He looked from Eric's body, now crumpled on the floor, to Eric's soul standing in front of him. Death was no great judge of human expressions, but Eric seemed somewhat unhappy at the moment.

"What the hell?" Eric sputtered. "What the hell?"

Death glowered at him and he fell silent, eyes wide.

"Eric Dean Silva, do you have any idea what you have done?"

"No!" Eric nearly shouted. "What happened to that thing?"

Death tried not to show his frustration. Humans had no perspective. They were always worried about the wrong things. Eric was still fearing a threat that had been annihilated, even though Death was staring him in the face at this very moment.

"The soul is gone," Death said. "Sent back into non-being."

Eric looked around wildly, spotted the soul of the boy sitting on the floor, and grabbed for it. He hugged the child against his side. The child submitted to this treatment without complaint. At the same time, Eric finally managed to spot his own body splayed across the floor next to the bed.

"Shit. Am I dead?"

"We shall see," Death said.

"Did you kill me?" Eric said. "Wait. I remember. I saw you before, when I fell out of the tree the day I was struck by lightning. How did I forget you?"

Death pulled the scythe out of the air and stood holding it, so that when Eric looked at him again, there was no doubting who he was.

"And who am I, Eric?"

Eric licked his lips, a nervous habit that was absolutely useless in his current form. "You're Death."

"And do you know what my job is, human? Do you know the entire purpose of my existence?"

Death was spreading it on thick and he knew it, but he needed the human to understand, to really and truly understand, what he had done. Death stalked forward until Eric's soul was pinned between the scythe and the monitoring equipment.

Eric was shaking his head. The terror in his eyes was right and proper.

"I am the guardian of human souls, the first and last friend of every living creature. My job is to guide souls safely from the here to the hereafter. Do you understand, human?" He let the word 'human' drip with contempt that he didn't really feel.

Eric's eyes were wide.

Death continued, "That is difficult to do when some mortal idiot is hijacking souls and trapping them between worlds."

Eric backed away. "I didn't…I mean that isn't…I…"

"Enough," Death bellowed.

Eric froze.

"What was your plan?" Death asked, knowing full well that the human hadn't had one. "When you bound this soul to yourself, did you intend to bait every specter on earth with the soul you've captured? Because that's exactly what you've done."

"There are more of those things?" Eric hugged the soul tighter. His eyes darted around the room as though he expected specters to pour through the walls at any moment. Of course, that was exactly what would happen if Death didn't get this situation under control.

"Thousands."

"What are they?"

"We will not discuss this here." Death stabbed his chin in the direction of Ryan's soul. "Take his hand." When Eric hesitated, Death shouted, "Do as you are told!"

Eric snatched Ryan's hand. Ryan didn't react.

"Do not let go."

Death grabbed Eric and jerked him sideways into the void.

Eric's knees collapsed under him, drawing both him and Ryan toward the ground. They didn't actually hit it because they were standing ten feet above on empty air. The specters couldn't reach them here. Death let go. Eric cried out.

"Quiet," Death said.

Winds howled around them, like starving dogs on a famine-driven hunt. They tore at Eric's clothes and hair and batted the soul like a balloon.

Death was gratified to see that Eric was paying close attention. He clutched Ryan's hand a little tighter. Death floated beside them, unmolested. The winds knew better than to taunt him when he was in his current mood.

Death swept the scythe before him, bisecting the clouds. The mist parted to reveal an empty blackened landscape that stretched in all directions. The ground was shattered, a desiccated lake bed. But there was no broken earth between the shards, just darkness, black and deep. It was the darkness children feared when they went to sleep at night. The darkness that woke adults in a cold sweat at two in the morning with no memory of what had brought them there. This was the proverbial darkness that tried men's souls.

"Where are we?"

"We are in the void between life and the afterlife."

Eric closed his eyes. "This is too strange," he said under his breath so Death knew he wasn't really supposed to hear it.

Death watched as Eric took a deep breath. It seemed to calm him, although he still didn't open his eyes.

"I'm not dead?"

"Not yet."

"Okay. Tell me about the specters."

If Death was capable of pity, he felt it for the specters. "They are lost souls."

"What did they do?"

"Don't misunderstand; this is not a punishment. This is a consequence. It's what happens when the order of things is disturbed. The woman you saw chose to walk alone. She spurned my help and refused my counsel. When you saw her, there was so little humanity left that I had no choice but to destroy her."

"Why was she there?"

Death noticed with approval that Eric had opened his eyes.

"You brought her there."

"Me? I didn't know that she existed."

"You brought her there by binding Ryan's soul to you. Specters are drawn to transitioning souls. When they find an unguarded soul they consume it, trying to make it a part of themselves. Trying to feel less alone."

There were tears in Eric's eyes, but he was standing up straight on the empty air. "I won't let them take him."

"You won't let them? Do you have the power to dispel lost souls? Do you have a weapon capable of reaping them?"

"No." Eric clenched his jaw. "But you do. You can keep him safe."

"I cannot."

Eric's face flushed with anger. "This isn't his fault."

"No. It's yours. You've bound the soul to you. Only you can protect it now. Only you can guide him to the afterlife."

"I don't know how! I don't know how any of this happened. I just wanted to save him. I thought I could save him if I just had a little more time."

"You humans and your obsession with time. Why

can't you see that the time spent worrying would be better used actually living those brief moments you call lives?" Death pounded his scythe against the air, which reverberated. Far below, the dust rippled. Death calmed himself.

"Will you help me solve a riddle, human?"

"I just wanted to save him." Eric looked up at the soul, blank-eyed and insensible. "What's wrong with him?"

Death went on, relentless. "The riddle is this: How does a weak, ignorant, average human gain the power of Death?"

Eric rose to his feet. "I don't know."

"You must know, because you did it. What happened to you the day the lightning struck?"

"I don't know." Eric shook his head. "I fell, and I died. When they brought me back I saw the ghosts, and then, when I saw this kid, bleeding to death in his own backyard, I thought, I can fix this."

Death shook his head. Useless. The human was useless. He didn't even have the wherewithal to save himself. "You must stand before the council," Death said.

"A trial?" Eric asked.

"An inquiry," Death said. "Will you help us solve this riddle, Eric?"

"You killed me," Eric said. "What choice do I have?"

"There is always a choice," Death said. "And you aren't dead, yet. I generally prefer not to kill humans. I merely collect them after they die on their own. For now, I've taken you out of your body, but it is most likely temporary."

"What happens when they find me dead on the floor?"

"Are you not listening? You are not dead. The other humans will see it as a coma. Your body will be cared for. Like a…like a house when the family goes on vacation."

"Okay," Eric said. "If it will help the kid, Ryan, I'll go."

Death smiled, a rare occurrence. Most humans who had seen it wished they hadn't. Eric would have been no exception, except that he was staring at the soul.

"Take my hand," Death said.

Eric reached out with his free hand and took the hand of Death.

CHAPTER THIRTEEN

Life Without Death

Death stepped them sideways into Cecil's chamber. Cecil was sitting at his desk. He was always sitting at his desk with the open book of the schedule before him. Death briefly wondered who besides himself ever came to visit the council. Was Cecil here for his benefit alone? If so, could they not have chosen someone a little less...Cecil-like?

"Master Death, once again you are not," Cecil hit the "t" like a cymbal, "on the schedule."

Cecil peered over his glasses. "And this time you've brought...guests. How nice. Shall I announce you, or would you prefer to barge right in?"

Death was annoyed. But now was not the time to show Cecil his place. There were deeper graves to dig.

He did allow himself to revert to his primal voice, a voice older than human memory. "You may announce us. This is the human the council has been so interested in.

Go and prepare them for our coming."

The voice had its intended effect. Cecil showed no inclination to argue. He hurried over to the door, opened it the barest fraction, and slipped inside.

When they were alone, Death turned to Eric. "Do as I say if you want any chance of returning to the land of the living."

"I thought you said you didn't kill humans."

"I said I don't usually kill humans. Some of them," he jerked his head toward the closed door, "have been known to do so out of mere boredom."

"Who are they?" Eric asked.

"They are the pantheon. Together they keep the balance of the worlds, but they are made by men. Remember that. They will try to make you feel like you need to answer to them, and of course you do. But in the end, it is you who created them. You see?"

"Not really."

Death glanced at the door. Cecil would be back any moment. He had no time to explain the intricacies of interdimensional politics to a human.

"Imagine yourself wearing a suit," Death said.

"Why?"

"Do you want to ask questions or do you want to live?"

Eric closed his eyes. His uniform pants became an ill-fitting grey suit. That would have to do. He looked down at himself in surprise. "How did I do that?"

Death ignored him. He was already in his humanoid

form, an average-sized male with a shaved head and no eyebrows. He'd never seen the point in hair. He shrugged away his coat to reveal a sharp black suit. It looked tailor made in a very expensive part of a very expensive town. His scythe shrunk down to become a lapel pin that glittered against the fine fabric.

The only thing that didn't change was his eyes, they were still empty holes into eternity. He turned them on Eric. Eric flinched and leaned toward the soul in a reflexive show of protection.

Death noticed this with approval. If he understood nothing else, at least Eric understood his responsibilities. What else could Death tell him that might protect him?

"Speak only when spoken to. Answer honestly. Some will know if you tell a lie, and they will not take kindly to it."

"Who are these people?"

"I told you, gods."

A hollow click announced the opening of the door. Cecil stepped through and beckoned them forward. "The council will see you now."

Death gestured for Eric to go first. The human's steps were slow and hesitant. He clutched the soul's hand tightly. Death followed along behind them, ready to catch Eric if he panicked and ran at the sight of the council.

It was dark inside the chamber, and this time it really was a chamber. Rough stone walls enclosed a wide, low room with a banquet table set sideways across it. The council sat like judges along the opposite side of the table.

In an attempt to spare Eric a view of their true features, the gods were each hooded. It was a prudent precaution. While the tableau certainly inspired fear, with its allusions to tribunals and inquisitions, there was nothing there to break a human mind.

The faint light came from flickering torches set in sconces on the walls. Hermes' podium had been set up beneath one of them. With the light behind him, he was nothing but a black silhouette in the deeper darkness.

The only truly bright spot in the room was a perfect circle of light in front of the council table. It seemed too bright for the scene and came from no discernable source. Death maneuvered Eric into the circle. The soul went with him, standing half in shadow, half in light.

Death noticed the heads of the council members tilting toward each other, whispering and listening. He couldn't hear their words, but he guessed what they were saying. Eric had been expected. The soul, however, was a surprise. They surely wondered what it meant.

Before anyone could start asking questions, Death laid his hand on Eric's shoulder. Then he spoke words in a formula no living human had ever heard. Their very utterance was like a spell, binding reality into new shapes. It evoked a time and god-honored tradition that had served for thousands of generations.

"This is Eric Silva, human born. I am his guide and guardian on this path. He is under my care and none shall harm him."

Osiris spoke his half of the spell. "So we have seen

and recognized," he said.

Death dropped his hand, leaving Eric standing in the circle of light. Ryan's soul had drifted so close that his shoulder nearly brushed Eric's arm.

"Do you know why you are here, Eric Silva, human born?" Osiris asked.

Eric stood at attention, back stiff, free arm straight, eyes staring at a point a few feet in front of him. "I'm here to help a child, sir."

Osiris cocked his head, in an unmistakably bird-like movement. "Is this the child in question?" He pointed his flail at Ryan's soul. Ryan was standing with its head tilted back, staring up into the light. Eric pulled at him protectively, but Ryan, as always, ignored him.

"Yes, sir," Eric said.

"I believe an explanation is in order, Lord Death."

If he had been capable of such a base emotion, Death would have been nervous. This needed careful handling, and even so, it might be the last nail in the coffin.

"The problem has…evolved somewhat since last we spoke," Death said. "This human managed to bind another human soul to himself."

The council erupted, an instant argument, all of them talking at once, arms waving. Xolotl's hood slipped and he jerked it back into place, but not quite quickly enough. Eric's face flinched. He had seen the dog face and feathers, but he remained standing at attention.

"And you allowed this to happen, Death?" Osiris said over the hubbub.

Death kept his voice calm, measured. Nothing would be gained from shouting. A cool head, that's what was called for here. "I allowed nothing. It happened. That is all."

Osiris laid his long fingers atop the table. "Perhaps we should not have expected you to handle this on your own."

Death stalked forward. "Perhaps you should not have. Perhaps you should have given it more than a passing thought. Perhaps," and the sarcasm dripped so heavily from the word it was amazing the floor did not dissolve under it, "you should take some tiny interest in where the humans come from. When was the last time any of you even set foot in the living world? Do you have any idea of the things that humanity has accomplished in just a few generations?"

The stillness among the cowled heads told him they were listening, which was just as well because he didn't intend to stop.

"Have you seen Van Gogh's paintings? Have you walked through New York City? Do you know what a computer is? The world down there is changing, and you are relics of the past. The average human has forgotten most of your names." So much for a cool head.

"Tell me, Osiris," Death added, "who tends your temple now?"

It was a stupid, reckless addition. He should have stopped while he was ahead. Now Osiris had no choice but to retaliate in kind.

"How dare you condescend to us?" Osiris snapped. "You walk among them, yes, but they don't know you. They run from you. They've built whole professions in hopes of escaping you."

"They fear me." The scythe jumped into Death's hands and sliced the air a millimeter from Eric's face. Eric stumbled backwards and grabbed for the soul, shielding it with his body.

"Parlor tricks," someone muttered.

Death stopped. The whisperer was right of course. That was a parlor trick, an illusion calculated to draw fear. There had been a time when he had ravaged the known world, taking one human for every one left behind. Villages fell. Death was there when Rome burned. He was there when Vesuvius vomited fire into the sky. He was there when the floods destroyed every living creature. Should he allow himself to lose his temper at mere bureaucrats?

The scythe disappeared. The form of the man in the black suit sharpened. He adjusted his cuffs. Eric rose, slowly, from his crouch.

Death waved his arm, attempting to erase the previous exchange. "I believe we may be getting off topic," he said. "This was about the human."

The council also seemed willing to move forward. They were not Olympians after all. They sat still and quiet as chess pieces. Finally, Osiris spoke. "Yes, you've brought him here. Now what do you expect us to do with him?"

"I don't expect you to do anything. You asked me to observe the human. I have done so. His ability is a problem, as you can see." Here he paused and nodded at the soul. "I, of course, would like this situation handled expediently so that I can return to my regular duties."

"I still think we should kill him," Xolotl said.

"And I still think you have the reasoning skills of a concussed troll," Freyja answered. Both lines were delivered calmly. If not for their familiar voices, Death would not have known which member of the council had spoken.

"It seems to me, Lord Death, that it is you who needs to deal with this problem," Osiris said. "We sent you to monitor the situation. It is your responsibility."

"Monitoring is no longer required," Death said. "I've brought the human here to be dealt with. As I told you before, I have my own duties to attend to. Even as we speak, more than a hundred humans are exhaling for the last time."

"I'm well aware of your duties, Lord Death. That's why I intend to lighten your burden." Osiris paused. "I move to suspend Death until this situation is resolved. Is there any discussion?"

"You can't do that," Death nearly shouted.

"In fact we can," Osiris answered. "Hermes, if you would read the bylaws."

The strained silence that followed held only the sound of pages turning. "And in cases when the threat to law and cosmic order is deemed extraordinary, this council shall be imbued with all power and authority as the chair deems necessary to bring about a suitable conclusion resulting in the restoration of all said cosmic order," Hermes read.

"Souls will be lost." Even as he protested, he cursed himself for ever agreeing to entrust his power to the council. It had seemed like the prudent choice at the time, but now…

Osiris waved away his concern. "They will simply stay in their bodies until such time as you can collect them."

"Death-san," Izanami said. "We do not wish to start a war. Let us not behave like Olympians, quarrelling over power. Instead we should strive forward with one mind."

Death weighed his options. He'd been telling himself for generations that he would teach the council a lesson. These jumped-up bureaucrats had no idea who they were dealing with. In the old days, when Death alone ruled over the passing of human souls, he'd managed just fine. And yes, humans died, and yes, souls were lost, but death was his and his alone.

If only the humans wouldn't multiply so quickly. If only they'd stop warring with each other. Maybe he could have continued to shepherd them. But there were so many now. So many souls crying out for guidance from there to the hereafter. He couldn't take them all, not without someone to manage the day-to-day administrative tasks. And so the council had come into being.

Even he had thought it was a good idea at the time. It would protect those souls who might otherwise pass through the cracks. It would keep him organized and hold him accountable. Even Death could make mistakes, though he was loath to admit it. He'd made one here. He wasn't sure exactly what it was, but he must have made one. What other explanation was there for this situation?

"Very well," he said.

"All in favor of suspending death until the crisis is resolved," Osiris said.

A chorus of ayes answered him. He began to turn away, but Osiris stopped him. "Your scythe, Lord Death."

If he'd had blood it would have boiled. As it was, he ground his teeth so hard that humanity shivered, both the living and the dead. Hermes stepped forward, hand outstretched to take the scythe from Death.

"No," Death said. "I will allow you your illusion of power, but I won't give mine away."

"Then what guarantee do we have that you will address the problem at hand?" Yama asked.

"My word, and that must be enough," Death said. "None of us wants to start a war," he repeated. True as it was, one look at Death said that he would happily finish one if someone else dropped the first bomb. His skin thinned until his skull showed through. With scythe in hand, he stood perfectly prepared to reap the entire council then and there.

"Of course, Lord Death," Osiris said, ever the balanced chairman.

Death turned and left the room. Eric and the soul trailed behind him. Cecil must have been listening at the door because he was nowhere to be seen when they stepped into his chamber.

As soon as the door whispered shut behind them, Death turned on Eric. "What are you keeping from me?"

Eric shrank from Death but still managed to step in front of Ryan, shielding him.

"Nothing. I don't know anything. I don't know why this happened. I don't know why he's still here. I don't know how to stop it."

Death paced. "Do you have any idea what you've done?"

Eric found a little courage. "Not really, but it sounds like nobody is going to die anymore. I realize that's not great for your business, but speaking as a human, it seems like a damn good idea."

Death stopped and suddenly his face was inches from Eric's. He was no longer a slightly disconcerting business man in a black suit. Now he was Death personified, tall and hooded, his empty eyes staring into Eric's deeply enough to read his soul.

"Do you think so, human? You mortals fear Death. You hate me. You try desperately to escape me. But when the time comes you will cry out for my help. You will beg for my ministrations," Death said. "When your flesh is torn and broken in a car crash, when your mind has come unmoored and you've forgotten not just the names of your children but how to button your pants, when your lungs fill with blood and every breath is agony, when decades of illness have worn you down to skin and sinew, you and all your brothers and sisters will beg for me.

"And what will happen when I do not come? Or worse, when someone else does? What if some ignorant human binds your soul to them and doesn't know how to break it free?"

Eric put his arm around Ryan. "I didn't mean to hurt him. I don't even know what's happening."

Death sighed and let himself recede to a more respectable form. "Neither do I. Let us remedy that situation. Shall we?"

~

Amelia was sitting at her desk, working through a math problem, when the phone rang six inches from her ear. She almost fell out of her chair in her scramble to pick up the damn thing and stop the noise.

"Amelia, it's your mother."

"Hi, Mom. I'm just heading out to class." She still had about ten minutes before she had to leave, but she also knew her mother was incapable of having a phone conversation that lasted less than fifteen. It was always best to have an exit strategy prepared.

"It's your brother."

Amelia's heart tightened in her chest. Ever since Eric's accident, she'd had nightmares that started just like this.

"What happened to Eric?"

"They found him on the floor of the ICU. He's in a coma."

Amelia slumped back in her chair. "I don't understand. What happened? What was he doing there?"

"They don't know. They're running tests now."

"I'm coming."

"No, stay at school. You have classes. I just wanted you to know what was happening."

Amelia's laugh sounded harsh even to her own ears. "Are you kidding? No. I'm heading to the train station now."

She hung up before her mother could catch breath to argue. Then she felt bad about it. Her mother was probably as upset as Amelia was, and Amelia hadn't even said I love you before she hung up. Oh well, she'd be there soon.

She snatched up the phone again and dialed Andy's number from memory.

It rang and rang, but nobody answered. Tears welled in her eyes, but she refused to let herself cry. She looked at the clock. He wasn't answering because he was already on his way to the airport.

Just in case, she tore a piece of paper out of the back of her notebook and scrawled a message to Tammy. "Brother sick again. If Andy calls, tell him I went home. —A"

When Amelia got back, Tammy was certain to give her the third degree about who Andy was and why he kept calling. That girl was a walking gossip mill, but at the moment Amelia didn't give a shit. She needed to be in the hospital room with Eric. Everything would make sense if she could just see him with her own eyes.

She stuffed some books into her backpack and headed for the door. At the last minute, she turned back to grab some extra socks and underwear. She didn't know how long she'd be gone, and she wasn't coming back until this whole mess was sorted out, however long that took.

CHAPTER FOURTEEN

A Dying Mind

Eric, Death, and the soul of Ryan stood in a field of orange poppies. The sky was blue and high above them. No clouds obscured the oversized disk of the sun. It shone brightly, but without heat.

"Where are we?" Eric asked.

"We're in a dream," Death said. "Now be silent."

That told him pretty much nothing. Eric looked around for clues and noticed the shadow stretching from horizon to horizon. It raced toward them, rolling over the field like an exhaled breath. Everywhere it touched, the poppies withered. It flushed out a flock of birds, which burst upward cawing and crying. They swooped toward Eric, who threw his arm around Ryan as though that would somehow protect him.

Looking to Death for rescue or explanation, Eric saw him raise his scythe to his shoulder, like a batter at the plate. He stared intently at the flock of birds and then, with a sudden sweep, knocked one from the sky.

The bird dropped at their feet, stunned, but still living. Death had struck it with the pole of the scythe, not the blade.

"What are you doing?" Eric shouted.

Death grabbed the stricken bird by the neck. Blue and purple flashed in the blackness of its feathers as it flapped its wings in protest. Death shouted in its face, "Fetch Morpheus. Now."

He opened his hand and the bird lost its battle with gravity. It plopped to the ground like a feathered sack of rotten potatoes. A hop and a flurry of wings sent it into the sky. It disappeared into the glare of the sun.

Behind them, the darkness was still advancing.

"Should we be running?" Eric asked. "I feel like we should be running."

"I do not run," Death said. He stood against the oncoming dark, unperturbed.

Eric felt terror rising. It made his knees weak and his head swim. He thought he might pass out. Only the soul's fingers clutching at his side kept him upright.

"Whose dream is this?" Eric asked.

Death turned toward him. "It's yours."

Darkness rolled over them. Eric collapsed to the ground, shielding the soul with his body, but there was no need. The darkness, great and terrible as it had seemed from a distance, fell like night. And like the night, it didn't hurt, it didn't snuff them out. It was merely a change of scenery. Eric looked up. Death stood next to him, silhouetted against the stars.

The terror had been so real a moment ago. Eric had been completely certain that if the sweeping dark engulfed them, there would be nothing left. And now here they were, safe. It wasn't even all that dark. He could easily see the soul, and Death, and even the blades of grass nearest his face. It was mostly color that had faded. The grass seemed bluer, the poppies inky. Death's bald head reflected light like the moon. But there was no moon, just billions of stars.

Feeling idiotic, Eric sat up. Ryan just lay where he had landed, like a toy knocked over and forgotten.

"What was that?"

"You are dying. Therefore, my world and the dream world have brushed against each other in your mind."

"That doesn't really help," Eric said. "And I thought you said I wasn't going to die."

Death shrugged. His attention was on the sky. "Everyone is going to die, sooner or later. Today, you're a little closer than most."

Eric shook his head. That didn't feel like an answer either. He checked on Ryan, who had managed to sit up with his legs splayed out and his head tilted back to look at the sky. Eric patted his arm, but Ryan ignored him.

"What's wrong with him?" Eric asked.

"The soul? You knocked him over."

"No. I mean, he's so quiet. It's like he doesn't know where he is most of the time. All the other souls I've seen were more alert. One even talked to me."

Death glanced down at Ryan. "The binding puts the soul in a kind of trance. He may become more alert with time. Then again, he may not." He looked back up at the sky.

Eric followed his gaze. A huge golden bird was drifting toward them. The size had to be an illusion. Its wingspan looked to be more than twelve feet wide. As it got closer, Eric realized that it wasn't a bird, but a man, a man with wings. An angel?

The angel alighted in a susurration of feathers. Eric gaped. The creature before him was like a Greek sculpture and nearly as naked. His body gleamed, as though followed by a spotlight. Eric could see the curve of every muscle, arms, legs, chest, torso. An artfully draped cloth hugged his hips and covered his embarrassment. It did very little to cover Eric's.

The creature looked down at Eric where he knelt amidst the suddenly vibrant poppies. It smiled. Eric could see it had fine black hair and eyes in two colors—one green, one blue.

"This is the human?" the angel said.

"It is," Death answered. "Morpheus, Lord of Dreams, this is Eric, human born."

Morpheus held out his hand. Something was wrong with it, but Eric found himself unable to focus on what that was. He let it envelop his. The fingers, there was something about the fingers.

Morpheus stared deep into Eric's eyes. "You've been hiding from me, Eric."

"I'm sorry." And he was sorry. He'd never been so sorry in his whole life. He felt like crying. "I'm sorry."

"And who is this?" Morpheus asked. He shifted his attention away from Eric and Eric felt as if the air had been squeezed out of him. He fell back on his heels.

"A soul," Death said. "Bound to our human."

"It's worse than I feared," Morpheus said.

"Yes, and they've suspended me until I solve the puzzle of why."

Morpheus raised both eyebrows. "Do they not realize what mayhem that will cause?"

"They think it's better in the long term," Death said.

"And you?"

Death's chuckle sounded like bones rattling. "I think we need to discover the answer quickly before things get even further out of hand," Death said.

"You haven't found anything?" Morpheus asked.

"Nothing. Nothing at all. He lives a perfectly normal, boring life. There is nothing special about him. He is exactly like the entire teeming mass of humanity, except that he can meddle where others can't. The reason why is a mystery."

Morpheus cocked his head and looked at Eric like a person considering where to put a piece of furniture that didn't quite fit in the new apartment.

"You could kill him, I suppose," he said.

Eric should have been afraid. Morpheus had said those words with no hint of pity or dread. Killing Eric would be like crushing a gnat beneath his perfect foot. But Eric felt only awe.

"No," Death said. "I won't win the game by overturning the board. The human is the key. We must discover what he unlocks."

Morpheus looked down at Eric, still on his knees in the grass. "You are a troublesome thing."

Eric wanted to cry. Between the accident and the ghosts and the boy with the gunshot wound, he hadn't slept, hadn't properly slept, in weeks, maybe months. And now he was apparently inside his own dream, which didn't make sense, and an angel looked at him and saw only trouble.

"I hoped you'd have some good news for me," Death said.

Morpheus shook his head and his wings rustled in the silent night. The sound made Eric sleepy for some reason.

"I've scoured my realm," Morpheus said. "There's nothing. All the seals are in place, the borders unbroken. No one should have been able to get in uninvited."

"And yet," Death said, gesturing with his scythe.

"Yes, I know." Morpheus anticipated the next question. "I have investigated my people most thoroughly. I assure you that if any of them had any part in it, I would know."

Death tapped his scythe on the ground, the way an old man taps his cane while thinking. "It seems we have no choice but to join forces, brother."

Morpheus inclined his head in agreement.

Death nodded in return, and continued, "Where does

that leave us? Or better, who does that leave us with?"

Eric let himself slide sideways until he was sitting on the ground. Nobody was paying any attention to him. Death and Morpheus were talking about things he couldn't understand. The soul was staring up at the sky. What was so interesting up there? Eric lay back in the grass. There were more stars than he had ever seen before. Maybe it was because he'd lived close to cities his whole life, or maybe there were actually more stars in his dream than in other places. Either way, they were beautiful.

He probably should have been upset. A minute earlier he had been. But now there seemed no point in it. The darkness had fallen but it wasn't all that bad.

~

In the ER of St. Luke's Hospital, Mr. Joseph Methia should have been dying. Both his kidneys had failed after years of alcoholism. His blood was filling up with poison. Despite a full regimen of pain medication, more, truth be told, than he should have been allowed in his current state, he was still weeping and writhing in agony.

The younger doctors, who thought they were starting to know something about something, had admitted that they didn't know what to do in this particular case and called in the older doctors, who were quite secure in the knowledge that they knew nothing. They asked each other how to proceed, what medications to give, whether they should move him to intensive care. But nobody asked the big question they were all thinking: How is he still alive?

They were still not asking that question when he slipped into a coma twenty minutes later. They moved him to intensive care and still nobody so much as murmured.

It wasn't until the intensive care unit ran out of beds that anyone spoke the words. And it did no good. No one had an answer.

CHAPTER FIFTEEN

A Fate Worse Than Death

Most likely, none of this was even real, Eric decided. He was clearly asleep. Maybe he'd never woken up after the accident at all. Maybe the weeks in a hospital bed and the months of physical therapy and the raving homeless guy and the kid with a bullet in him had all been part of one big, dying dream, the last SOS of failing neurons.

"Eric, get up," Death said. His voice was impossible to disobey, and Eric found himself standing before he even registered that he'd heard the words.

"Must we take him with us?" Morpheus asked. "He might pose a liability."

"He's coming with us," Death said. "If I'd kept a closer eye on him, perhaps none of this would have happened. And tone down your glamour, please, or he's going to keep gawping at you."

Ryan inched over and curled his fingers around Eric's, the way a child might reach for his parent without even glancing up. Eric had done that once in a grocery store. Even though he'd been only four years old at the time, he remembered distinctly the feeling of terror when he looked up and realized that the hand he was holding was not his mother's but that of a stranger. The woman had smiled down at him. "Why hello there," she'd said. "Are you lost?"

"I abso-fucking-lutely am," Eric muttered.

If he was going to get unlost, he was going to have to start paying attention. Eric forced himself to tune back in to Death and Morpheus' conversation.

"Oh please let it not be Agni," Death was saying. "I can't bear another game of hide and seek."

"Is Agni a kid?" Eric asked.

"Agni is the fire god born of the Hindu people. He finds it amusing to hide from gods and men."

"And you think he did this to me?" Eric asked.

"It's possible," Death answered. "At this point anything is possible."

"I'm not running off to Asgard and Narnia and who knows where, accusing gods of we don't even really know what," Morpheus said. "We need some evidence."

"And how do you suggest we find it?" Death said.

"Use the human."

Morpheus' initial charm was quickly wearing thin.

"Do you gods even care about humans?" Eric asked. "Aren't you supposed to watch over us?"

"Lord, what fools," Morpheus said, rolling his eyes skyward. "You humans created us. It is you who bear the responsibility for us, not the other way around. You made us to do jobs, to tend the fire, to build your dreams, to guard your crops. Of all the creatures in your universe, you are the only ones who believe that the things you make are greater than you are."

Death's voice cut like a scythe. "Morpheus, that's enough."

Eric felt the eyes of Death on him. Death shook his head. In disgust? Amusement? It was hard to tell.

Morpheus' grin was like the sun bursting through a cloud bank to set the rain ablaze. He drew close to Eric.

"I've seen your dreams, you know. I built some of them with my own hands."

He lifted those hands and splayed out his twelve fingers. Eric stared. The idea of this creature, this god, touching his dreams embarrassed him deeply. He felt a blush starting from the depths of his gut and tried to put on a brave face. He drew himself up.

"I hardly ever dream," Eric said.

This time Morpheus laughed. "Humans. They think they know themselves. It's adorable."

He looked at Death, as if expecting him to concur, but Death made no comment. So Morpheus continued, "Of course you dream. You dream in your sleeping and sometimes even in your waking. You dream about your desires, and your fears, and the hopes you've never spoken and wouldn't even know belonged to you if they licked your ear and called you tiger. But you forget them. Repress them."

"It doesn't matter," Eric said. "Dreams aren't real."

Morpheus laughed again, and his mouth opened wide, wider than his face, spreading, spreading until Eric could see nothing but teeth, and behind those, a tongue like a snake. It lashed out and caught him, throwing him up into the air and letting him fall toward the gaping mouth which was now big enough to swallow him whole.

Eric shrieked like the terrified child he had been so long ago, when night terrors had woken him at least once a week for more than a year. Eric fell through the illusion of the tooth-lined pit and thumped to the ground. He realized, in that moment, that it must have been Morpheus bringing him those terrible dreams night after night all those years ago. How could he ever have thought this monster was an angel?

Morpheus fell down on top of him. Pinning him there with a forearm against his throat. The god was beautiful again, superhuman and almost painful to look at in his splendor. But he forced Eric to look, holding him with the blue eye and the green. Eric decided then and there that he didn't like Morpheus and could not trust him.

"Feel your heart beating? Feel your blood pounding? Feel the rush of adrenaline making every hair on your body thrum? That's happening to you now, in the real world. As we lie here so cozy together inside your dream, a nurse is running toward your room, wondering why your vitals just spiked. I am as real as you are human."

"Morpheus," Death said, his voice sharp.

Morpheus grinned. "Tell me again that dreams aren't

real."

Eric struggled against the god, who seemed so much heavier than his current form would suggest.

"This isn't helping, Morpheus," Death said.

Morpheus disappeared. Eric scrambled to his feet, gasping. He glanced at Ryan, who was standing nearby, staring at nothing with his usual dull expression. Then he looked at Death. A large bird, some kind of owl, had settled on Death's shoulder.

"What the hell was that?" Eric gasped.

"A warning," Death said. "Never underestimate a god."

The owl preened its feathers with the side of its beak. Death shrugged, but the owl only clung tighter.

"Lord Morpheus," Death said in the careful tone of someone trying hard not to lose their temper, "would you be so kind as to lead the way? Please."

The owl rotated its head the wrong way around to peer at Eric, then suddenly took wing.

Eric gaped after it. Death stalked in the direction the owl had gone. "Come, Eric. There's work to be done."

At first, Eric didn't move. He was trying to take calming breaths and keep the image of ten billion sharp teeth from appearing every time he blinked. Ryan wandered over to him and picked at his sleeve. Eric closed his hand around the boy's and followed Death.

"So," he said, after he'd had a moment to calm down, "he's an owl now?"

"No, he's a god. He only looks like an owl."

"Right. Of course," Eric said. "And where are we going?"

Death manufactured a sigh to make it clear that he thought Eric was an idiot. "We are inside your dying dream. Not much is happening because you're dying very slowly, but as Morpheus explained, all dreams are connected. From here, we can visit every dream you've ever had."

"Why would we want to do that?"

"Because it's easier than going door to door asking gods if any of them are currently working on the overthrow of the interworld order."

"I don't understand."

"They may not operate in the world you know, but dreams can affect it. If a god who doesn't belong in Dream is meddling there…it could do a lot of damage. That's why Morpheus is somewhat overheated at the moment."

The owl dove, narrowly missing Death's head. "I have excellent hearing in this form," it shrieked as it swept back into the sky.

"And understandably so," Death added, not missing a beat.

"Okay, dreams affect me, I affect the world. Sure. I can see that. But what do you expect to find? I don't remember my dreams."

"You wouldn't. They've been taken, at least, some of them have. That's the second reason why Morpheus is so justifiably upset. Someone trespassed in his realm and stole what was his and his alone."

"Aren't my dreams mine?"

Eric heard the sound an owl would make if it could laugh. It was a far-off sound, but still off-putting.

"Dreams belong to the Dream Lord. He grows the raw materials for their making and weaves them with his own fingers. They are merely on loan to you."

"Like library books?"

Death waved the comment away. "The point is, we hope that by inspecting what was left we can discover what is missing. We'll do this by going into your dreams and looking for what is out of place."

Morpheus dipped one wing and spiraled in overhead. Eric ducked involuntarily. The Dream Lord landed on Eric's shoulder and dug sharp talons into his flesh, hard enough to suggest that they could draw blood if they wanted to. That raised an interesting question, or a question that would have been interesting if it was a hypothetical concept and not the reality Eric was about to face.

"Is this going to be dangerous?" he asked. "I mean, I've had some pretty bad dreams in my life. If we're going to revisit them, can they hurt me?"

Death cocked his head ever so slightly, suggesting that he didn't know the answer. Morpheus shifted his weight on Eric's shoulder.

"It's not dangerous for me, or for Lord Death, because we are better than human. And it probably isn't dangerous for the soul. He doesn't seem all that aware of his surroundings. But for you...perhaps," Morpheus said. "You must have heard that if you die in your dream you die in real life?"

"It's true?"

"Of course. You are you, wherever you are."

"But I can't die right? Death is on suspension or whatever until we get this mess sorted out."

"There are fates worse than death," Morpheus said.

~

It took a while for anyone to notice that the dying weren't passing on. After all, life is resilient. There was once a Czechoslovakian airline stewardess who fell 33,333 feet and lived to tell the tale. A Uruguayan rugby team lasted seventy-two days in sub-zero conditions after crashing into the side of a mountain. In Virginia, a forest ranger was hit by lightning seven times during his thirty-two-year career. Which just goes to show that it's not as hard to cheat Death as everyone seems to think, but it helps if he's in a gambling mood.

One in a million chances are bound to happen sooner or later. And when all else fails, there are always miracles. They happen every day. Every nurse and doctor has at least one story of that patient who could not possibly have lived, but somehow did. What else could you call that but a miracle?

When the intensive care ward where Ryan lay in a

drug-induced coma made it through the day without losing a single patient, the doctors congratulated one another. When they made it three days they started joking about calling Guinness World Records.

By day four, things were getting serious. They were running out of painkillers, for one thing, and they were also running out of room. People weren't dying, but they were still getting hurt and having strokes and shooting each other at the same rate as they always had. Injuries were just as damaging, but even the worst cases didn't seem to be lethal. Extra supplies were impossible to find, and patients couldn't be sent out to other hospitals. Those were full too.

Hospitals operate on a twenty-four-hour clock. Illness has no concept of time. Babies are born whenever they please. And there are always those idiots who chose three a.m. to say "here, hold my beer" before doing something immeasurably stupid that inevitably lands them in the Emergency Room. So hospitals never completely shut down, but they generally have their quiet hours. Between midnight and five a.m. the lights are turned down low and all but the most demanding patients fall into a fitful sleep. During those hours, the corridors become echo chambers. A single nurse, in her rubber-soled shoes, can set up a squeak that reverberates from the north wing to the south. A cart of medical supplies inexplicably transported in the dead of night sounds like a dozen stewpots falling down stairs and wakes every patient on the floor.

But it was 2:53 a.m. and the hospital was wide awake.

The medications that doctors relied on to keep their dying patients decently high and free from pain were running out, and they had to prioritize. As a result, the halls echoed with crying and gnashing of teeth. Those in less pain were kept awake by those who suffered, and their complaints added to the cacophony.

The entire staff had been put on double shifts to handle the increased demand. They were exhausted. Some of them slept in the locker rooms or on the floor of the break room instead of going home. That way they could talk about what was happening. Their only leisure activity became the trading of stories.

"I heard that up in Boston they had a fireman brought in with third-degree burns over ninety percent of his body," an intake nurse whispered to a half-asleep audience. "They had to put him in the morgue so he didn't keep the other patients awake with his screaming."

Another nurse leaned forward, dark circles under her eyes. "My friend works at Maine Medical Center, and she says that way up north they had a guy brought in who'd opened up his femoral artery with a chain saw. He bled out completely, but was still alive when they brought him in."

Nobody bothered telling her that was impossible. Each of them had seen something equally strange in the last few days.

"I won't tell you about the suicide that came in yesterday," a first year resident said. "A gunshot wound to the head is supposed to kill you. You know?"

~

Andy knocked on the door of Eric's apartment. Nobody answered. He banged louder, then stuck his ear against the door, listening for sounds of movement. Nothing. Eric must be at work. Damn it. Amelia hadn't answered when he called, and now Eric wasn't home either. What was the point of making plans if everyone forgot about them?

Andy looked around. The hallway was empty. White walls, cheap industrial-grade carpet in a pretty standard grey-brown color. One window at the end of the hall to let some light in. He'd slept in worse places. Better just camp out here until Eric came back. If he took too long, Andy could find a pay phone and call Amelia again. He set his pack down on the floor and sat down next to it, his back against the door.

During his time in the Marines, Andy had learned a couple of really valuable skills. One of the more socially acceptable was the ability to fall asleep literally anywhere at almost any time. You never knew when you'd next have an opportunity to sleep, so you took them when you got them. He leaned his head against the doorframe and fell almost instantly into dream.

A couple of hours later, he was awakened by Amelia's voice saying his name.

Andy sat up immediately. That was another skill the

Marines had taught him, flipping from dead sleep to full wakefulness in a breath.

"What are you doing?" Amelia asked.

It had been over a year since he'd last seen her. Somehow she'd gotten more interesting in that time. When he'd left she'd just been his friend's kid sister. Now she was...something else. He wasn't sure exactly what, but he was curious to find out.

Amelia stared down at him like a scientist looking down a microscope at an unexpected strain of bacteria.

Andy tried to look awake and alert. "I was waiting for Eric."

"I tried to call you," she said. "You must have been on the way to the airport already."

The realization that something must be up finally permeated Andy's brain. "What happened?"

Amelia pressed her lips together. "Can we go inside?"

She took a step back, giving Andy enough room to scramble to his feet. His bag was still in the doorway, but she just reached across it and unlocked the door to Eric's apartment.

She stepped over his pack and through the door. Andy bent to pick it up. When he straightened, he held back a whistle. The apartment was a wreck. Empty pizza boxes and takeout containers were littered randomly across the floor. The counter was a standing army of beer bottles and soda cans. Laundry lay wherever it had been dropped, or possibly thrown. An overflowing laundry basket was tipped over near the couch, clearly dug through by someone in a hurry to find a particular shirt or sock. In the middle of the coffee table stood a boot with nothing else around it.

Eric had never been the neatest man in the world, but he'd never been a pig either. He'd throw trash away and kick his clothes into a respectable pile in the corner of the room like any other guy. This was a whole new level.

Amelia was clearly affected by the sight. She turned her head from side to side, surveying it all, then crossed her arms across her chest, like she was afraid to touch anything. Andy had to nudge her forward so he could close the door behind them.

"What happened to Eric?" he said.

"He's in the hospital again. I just came to get some things. I didn't want Mom to come, because I knew Eric likes his privacy. And Mom can be..."

She trailed off, but Andy could fill in the blanks. He knew exactly how Eric's mom could be. She was a big ball of anxiety with a veneer of judgement.

"Why is Eric in the hospital?"

Amelia shrugged. With her arms still crossed the gesture made her look like she was warding off a chill.

"They don't really know. They just found him passed out in a random hospital room. There doesn't seem to be anything wrong with him. But they can't...He won't wake up." She turned her head. Now Andy could see her face in profile. She was trying not to cry.

He wanted to hug her, but he didn't know if that would help or not. Suddenly he realized he hardly knew her at all. Yes, she'd written him letters in boot camp and they had this cute little phone thing going on, but how well did he know her really? She was just his friend's kid sister who had called him once to share some bad news.

Andy stood just inside the door, his pack in one hand, his free hand curling into a useless fist. He didn't know what to do here. He didn't even know what he was doing here. He shouldn't have come. He tried to think of something to say, something that didn't sound callous or careless, or like he thought this was all some big joke.

"Where does he keep the trash bags?"

Somehow, those seemed to be the right words. Amelia dropped her arms to her sides and he saw the tension in her shoulders relax just a bit.

"Under the sink maybe?" Her voice was almost steady. She began to pick her way across the room. "Let me go pack Eric a bag, and I'll be back to help you."

When she'd disappeared into the bedroom, Andy sighed. Not his smoothest moment, but they seemed to have gotten past the crisis point.

CHAPTER SIXTEEN

No Place Like Home

There were fates worse than death. Death knew that all too well. And one of them was being lost in the void without a guide. A soul unguided could be lost forever and often was. If Death had been capable of shame, he would have felt quite a lot of it over the sheer number of souls that had been lost before the gods had stopped bickering enough to form a decent governing system for these sorts of things.

Back in the dark times it had been every soul for himself. Death had reaped and run as it were. But now there was a system, a structure to the whole thing, and Death took pride in the fact that it had been nearly six hundred years since he'd lost a man. Even the world wars hadn't broken his streak.

So Death felt a certain measure of apprehension at what they were about to do. If they lost Eric, that would be bad enough, but to lose Ryan as well…

Still, what choice did they have? This situation demanded resolution, and Death was good at resolving things. Death grasped Eric's shoulder, the one that didn't currently have a god in the shape of a bird roosting on it.

"Eric, you've bound this soul to yourself. Whatever befalls you befalls him as well. Remember that."

Death watched as Eric looked down at Ryan. He was still holding Ryan's hand, but the soul had pulled away from him, like a dog straining on its leash. Eric tugged gently and Ryan drifted back toward him to settle at his side.

"Great," he said. "No pressure. So where are these dreams?"

"That spot where the grass changes color," Morpheus said.

There was such a spot just ahead, a perfect circle of darker grass. It looked as though someone had cut out the sod and replaced it with sod from another field.

"Step into the circle."

"I'm fairly certain that nothing good ever happened following the words 'step into the circle,'" Eric said, but he did as he was told.

~

In the parking lot outside Eric's apartment, Amelia led Andy to a silver 1984 Pontiac 6000. As she opened the trunk she said, "This is going to sound crazy, but can you take off your boots before you get in? It's Mom's car and she's..."

"Yeah, no problem," Andy said. He dropped his bag in the trunk and walked around to the passenger side. Amelia had already popped the door locks.

She pulled off her Mary Janes and stuck them in her purse. Andy sat down in the passenger seat and set to work unlacing his boots enough to take them off. It wasn't a quick process.

Watching him, Amelia started to giggle. "Hang on a sec. Don't move."

Andy froze. "What?"

"Just wait." Amelia reached into the backseat, her body brushing against Andy's arm for just a moment. She smelled like vanilla. He heard a rustling noise, and she came back with a copy of *Popular Mechanics* rolled up in her hand.

"Here, just put this on the floor."

"I can't put my feet on your magazine."

"It's fine. I already read that one twice."

Andy opened the magazine, laid it on the pristine carpet, and then set his feet on it gingerly. He shut the door as Amelia started the car.

"So," Andy said. "You still read *Popular Mechanics*?"

"Yeah, why shouldn't I?"

"You should. I mean, there's no reason why you can't. I just remember you reading that when we were in high school."

"They make new issues every month, Einstein."

Andy chuckled at that. "Yeah, what was I thinking?"

Amelia drove in silence for a minute. She hadn't even turned on the radio. "Eric isn't okay," she said suddenly.

Andy wasn't sure how to respond to that. Eric was in the hospital. People didn't usually sign up for a bedpan and an IV drip because they were doing great. He struggled to find a non-sarcastic way to say that, but Amelia went on before he managed it.

"I mean, he hasn't been okay for a long time. It's not just the accident. Even before that, he was drawing into himself. Not answering the phone. Not visiting." She blinked back tears. "That apartment. That wasn't Eric." She sighed. "I'm not saying it right."

"No, I know what you mean. I don't know how well you remember, but Eric changed a lot after your dad died. The last few months have felt a lot like that."

Amelia nodded. "He struggled back then, and he's struggling now. Lately, it's like he's trying to save the whole world, no matter what it does to him." Her voice hitched at the end.

She stopped at a red light and turned her face toward Andy. "I should have done something sooner. I should have seen something was wrong."

He wanted to tell her that wasn't her job. He wanted to say that big brothers were supposed to take care of little sisters, not the other way around. But he felt a little of the same guilt. He should have come home sooner. He should have known Eric wasn't okay.

"We're doing something now," he said.

Amelia smiled a soft little smile. "I'm glad you're here, Andy."

All of his doubts evaporated in an instant. If him being here made her glad, then here was exactly where he wanted to be.

"Me too."

~

Suddenly, Eric was home. Not in the apartment where he lived now, but in his childhood home, the one that would always be his. He and Ryan stood in the middle of the kitchen. There was the chipped green and white linoleum. There the wood paneling around the refrigerator. Every detail was perfect, right down to the ugly hand-crocheted dish towels his great-grandmother had made while she was in the nursing home.

The details were perfect, but somehow the whole wasn't quite right. The ceiling was too high, the walls too far away. It might have been because Eric was smaller all those years ago when they lived in the house on Dartmouth Street, but the overall effect was ominous.

He hadn't set foot in that house since he was a teenager. After his father died his mother had sold it to a nice young couple with two-point-five kids and a dog. All they'd lacked was the white picket fence. Eric had been angry about it at the time. He hadn't really been able to explain why. He'd just stomped around the house, slamming doors and refusing to pack his room until his mother did it for him. It had taken years for him to realize what the real problem had been. It wasn't just that he was being forced to leave the only home he'd ever known. That was part of it. But there was something worse too. It was the injustice of this perfect whole family stepping into the place where his had once been.

He guessed that his dream of the house was set in a time before his anger. This was the house as Eric remembered it when he was six or seven. Before his mother replaced the ugly wallpaper in the dining room, before he kicked a soccer ball not just into, but through the window on the front door and she'd replaced it with double-paned glass that the salesman claimed would stand up to a hundred soccer balls.

"Why am I here?" Eric asked.

Morpheus fluttered over and perched on the back of a dining room chair. His talons left scratches in the polished wood and Eric winced. His mother would be furious.

"This is your dream," Morpheus said. "You tell us."

A voice called Eric's name. It was a voice he recognized, but he couldn't quite place it. He tilted his ear toward the sound. It was coming from upstairs.

"Down here," Eric said.

Nobody answered, but he heard footsteps cross the upstairs hall and then start down the stairs. It was a heavy tread, too heavy to be his mother.

"Dad," he said. This was a dream. In a dream his dad could still be alive. "Dad!"

He ran down the hall, dragging Ryan with him. The soul tried to hang back, but Eric was bigger, stronger, and too excited to pay much attention to Ryan.

"Dad!"

Eric skidded to a halt at the bottom of the stairs. Something was coming down, but it wasn't his father. At least, it wasn't his father as Eric remembered him. It was a corpse. Rotting flesh hung from exposed bone. What little skin it had left was turning black with a tinge of green. The corpse smiled, revealing not just teeth, but also sinew and blackened gums.

Eric screamed and scrambled backward, away from his father's mobile corpse. He should have known this was coming. He'd had this dream before. It had endless variations, all of them equally macabre. But in the dream he never remembered until it was too late.

He ran for the front door, the door they never used because they were from New England and everybody knew that front doors were only for show and occasionally for moving large pieces of furniture in and out of the house. It was locked, of course.

He twisted back the dead bolt, fumbled with the handle. All the while, he could feel the corpse at his back. The smell of rotting flesh filled his nostrils and made his stomach heave. He knew that smell. Once he'd been called for a man passed out in a car only to discover the guy had been dead three days, broiling in the summer heat.

Eric finally won his battle with the locks, certain the

zombie was just behind him, ready to throw its rotting arms around him. He threw open the door and burst out…

Not into his front yard, with the apple tree and the three cement stairs, but into the open field. Blood-colored poppies bobbed and waved around him.

"Eric, the soul!" Death said.

Eric swore and stepped back into the circle. He was in the kitchen again. He sprinted down the hall. Ryan was parked against the window next to the front door. He seemed oblivious to the animated corpse, which was further away than Eric had feared but still too close for comfort. It had almost reached the bottom of the stairs. Eric ran right past the zombie, seeing more suppurating wounds than was good for him. He grabbed the soul by the shoulder and dragged it back through the door.

Safely in the field, Eric swung around again to see if the thing had followed them somehow, but there was only Death, with Morpheus still in the form of an owl perched on his scythe. Above them, the stars blazed in a glittering band across the sky.

"What kind of sicko are you?" Eric shouted at Morpheus. "There's not enough ugly in the world? You have to give me dreams full of rotting corpses."

He was panting, and his knees felt weak. If Morpheus had been in human form, Eric probably would have punched him. Since he would feel stupid hitting a bird, he only glared.

Morpheus spun his head around 180 degrees. "Don't blame me," he said. "The ideas come from your subconscious. I just give them form."

"Well fucking skip that one next time."

Morpheus stuck his tongue out at Eric, a thing that Eric hadn't expected a god would do or an owl even could do.

"Uppity human." He shuffled along the blade of Death's scythe.

Eric looked at Death for some support. Death just shook his head as if to say, don't look at me, he does what he wants.

"Did you see it?" Eric said.

Still, Death said nothing.

"If you're done whining, maybe we can talk about what's actually important here," Morpheus said.

"And that is?"

"You must be more careful, Eric," Death said. "You very nearly lost the soul back there."

"You said the dreams couldn't hurt him."

"Probably couldn't hurt him," Morpheus added.

"Probably?" Eric said.

"Nevertheless," Death said, "being separated from you means his soul is untethered. In a very short time it would begin to drift. The soul is drawn to the void, and in the void there are more specters than on earth. Without you, Ryan stands no chance."

Eric looked down at Ryan, just standing there, staring off into space, completely oblivious to the arguments going on around him. He felt guilty. This kid was his fault. He adjusted his grip on Ryan's hand.

"The more important point is, what was out of place?" Morpheus said. "In your dream, what wasn't there that should have been?"

Eric felt like crying. He was supposed to play a game of spot the difference like a kid with a *Highlights* magazine when he'd just been standing a foot away from his father's rotting corpse? He couldn't do it.

"Nothing. I don't remember. It's been years since I lived in that house. I don't remember everything in it."

Eric pulled Ryan a little closer. He hadn't meant to abandon the kid, he'd just been scared. "Plus, you made the damn thing. Maybe you left something out. How should I know?"

"Think, Eric," Death said. "Was there anything in that dream that struck you as odd?"

"There was a zombie on the stairs. I think it was my dad, had been my dad. Not sure what exactly counts as odd in that context."

Morpheus huffed and ruffled his feathers. "This isn't getting us anywhere," he said. "We need to find another dream."

He launched himself into the air. His wings churned, gaining lift, and then he spread them and drifted away on invisible air currents. Death stalked off after him. Eric was left holding Ryan's hand, feeling useless and guilty. He wanted to help. He just didn't know what they expected from him.

The last thing he wanted to do was think about that dream, but something was tugging at his memory, something that happened before the body on the stairs.

He rushed to catch up with Death, towing the soul behind him like a deflating balloon.

"There was something," he said, when he reached Death's side. "But it's probably nothing."

"At this point, Eric, even nothing might be something," Death said without looking at him. He was glancing upward at Morpheus silhouetted against the stars.

"It might just be memory playing tricks on me, but the voice that called my name, it didn't sound like my father's voice."

Death turned his cowled head to stare at Eric. He stopped walking. "You said the zombie was your father."

Eric paused too. The soul drifted to a stop half a pace ahead.

"He was," Eric said. "But that voice. I don't think it was his." The more he thought about it, the more certain he was. The voice that had called his name was not his father's voice.

"Whose was it then?"

"I don't know. I thought it was a voice I recognized, but I can't place it."

Death tapped his fingers against his collarbone, making an audible clicking noise that set Eric's teeth on edge. He was apparently thinking.

"It might be nothing," Death said slowly. "Then again, it might not be. We'll have to keep looking."

"Why do I get the feeling I'm not going to enjoy this?"

Eric said.

Morpheus landed heavily on Eric's shoulder. Eric let out a little puff of air that might have become a shriek if he hadn't stifled it.

"Calm down, human. Some would count themselves blessed to be touched by a god."

"Yeah well, I guess I'm just an ungrateful bastard," Eric muttered.

Morpheus actually laughed at that. "And just when I've found another gift for you." He flapped his wings, which caused Eric to turn his head and see another dark circle in the grass.

"Is this a good dream or a bad dream?" Eric asked.

Morpheus nipped Eric's ear. "Just go."

CHAPTER SEVENTEEN

War is Hell

When Andy followed Amelia into the hospital room, Eric's mom was sitting beside his bed. She wasn't doing anything, just sitting there, her eyes on Eric's face. Her cheeks were hollow, her mouth drawn into a thin line.

She flinched when Amelia said, "Mom?"

"Amelia, honey, there you are. You were gone so long." Her face reconfigured itself into a more pleasant expression, but Andy saw the strain in the corners of her eyes.

"We wanted to make sure Eric's apartment was okay. We don't know how long he'll be here."

"Yes," Mrs. Silva said.

The weight in that word made Andy once again regret ever coming back to Massachusetts. He didn't belong in the middle of this family tragedy, even if Eric was his best friend. But Amelia hooked her arm through his and pulled him forward.

"Mom, you remember Andy Templeton?"

"Eric's friend from high school. Of course I remember. Nice to see you again, young man."

Mrs. Silva always defaulted to politeness when she was worried. Andy hurried around the bed to take her outstretched hand. He knew she'd never really liked him.

"You too, Mrs. Silva. How's Eric?"

Her eyes fell to her son's face. He looked like he was sleeping. Andy half-expected him to open his eyes and shout "gotcha!"

"The same. Healthy as far as anyone can tell, but unresponsive."

Andy didn't know what to say to that. Luckily, Amelia jumped in and saved him.

"Mom, you need some rest. Why don't you head home for a while? Andy and I will stay here with Eric."

Mrs. Silva's eyes darted from Amelia to Andy. Her mouth twitched like she was about to say something, but she sighed instead.

"You're right, dear. Call me if anything changes?"

"Of course." Amelia handed her mother the car keys.

When Mrs. Silva had gone, Amelia perched on the edge of the chair her mother had vacated.

"Hey, Eric," she said. "Andy's here with me."

"Can he hear you?" Andy asked.

Amelia shrugged. "Nobody knows. But if he can, I want him to know he's not alone, you know?"

"Yeah," Andy said. "That makes sense." He pulled a chair over and set it next to Amelia's.

If Eric hadn't been sick, this would be super weird. Here he was sitting at Eric's bedside, watching the slow rise and fall of his chest and hoping he'd open his eyes soon. It made him feel like a creeper.

There had to be a way to make this less awkward. "Hey, man," he said. "I never got to tell you about my field campaign…" He tried to tell the story exactly as he would have if Eric was sitting across from him in his living room instead of lying in a hospital bed, wired up to machines. As he talked, he was aware of Amelia, watching him intently and laughing in all the right places.

~

Eric found himself in the middle of a dense jungle. The air was hot and so humid that he felt half-drowned just from breathing it. He wore the uniform of a Marine. His pack was heavy on his back.

Planes overhead. The rattle of guns. A distant explosion as a land mine detonated. All around him men were screaming, bleeding, dying. Louder than the gunfire, louder than the wrath of war. He had to help them. He ran to the nearest man. It was Andy Templeton. The hole in his belly was as big as Eric's fist. Eric could see his organs, red and slippery with blood.

Tempe grabbed Eric's uniform and pleaded, "Don't let me die, doc. Please, please, don't let me die." His eyes were wild, his skin yellow and blotchy. Eric could smell fear on his breath. Tempe fell back, gasping.

Eric opened his pack. It was full of small rectangles of paper. He dumped the pack out on the ground. No drugs. No disinfectant. No bandages. There was nothing but paper. He seized a piece and read it. It was a plane ticket.

"This is your ticket home, buddy," Eric said. He pressed it into Andy's hand but Andy couldn't hold onto it. It fluttered to the ground like a dying leaf.

Eric knew then that it was hopeless. Andy would never get home. He was losing blood with every heartbeat. Eric had to stop the bleeding, had to stabilize him. But there was nothing, no supplies at all. Not even a pain killer.

Andy was weeping now. "Why won't you help me?"

Eric looked down at his friend, bleeding and dying in the mud. He tore off his top and pulled his sweaty, dirt-smeared undershirt over his head. It wasn't a good solution, and it certainly wasn't sterile, but it would stop the bleeding. It would close the hole and cover the organs that should never have been exposed to harsh sunlight in the first place.

He pressed the balled-up shirt against Andy's stomach, pressed hard, until Andy cried out in pain. Eric's heart broke a little as he did it, but he pressed harder. It was the only way. He strained his ears for the sound of a chopper, the sound of salvation. But all he could hear was the rest of the platoon, who screamed and cried and died, and the bombs that kept exploding and the screaming that never stopped.

Death leaned down until he was almost level with

Eric's ear.

"What is out of place?" he asked.

Eric looked up, bleary-eyed. He'd forgotten Death was there. "Don't take him," he said.

"This is a dream, Eric. Remember."

"What?" Eric tried to focus. There was noise all around and Eric couldn't stop the bleeding, but he had to focus. Death was telling him something important. They were here for a reason. Now what was it?

"A dream," he said. "Right."

The bombing was getting closer. Eric felt each shell as it confronted the ground and made it tremble. Something exploded close enough to send dirt and bits of vegetation flying all around them. It fell in an unsteady rain on Eric's bare shoulders.

Death held out his scythe, blocking Ryan from wandering toward the noise. A disembodied soul had no fear of anything, it just drifted toward whatever caught its interest. That could be a shiny rock or an impressive explosion. It was all the same to the soul.

"Pay attention, Eric. You're supposed to be noticing what isn't here."

"My friend is dying," Eric shouted.

"He isn't though. Nobody is. Not until we fix this. And in the meantime there's a little boy right here who is entirely dependent on you."

Eric kept pressure on the wound, but he also kept his eyes away from Andy's face. It made it easier that way, easier to believe that this was all a dream, that his friend wasn't dying in front of him, that he wasn't helpless in the face of Death. Except he was, wasn't he? Death was the one pulling the strings here, Death and that damned bird.

Eric looked around for Morpheus but his eyes landed on Ryan. He was still trying to walk away from them, despite Death's scythe blocking his path. Eric reached out and grabbed Ryan by the hand. Eric looked into the little boy's vacant face and made a heroic effort to focus.

"I've had this dream before," Eric said.

"Yes, but this one is different. Tell me how."

"The sergeant," Eric said. "There's usually a sergeant, running around telling me what a horrible job I'm doing."

"Good. Very good. We can go now."

Crouched there on the ground, one hand holding his friend's organs in place, the other holding a lost soul, Eric begged for Death's help.

"Please. We have to take him with us. If you grab his feet—"

"He isn't real."

"We could carry him out, no problem."

"He. Isn't. Real."

Morpheus swooped down out of the sky, changing as he landed so that he hit the ground in fully humanoid form. He was wearing full combat gear. One blue eye and one green stared out at Eric from beneath a khaki green helmet.

"Human. Look at me. You never even saw combat did you?"

Eric looked around. He was seeing it now, in all its

bloody awfulness. He'd never understood how anyone could think that there was glory in war, or honor. It was just one big accident scene with too many casualties and not enough ambulances.

"No," he said. "I was only five when we pulled out of Vietnam."

Morpheus leaned close enough for Eric to realize that the god wasn't breathing, and why should he? He didn't have lungs. He wasn't real. None of this was real. Morpheus searched Eric's face.

"Then why are you so afraid?" Morpheus asked.

"I'm still dying," Eric said. "This, all of this, is just the last gasps of a dying brain. A near-death experience."

"That," Death said, "is entirely a matter of perspective. Now if you're quite finished."

Eric looked around, keeping his eyes on the tree line to avoid seeing the bodies all around them. "How exactly do we get out of here?"

"We walk," Morpheus said. "The dream only extends as far as your memory."

"I told you, I never saw combat."

"No, but you saw a movie about it once. That's enough."

Eric thought that it certainly was. He stood up. He picked up Ryan, resting the child against his hip, his legs dangling down on either side. He wasn't heavy. And again, why should he be? He wasn't actually a boy. He was a soul, without substance, but still the most precious thing in Eric's world. He couldn't save Tempe, but he could save this kid.

Eric turned his back on the battle, on the screams of dying men, on the sweat and the blood and the gore, and walked toward the tree line. He'd read about men in combat doing this very thing. They'd drop their weapons and just walk away. Sometimes they were found days later at the bottom of a spear-lined pit or among rescued prisoners of war. Sometimes they were never found and their families held funerals over empty caskets. He'd always thought those men were cowards, but maybe they had just been trying to escape a bad dream.

It worked for Eric. As soon as he stepped under cover of the trees, they disappeared, and he was standing in the field which was somehow inside his own dying mind. He tried not to think about it because it made him feel like he was slowly unraveling. Instead he looked down at himself and noted that he was fully dressed and completely clean, as though the last few minutes hadn't happened. And he guessed they hadn't. Not really.

First he set the soul gently on its feet. Then he sat down on a patch of grass between two bobbing poppies. He felt better closer to the ground. Especially if he didn't think about the fact that it wasn't real ground.

"Is this getting us anywhere?" Eric said to no one in particular. "I don't feel like this is getting us anywhere. I feel like I'm just watching a highlight reel of my all-time worst dreams. That's not really what I call fun, so it'd be nice to know it's at least useful."

"I'm not sure yet," Morpheus said. He was still

humanoid, his eyebrows furrowed together in thought.

"It's clear that someone has been meddling with your dreams," Morpheus said. "Even you noticed it when you were in them, but he removed himself from them so you couldn't remember him when you woke. The question is who is he? I have my suspicions, but thus far, nothing concrete."

"So more dreams then?"

Eric got to his feet. He didn't want to, but he did. Ryan had wandered farther afield than usual. Eric jogged off to retrieve him. The other two waited where they were. Death, patient as the grave, Morpheus, significantly less so.

As Eric returned with the soul in tow he wondered what the kid thought of all this. He didn't seem to be registering much of what was going on around him, but who knew what was going on inside his head. He might be scared stiff and just not be able to show it.

"Is he aware of all this?"

Death shook his head. "Not enough to remember. It's all instinct and no real consciousness. He will startle at a loud noise, and his eyes might follow a shiny object, but he's not capable of much more than that."

"Good. I'd hate to think that the poor kid was seeing my nightmares. They scare the shit out of me. I don't know what they'd do to him."

Morpheus snorted. "He has bad dreams of his own to worry about. He doesn't need yours."

That wasn't particularly comforting.

CHAPTER EIGHTEEN

A Dream of Days Gone By

Eric had heard people say things like "may all your dreams come true" or "have the life of your dreams." They were the kind of empty platitudes he'd never thought much about until now. Now that he was actually seeing and remembering his dreams, he thought that the people who said such things must be either idiots or sadists. If the last couple of experiences were anything to go on, having your dreams come true would be the worst punishment imaginable.

When they reached the next dream spot, Eric wavered just outside the circle.

"We need to keep moving, Eric," Death said.

Morpheus didn't waste time on words. Eric felt a six fingered hand on his back and heard Death say.

"Was that nece—"

And then he was inside the dream. Eric braced himself for another nightmare. Except that this one wasn't. It wasn't a nightmare at all, at least, not yet. They were standing on a mountain. He'd climbed it only once, many years ago, but the view from the top had seeped into his heart and become a part of him.

It had been summer vacation. His parents had taken him and Amelia to Maine, where they'd stayed in a cabin on a lake and shopped at a little general store that sold bait and galoshes next to tie-dye tee shirts and little plush moose next to milk and eggs and a soda called Moxie. It came in an orange can.

Eric had begged to have one, and even though his mother almost never let him have soda, she gave him thirty-five cents to buy it. His parents had laughed at the face he made when he took the first sip. It had tasted like Dr. Pepper laced with crushed aspirin and iodine.

On the third day of their vacation, they'd driven into Acadia National Park and left their car at the base of Cadillac Mountain. His mother had wanted to drive up, apparently there was a road, but his father said it would be good for the kids to get a walk in. Amelia had spent the whole walk trying to identify plants using the pictures in her *Outdoor Adventurer* book.

When they reached the top, even Amelia was impressed. The scene was breathtaking. Nine-year-old Eric had never been up so high. He'd stood near the edge of the cliff and looked down at the ocean below. It seemed like he was in another world entirely. There were no people here, no roads, no cars, no three-story walk-ups or barking dogs on chains. Sunlight glinted on the water. Pine trees held conferences on the islands below. The real world seemed so far away, hiding on the other side of that bluish haze.

His mother had fussed at him not to fall, but he hadn't been afraid. The air seemed so much more solid here. For a moment he'd had the wild thought that if he ran and jumped and spread his arms, he could fly over the rocks and over the trees and out over the ocean and he'd never have to land and he'd never get tired, because the wind would carry him wherever he wanted to go.

He hadn't tried it. Even a nine-year-old knows on some level that he is mortal. He knows that what goes up must come down, and that those trees that seem so small and the water that seems so welcoming are really very far away. Between him and them is nothing but the very thinnest air.

As an adult, standing on the memory of that mountain, Eric knew equally well that he could in fact jump from the cliff and glide off into the distance. He had done so in his dreams on more than one occasion. Eric wondered if he should jump this time, but there was Ryan to think of.

Ryan had drifted as far as their joined hands would let him. He bounced there like a balloon caught by the wind. Eric opened his hand. This wasn't a bad dream. There was nothing here to hurt Eric and therefore nothing that could hurt the soul. There could be no harm in letting Ryan wander around a little. It would be good for the boy to get a walk in.

They were alone except for Death and Morpheus, who had apparently decided he preferred being a bird and had turned back into an owl. He was drifting low overhead, riding the wind. Eric wondered if he could do other animals too. If so, there must be some significance to the owl thing, because it certainly didn't make much sense out here in the full daylight.

Meanwhile, Death was standing close to the edge, his long black jacket whipping in the breeze. He looked incredibly out of place. Maybe it was the sun, shining on his bald head, making the skin seem translucent so Eric would have sworn he could see through to the skull beneath. Maybe it was the way his bony shoulders hunched in his jacket. It was the posture of someone guarding himself against pouring rain. It didn't make sense. How could anyone hunch against this view?

Both Death and Morpheus seemed lost in their own worlds. It was a welcome reprieve from their usual prodding and meddling. Eric made up his mind that he would jump and see where the wind took him. But first he should check on Ryan.

The soul hadn't wandered far, just up the ridge and around a knee-high rock. Eric took his time climbing over to it. There was no rush. As Eric approached, Ryan crouched to look at something. This was the most like a normal child that Eric had ever seen him. Maybe the mountain air was doing him good.

"What are you doing, buddy?" Eric asked.

Of course Ryan didn't answer. He didn't even look up. Eric stepped close enough to bend and take his hand. In the process, he saw what had caught Ryan's attention. A tiny golden feather, lying in the shadow of a rock.

The sight of it stirred a memory that Eric couldn't quite catch. It felt like trying to remember a name when you knew for certain the first letter was probably B or D and it definitely ended in a y or maybe an a. He would remember it soon, certainly.

Eric picked up the feather. It was very small, no longer than his thumbnail and maybe half as wide. He closed it in the palm of his hand to protect it, afraid that the wind might take it before he could inspect it properly. With his other hand, he caught hold of Ryan's sleeve and guided him back toward where Death was standing.

"I found something," he said.

"Are you sure?" Death answered. "There seems to be very little happening in this dream."

"I don't know if it's important, but it feels like it is," Eric said.

The feather felt warm against his palm, and that didn't seem right. Feathers didn't usually give off heat. It was also too heavy. It seemed to weigh maybe as much as a penny when it should have weighed very nearly nothing. He cupped his other hand over his fist and opened them both slowly, taking care to keep the feather deep in his palm where the wind couldn't steal it away.

"I almost remember—" Eric began.

But he was cut off by Death who bellowed,

"Morpheus."

The god-bird dropped from the sky like an anvil, catching himself at the last moment with a flare of his wings, and landing lightly on Eric's shoulder. Eric flinched and closed his hand around the feather. He was so close to understanding something, something important, he didn't want it to disappear before he could fully grasp its meaning.

"Human, show Morpheus what you've found."

"Ryan found it actually," Eric said. He opened his hand.

Morpheus screeched. The sound, high and piercing and oh-so-close to Eric's ear, made him jerk away, which earned him a painful moment as talons squeezed against his shoulder to keep Morpheus from spilling toward the ground.

"That sneaky, no-good trickster. How dare he come into my realm and meddle with my creations. That, that…Roman." Morpheus spat the word. "I'll stuff that..." here he said a word that Eric had never heard before, though the meaning was perfectly clear, "...caduceus down his..." another word that practically made Eric's ears ring, "...throat snakes and all."

Death hadn't said anything yet, and Eric looked to him as the cooler head. "Who are we talking about here?"

"Morpheus, show him."

"I won't. I won't defile myself in the form of that, that—"

"My Lord, please," Death said, in a tone that

demanded compliance.

Morpheus fell from Eric's shoulder, changing as he did so. It was the most graphic transition Eric had seen. He didn't just flit from form to form as he had done from humanoid to bird and back. This time, he almost seemed to relish all the grotesque shapes that came between.

When he finally settled on a shape it was roughly that of a man. Roughly. He had a head and beard of curly dark hair, pale skin with a slight olive undertone, and dark eyes framed in even darker eyelashes. He was wearing a toga that exposed most of his chest and a good deal of thigh. He also had wings, four of them, one on each ankle and two nestled in the curls of his hair. They were golden and covered in tiny feathers that matched the one still clutched in Eric's hand.

Memories flooded back in a crushing tide. Eric actually stumbled with the force of them hitting all at once. Death had to catch his arm to keep him upright.

A golden figure striding through his dreams night after night, standing between him and the walking corpse, bringing in supplies for the platoon, catching him when he jumped and guiding him swooping and gliding through the air and across the sea.

He had been there when Eric lay stunned in his hospital bed. It was he who blew away the morphine fog and told Eric he would live. It was he who whispered soothing words when the pain was enough to reach Eric even in his dreams. It was he who pushed Eric to greater heights, greater feats, shouted encouragement, lent a helping hand. He was there in every dream, the winged god, standing between Eric and his nightmares or coaxing greater joy out of his pleasanter dreams. And he, most importantly, who had shown Eric how to bind a soul.

They all fell in on him at once, every one of Eric's dreams for the last four months, swirling and spinning over each other in a mad rush out of the darkness. Eric felt like a bead in the middle of a kaleidoscope, refracted in every direction until he lost track of which one was him.

In the end they all came together. Every dream ended the same way. The golden man had turned to Eric and said, "Here, you are hungry, eat."

And Eric, finding that he was ravenous, would eat all that was offered him. Eric opened his eyes and looked into the eyes of Death. For once, he didn't flinch away.

"I remember. I don't know his name."

"Mercury. One of the slothful Roman gods. He is their messenger, so he can go very nearly anywhere he pleases."

Death released Eric to stand on his own.

"And he was once tasked with leading souls to the underworld," Morpheus said. He'd become himself again, or at least the humanoid form of himself. "A task he apparently seeks to take on again."

"We don't know that, Morpheus. It may just be a foolish Roman prank."

"He kept giving me food," Eric said.

Both Death and Morpheus turned at the same time to stare at him. It was unnerving and this time Eric did flinch away from them.

"He did," Eric said.

In a slow, deliberate voice, Death asked, "What kind of food?"

"It was like…celestial trail mix I guess. You know, nuts and berries but sort of golden. They tasted like honey and…is it possible to taste sunlight? I know it isn't. But they tasted like sunlight anyway."

Morpheus rounded on Death. "And you called it a prank!" he shouted. "This is no prank. He's feeding ambrosia to humans. How much would he have to eat to become a demigod?"

"He's not a demigod, he's merely a gifted human."

"Do we know that?"

"A change of diet does not make a human a demigod."

"He's bound a soul."

"There's nothing heroic in that," Death said. "And standing here arguing about it will not solve this issue. Human, collect your soul."

Eric jogged over to Ryan, who was standing a few feet away staring at the sky. Eric looked up to see what had caught his attention, but there was nothing there, just blue sky and the occasional wispy cloud.

"I don't understand any of this," Eric muttered. He took Ryan by the hand and led him back to where Death was waiting. The scythe was out again, and Death was tapping it impatiently against a rock while he half-listened to Morpheus, who was still raving.

"And what if he's contagious? Prometheus gives a

couple of humans fire and the next thing you know they've got the industrial revolution, and air travel and those damned television sets. Not to mention—"

Death snatched Eric as soon as he was near enough and stepped.

CHAPTER NINETEEN

Knocking on Heaven's Door

Eric was momentarily blinded by a bright white light. Was this finally it? Was he dead? But no, he could feel Ryan's hand in his, small and cool. Death's sharp fingers still gripped his shoulder. Beneath his feet, Eric could feel slightly springy ground. He realized all this and knew he wasn't dead, not yet. Death had just transported him somewhere else.

Gradually, his eyes began to adjust. At first he thought he was seeing things. Eric and the soul stood before the gates of heaven. Pillars of cloud stretched eight feet tall, supporting a cloud arch. Within the arch shone a gate of white light.

Eric reached out and touched a pillar. He didn't dare reach for the gate. The pillar was springy like the ground and his hand came away damp. Finally putting two and two together, Eric looked down at his feet. He was standing on a cloud. A cloud so big, it might cover the whole earth, and so white and fluffy it could have come out of a Care Bears cartoon.

Eric was no scientist, but he'd made it through middle school science class. He knew you couldn't stand on clouds. He stamped his foot experimentally, which caused a tremor similar to the result of dropping a heavy object on a mattress. Ryan startled away from him.

"Sorry," Eric said, but Ryan was already staring off into space. Once again, Eric wondered how much Ryan understood. He didn't seem to notice much of what was going on around him, except when he did.

"Where are we?" Eric asked.

Behind him, he heard Morpheus chuckle.

At that moment, a figure stepped through the gate of light without causing so much as a ripple. It was humanoid: two arms, two legs, a head. Eric wasn't sure if it was a man or a woman or something else altogether. It might have been a hallucination, because the eyes that looked at them from its soft face spilled golden light. Eric felt his knees go weak. What was this creature?

"We come in peace," Morpheus said, and this appeared to be some kind of joke, because the creature threw back its head and laughed. The sound was like a wind chime store in a hurricane. Eric covered his ears.

"I'm sure you would if given half a chance," the creature said.

As it drew closer to them, Eric wondered how he had been so easily fooled. At first glance this woman, and now it clearly was a woman, had seemed like the most beautiful creature. Up close Eric could see she was fairly plain, almost boring really. Her white hair wasn't white at all, but a pale blonde, and her eyes spilled nothing. They were honey brown. She was pretty enough, but not someone you'd look at twice. Eric wondered why he'd originally found her so appealing.

"Let us in Eirene," Death said.

The woman pouted. "Hmph," she said. "He flirts with me, and you call me by my sister's name."

"Don't be childish. And you should count it a complement to be named among the Greeks."

Eric had no idea what they were talking about.

"Hardly," Eirene's sister said. "Those stuffy Greeks wouldn't know a good time if it drank from their cornucopia, my sister included. Incidentally, I'm missing the party while I'm talking here with you."

"I would happily escort you, Lady Pax," Morpheus said and stuck out his arm.

Pax hesitated. "Morpheus, you old charmer. You've brought along some humans. Jupiter might not like that."

"The hypocrite," Death muttered.

"We can stay out here if that's better," Eric said.

He was getting tired of being dragged along. He'd solved their riddle. Now he and the soul could just as easily wait here until Death had done whatever he was going to do and then they could go home.

"He's not exactly a hero is he?" Pax said, drawing close to Eric.

When she stood near like this, her beauty came back.

The golden light poured into him. Eric stood transfixed, like a deer in the beams of an oncoming semi.

"Thus far, no," Death said, "but the end of his story is not yet written. He is, in fact, the reason we are here. Someone has been meddling with his mind."

"Well that isn't so hard," Pax said. "Humans are very simple creatures. All you have to do is rain on their holiday, or blow out the light they're using to read, or make a jar difficult to open, and you can set them off for hours." She giggled. "They're like children really."

Death grimaced. He didn't seem to know quite how to handle Pax. Morpheus, on the other hand, did. He smiled a charming smile. "If you let us in, I'll give you a crown of flowers for your hair," Morpheus said.

Pax clapped her hands together. "I want narcissus, and amaryllis, and oleanders."

Morpheus made a deep bow. "Of course, my lady. Whatever you wish."

He plucked the flowers out of the air one by one. His twelve fingers wove deftly, crafting a flower crown in moments. When it was complete, he set it with great solemnity on Pax's head.

"Oh, Flora will be so jealous," Pax said. "Come let's show her now." She linked arms with Morpheus and skipped toward the gate.

Eric watched them pass through the light. He hesitated. He'd meant what he said about staying out here. There was no way he could be of any use inside.

Death tapped the heel of Eric's foot with the butt of

the scythe. "Step into the light."

"I don't think…"

"It won't hurt you. Move. We have business to attend to."

Eric inched forward. Death huffed and pushed past him. Eric stopped. He thought maybe Death had decided that Eric was nonessential on this mission after all. Then a familiar pale hand reached back through the gate of light and beckoned Eric forward. He sighed and stepped into the light.

It didn't hurt. It was just light. Stepping through it revealed a room carved out of a cloud bank. The columns that rimmed the wide open hall appeared to be holding up the blue sky and nothing else. A dozen or more couches clustered around what looked like a square pool. It shimmered. Gods and goddesses, at least that's who Eric assumed they were, lounged on the couches and sometimes on each other.

Morpheus and Death strode inside as though they owned the place. Eric lagged behind.

"Well met, Lord Jupiter," Death said. His voice tolled across the space, stopping conversations in mid-sentence.

The lyre music stopped abruptly, leaving an echoing silence where the notes had been. A small group had been playing dice, and the clatter as the roll landed was as loud as a landslide. Every eye turned to look at Death.

He hadn't shouted. Death would never shout, but he tended to speak in a way that could not be ignored.

"I doubt it," Jupiter answered.

He sat up slowly, stretching his great arms, like an eagle set to glide. He moved with an easy strength that mesmerized, even as it raised tiny alarm bells in the most animal parts of the brain. Eric felt the switch on his fight or flight response stick halfway. He felt rooted to the spot, and Jupiter hadn't even looked at him yet.

"What brings you to Olympus, old friend?" Jupiter asked. "Somehow I doubt you're here to join the party."

There was no party at the moment, just silence as the assembled gods watched their lord parley with Death. Eric tightened his grip on Ryan's hand. Now did not seem like the time to let him go wandering off.

"Somehow I don't get invited to many parties," Death said.

"Don't be modest, people are always dying to see you," Morpheus said, his tone perfectly flat.

Laughter scuttled through the assembly. Death gave Morpheus a poisonous look.

Jupiter chuckled. "Well said, Dream King. You have a wit."

"I have the wit to wile, lord. But now I'm at wit's end," Morpheus said.

"Is that why you've brought a human to Olympus? He is no hero. He should have been struck dead at the door."

Jupiter strode toward Eric. His footfalls thundered. They shook the clouds. Eric clenched his teeth. Everyone kept pointing out that he wasn't a hero. It irked him. He wasn't trying to be a hero.

Except maybe he was. Wasn't that what had gotten

him here in the first place? Was he playing hero when he tried to save Ryan, to keep one kid from dying and one brother from feeling like a murderer? Was that heroic? It didn't feel like it was. He hadn't charged in guns blazing and challenged Death to a duel, he'd just grabbed the kid by instinct and now here they were surrounded by the gods of Rome and he had no clue what was going on.

Which just brought home to him what a phenomenal, monumental screw-up he was. He'd nearly died trying to save some kid—who died. He'd stumbled around like an idiot for the last few weeks and somehow managed to upset the very fabric of reality enough that the gods themselves had to come see what was going on. And to top it all off, he'd left a world full of suffering people to languish in pain while he sorted out the mess that he had made. He wanted to scream or bash his head against a pillar, except that it would probably just go straight through. The pillars were also made of clouds.

Jupiter looked down at him. "You could have picked a prettier one," he said.

"His looks are not what brings him here," Death said.

"No. I can see that you brought him here. The question is: why? Now come and drink with me and we'll discuss it." He returned to his couch where two soft-limbed young men were waiting, one to fill his cup and the other to offer him a tray of celestial trail mix.

"Do not eat or drink anything," Morpheus muttered to Eric. "You've done enough damage already. Just sit quietly and keep an eye on your pet."

"He isn't a pet," Eric said.

Morpheus waved the comment away. He followed Death to the couch that had been cleared for them.

Nobody bothered to clear a spot for Eric. He sat down on a handy lump of cloud within earshot of Jupiter and Death. Almost anywhere would have been close enough. Jupiter had a voice that carried like the roll of distant thunder.

Eric tugged at Ryan's hand. The soul drifted forward and then stopped when a golden apple caught his eye. Eric tugged again, and finally resorted to pulling Ryan into his lap, where he sat, if not happily, then at least still. Eric felt like a babysitter, or worse, like a child told to mind a doll as though it were alive. Then he felt disloyal. It wasn't the kid's fault that they were here.

Death was telling Eric's story to Jupiter and his court. It was not a flattering account. To hear Death tell it, Eric was a bumbling fool with no understanding of the world and no sense of what was truly at stake. At best he was a pawn, at worse an ignoramus.

Eric told himself to man up. He could hardly argue the point. He still didn't really understand why he was here or why Mercury had been visiting his dreams with a packed lunch or why that mattered in the grand scheme of things. He was a pawn and an idiot and he was certainly, certainly not a hero.

Around him, the chatter of the party had resumed. Someone started playing a delicate stringed instrument in a way that suggested the person was none too familiar with strings, or maybe didn't have thumbs, it was hard to tell. The clatter of the dice came back as well, and with it the cries and hissing of gamblers as they won and lost.

Eric sat there, unwanted and unheeded, with only his soul for company, and wished he could go home.

"It can't be," Jupiter said.

"It can and you know it," Death said. "This isn't the first prank he's pulled."

"Oh, I wouldn't put it past him. All of my children are clever," Jupiter said with a proud grin. "Even the girls. But it couldn't have been him. He's been chained to a boulder at the bottom of the sea for the last three hundred years. He tried to steal something from my dear brother. Neptune is a loving uncle, as uncles go, but he's fickle, you know. And you wouldn't like to be around when he is angry."

"He could have slipped away," Morpheus said. "Locks were never any challenge for him as I recall."

Jupiter swallowed half a cup of wine in one swig. "The locks are not the issue," he said. "These are chains forged by Vulcan in the heart of the volcano. They'd hold Death himself if we could catch him."

The look that Death turned on Jupiter suggested that he was not above reaping a god if the opportunity arose.

"No offense meant," Jupiter added.

"Have you checked recently?" Morpheus asked, leaning forward to break the aggressive eye contact between Death and Jupiter. He was weaving a second crown of flowers for Pax's friend. Both goddesses were sitting at his feet, watching with soft, adoring eyes.

Other gods had gathered close as well. They seemed enthralled with the creation process. Morpheus' fingers fluttered, plucking dreamstuff from the air and forming it into the most elaborate flowers with just a twitch and stroke. Eric thought he should be amazed by it—he certainly would have been a day ago—but he'd seen so much in such a short time, and he was exhausted. It was possible that nothing could surprise him anymore.

Ryan was growing restless, straining against Eric's grip. He let go. They were in Olympus, right? That was basically like being in heaven. There were no specters here.

Ryan wandered over to where two gods were playing a game like checkers, with gold and silver pieces and an obsidian board. Eric drifted slowly after him. Events were unfolding around him, but he had no more influence than Ryan. Why was he even here?

Just then, Ryan reached out and touched a piece. He liked shiny things Eric remembered, too late. Eric started toward him. One of the players, dressed in armor and with a sword sheathed at his side, backhanded the boy. Ryan did a full somersault before landing flat on his back. A group of gods scattered like pigeons. Eric swept through them.

"What the hell is wrong with you?" he shouted. "He's just a kid."

He knelt down next to Ryan, who was already trying to stand up. Eric restrained him, checking for broken bones. The hand that hit him had been armored.

The same huge hand grabbed Eric by the back of his shirt and lifted him into the air. He found himself swaying softly in the grip of a red-faced god with eyes carved out of flint heated to a red-hot glow.

"Surely you were not speaking to me, mortal. I must have misheard you with my focus so intently on the game."

Eric knew he should just swallow his pride and apologize. This was a god holding him three feet above the ground with no apparent effort. A god who carried a great deal of armor and weaponry just to play board games. Eric knew he should shut up, but sometimes he had no sense of self-preservation. And he was tired, so incredibly tired.

"You didn't have to hit him," Eric said.

The god dropped Eric, who immediately scrambled to his feet.

"And what is he to you?" the god asked.

"It's complicated," Eric said.

The god looked down on Eric from his great height. His shoulders were as broad as a bookcase, and he cast a shadow that was much too large for him. Eric was standing in it.

"Is he your son? Your nephew? Your slave? Your lover? Explain yourself."

"He's my…my brother," Eric lied, because it seemed easier than the truth. "I'm bound to protect him."

The god nodded. Eric had said the right thing at last.

"And so you shall," the god said. "Name the mode of combat."

"What is going on here?" the voice of Death demanded.

"The human has challenged Mars," said the other player in the tone of a stage actress delivering a vital line. She also wore armor, but hers was more delicately detailed, with the head of an owl shaped into the breastplate. Her black hair was plaited into a single thick braid that fell almost to her waist.

"No. I didn't," Eric said. "I didn't mean to anyway. I just didn't want him to hurt the kid. It was a misunderstanding."

"The god of war does not misunderstand," Mars said. "You challenged and I accept your challenge. Now name your mode of combat."

Eric looked at Death, who just shook his head. "I cannot help you. You've set your challenge. Now you must win or be shamed."

"Can't I just forfeit?" Eric said.

"Have you no honor, mortal?" Mars said.

"If you are defeated, you will be killed by Mars," the other player said. "If you forfeit, you shall be executed as a coward. But if you win, Lord Mars must grant you a boon."

"So my choices are die one way, die another way, or win against a god? That isn't fair," Eric said.

"You should have thought of that before you challenged him," Death said. "Now do as he says, choose your challenge."

Eric moved closer to Death, so they could speak with some semblance of privacy. "I'll lose," Eric said.

"Almost certainly," Death said.

"Can't you do something?"

"Honestly, human, you have caused me enough trouble already. I'm not going to start a feud with all of ancient Rome over your foolishness. We've found the answer to our problem. Death will come back into the world. You will die like all the others."

"I can't do this."

Death shrugged. "Probably not."

Eric looked over at the god, still angry, waiting impatiently beside his ransacked game board. His opponent was resetting the pieces, but at least one had gone missing. A few of the nameless and barely dressed boys were on hands and knees looking for it.

Morpheus sauntered up. He seemed to be in his element here. This was the longest Eric had ever seen him remain in human form. Pax was still trailing along after him, wearing her crown of flowers with her neck straight and her chin raised. No one could possibly fail to notice how fine a crown it was.

"What about you," Eric said to Morpheus. "Can you help me?"

"Against Mars? Perhaps. What's in it for me?"

Eric was getting angry. They'd dragged him up here and put him in a situation he couldn't possibly understand, and now they wouldn't even help him.

"What do you want?" he asked.

"From you? To be left alone mostly. The tour of my work was interesting, but I find the company tiresome."

"I didn't ask to be here," Eric said.

'And yet you are, and now you must deal with it," Morpheus said. He paused, then seemed to come to some sort of decision. "Challenge him to a footrace. It's traditional, and he's not known for speed, so it's sure to annoy him."

"How is that a good thing?"

"It will at least be amusing to watch."

Eric gave up. "Fine," he muttered. "Fine."

He turned to face Mars. "I challenge you to a footrace."

"A coward's challenge," Mars said.

"You only say that because you're slow," said Pax. She clearly had no love for Mars.

Mars ignored her and removed his gauntlets. He was taking this seriously.

Eric thought about forfeiting. He was going to lose anyway. What was the point? But hope was a powerful thing. He couldn't choose death when there was the slightest possibility of life before him. He'd have to run.

"Where are we racing?"

Mars waved his hand and some of the floor clouds rolled away. Far below, so far that a blue haze drifted between them and it, was the ground. It reminded Eric of the view from Cadillac Mountain, except that he was certain that here the fall would kill him.

"We will run between the olive trees," Mars said. "Minerva, will you see fair play?" His opponent, who had given up on resetting the board now that a more interesting game was afoot, nodded.

"I need someone to watch the soul," Eric said. "I can't run with him."

He looked around for Death, but Death was gone and so was Morpheus. Eric was alone.

CHAPTER TWENTY

With the Fishes

When Amelia's mom returned to the hospital, Amelia was pleased that Andy immediately jumped up and offered his chair. Eric had tried to paint him as some kind of wild man, but Amelia knew he was a good guy really. Just having him here made her feel like she'd finally caught her balance.

When the nurse came around to tell them visiting hours were over, Mrs. Silva was having none of it.

"You kids go. I'm going to stay here with Eric."

"I'm sorry, ma'am, everyone has to go home at the close of visiting hours."

Mrs. Silva's eyes narrowed. She clutched Eric's hand tightly. "He. Is. My. Son."

Amelia understood where she was coming from, but she could also see that the nurse was just trying to do her job. She tugged at her mom's arm.

"Come on, Mom. Eric needs to rest."

Her mom turned to look at her, eyes watery. "What if he wakes up alone?"

"We'll check in on him throughout the night," the nurse said. "And we'll call you if anything changes."

Mrs. Silva set her mouth in a hard line. "Fine," she said and marched out of the room.

Amelia hung back long enough to say thank you to the nurse. She was doing the best that she could.

By the time she and Andy caught up, her mom was already halfway down the hall.

"Where are you staying, Andrew?"

"I'm not sure, really. I was planning to stay with Eric, but that doesn't look like it's going to be possible."

"You can come stay with us," Amelia said, too quickly.

Mrs. Silva cleared her throat.

"Oh no," Andy said. "I'll just grab a taxi to the nearest Motel Six."

"That's stupid. Come home with us," Amelia said before her mother could get a word in. "Hotels cost money and you've already come all this way."

Amelia saw the twitch in her mother's jaw, but pressed on anyway. The thought of Andy alone in some crappy hotel room after he'd come all this way to see them, to see Eric, made her hands clammy. "There's no food in Eric's house and you have a spare room."

"Eric's room," Mrs. Silva said.

"Yes, and he's Eric's best friend."

"Fine," Mrs. Silva said. "Fine."

~

Death and Morpheus walked along the bottom of the sea. Fine sand crunched underfoot. Overhead, the surface of the water shimmered. A small school of silver fish spotted them and darted away, trying to look larger than they were by swimming close together. Morpheus flexed his fingers, but Death held up a hand. Morpheus was in a foul mood. Anything he made here was bound to upset the local sea life, which would, in turn, upset Neptune.

Neptune, of course, knew that they were there, but he hadn't shown himself yet. He was moody and didn't like to socialize. That was fine. In fact, it was what Death liked most about him.

They walked until the shimmering ceiling disappeared, deep into the cold shadow of the ocean. It was darker than a midnight cloud bank, but both Death and Morpheus thrived in the dark. They found their way across the ocean plain easily. Fish flew overhead like birds and the long tendrils of seaweed swayed like palm branches in a soft breeze. It was no different than a late-night stroll on land, except that they moved more slowly against the pressure of the water.

Approaching the cliff face Jupiter had named, Death half expected Mercury would not be there. But the trickster god was cleverer than that. He stood where he was meant to be. Shackles of rust-stained iron circled his wrists and ankles. A heavy collar encased his neck. He slumped against the rock, doing a convincing impression of a petulant child.

Morpheus was on him in a moment, pushing him back against the cliff. He'd allowed his glamour to slip, revealing a massive hunched figure with arms that nearly touched the ground and knees that bent backwards. His ragged wings trailed behind him like a wave of darkness.

"You dare meddle in my realm?" Morpheus shouted. "You upstart Roman. I'll kill you now and take Jupiter's wrath."

"I don't know what you're talking about, sandman." Morpheus' loss of control would have terrified a human. It only amused Mercury.

The back of Morpheus' hand striking his face was less amusing. The long talon that stuck out like a sixth finger raked across Mercury's cheek. The resulting gash bled liquid gold into the deep sea currents. Enraged, Mercury struggled against his bonds.

Morpheus wound up to hit him again. Death caught his arm and spoke to him in his most commanding tone. "Calm yourself, brother."

Morpheus growled like a hunting dog frustrated by an inconvenient fence, but he let his hand drop. He stalked away, grumbling. In the few minutes while he regained control, Mercury was clever enough to keep his mouth shut. At length, Morpheus recovered a more presentable form.

"What are you trying to accomplish?" Death asked

Mercury.

"I don't know what you're talking about."

"You think this gives you an alibi," Death said, prodding the chains with the end of his scythe, "but I've seen you wiggle out of worse. You're the messenger god, you go where you please, don't deny it."

"I still don't know what you're talking about. If I could be somewhere else, don't you think I would be? I'm missing the party."

"It's always a party with you Romans," Death said. "A party or a war."

"Well it's always a funeral with you," Morpheus said. "So you've no room to judge."

Bandying words was getting them nowhere. Besides, it wasn't Death's strong suit. He tended more to action than to argument. Clearly a new tactic was needed. Death plucked the feather from the water. "Do you deny that this is yours?"

Mercury shrugged, making his chains clatter together. "That depends on where you found it, but it's hard to say. I'm not the only one with golden feathers. And you still haven't told me what I am supposed to have done."

Morpheus, still keeping his distance, clearly not trusting himself to stay in control, shouted at Mercury, "You broke into my realm, you vandalized dreams, you fed a human ambrosia."

Death raised a hand. Morpheus turned away again. He'd begun pulling dreamstuff from the water and shaping small angry beasts, like bumblebees crossed with miniature bulldogs. They buzzed around his head for just moments before bursting in a shower of bubbles.

Mercury chuckled dryly. "Someone certainly has been busy. And brazen. But tell me, aside from the sheer fun of it, what's to be gained from such a course of action. I like humans well enough, but feeding one ambrosia? Why?"

"You tell me," Death said. "It's possible you thought you could disrupt the order of things. I know how you love to prove your cleverness. Or maybe it was something more, maybe you sought to usurp my power."

"I haven't done any of those things," Mercury said. "And I hardly think the power to be grim is one that I'd seek out willingly."

"I will have you know that I can be quite witty when I choose," Death said.

Mercury laughed aloud at that one. Death sighed. People were so closed-minded, even if they happened to be gods. He changed tactics again.

"Why are you here?" Death asked.

"My uncle Neptune caught me trying to steal his trident."

"So that's your alibi? I couldn't have disrupted the order of the universe because I was busy stealing?" Morpheus snapped.

"It's not an alibi. It's just a fact. I've been here for three hundred years give or take. Ask my uncle."

"I'm sure Lord Neptune has better things to do than to watch you every moment of the last three hundred years. Surely a clever trickster like you could have slipped away for a time without him noticing."

That was a direct appeal to Mercury's pride. Death could see it had worked. If you wanted to get something out of a Roman, it was always best to flatter them. Threats just made them laugh and any attempt at eliciting sympathy was met with stark incomprehension.

"I'm sure I could, if I put my mind to it. There's never been a trap yet that could hold me for long. I simply haven't bothered to attempt it. The salt water is good for the skin you know, and it is rather relaxing down here."

One of Morpheus' creatures buzzed by Death's head and exploded in Mercury's face. He cursed and tried to wave away the bubbles, but the chains kept his hands from reaching high enough. Death was beginning to think that Mercury was telling the truth for once.

CHAPTER TWENTY-ONE

Footrace

Someone touched Eric gently on the shoulder. He looked up at a goddess. She was taller than him. Everyone here was, except for the serving boys. At first, he wasn't sure what to make of her. She was wearing a simple shift, but the ringlets of her hair were held out of her face by a golden diadem and she carried herself with the straight back and high chin of a queen.

"I will watch the boy while you run your challenge," she said.

Uncertain whether he should trust her, Eric searched her face for some sign that would tell him what to do. Everyone on Mount Olympus seemed at best careless and at worst ruthless. Letting Ryan out of his sight seemed like a bad idea. What if something happened to him?

But something had already happened to him. He'd been assaulted by a god and Eric had done nothing to stop it. Ryan would probably be better off in the hands of someone who knew the rules of the place. Besides, her eyes were soft and kind. She took the soul by the hand and Ryan went along with her willingly, with no indication that he wanted to wander away in search of shiny objects.

"Thank you, ma'am," Eric said. "He seems to like you."

"You don't know who I am," the goddess said.

Eric shook his head. "I'm sorry. I'm not up on my Roman mythology." That was probably a rude thing to admit, all things considered, but it was the truth.

The goddess' sigh was heavy. Apparently she was used to human ignorance. "I am Juno, queen of the gods and mother of many," she said. "Your brother will be safe with me. At least until you lose."

"I'll win if I can," Eric said, but he couldn't make his voice sound all that convincing.

"You can't," she said. "But it is noble of you to try." She sighed again. "Mars is the most hot-headed of all my children."

Eric tried not to let his surprise show. She and Mars looked to be the same age. It was hard to believe that she could be his parent, but he guessed these things must be different for gods.

"Thank you," Eric said. "I'm sorry I didn't know your name."

The goddess shook her head. "I don't know what humanity is coming to. Not so many hundreds of years ago, the youngest of children knew my face by heart.

Time is so much crueler than Death. Death comes looking for you, but Time merely forgets you ever existed. He has a terrible memory."

The voice of Mars boomed over them. "How much longer do you intend to stall, human?"

Minerva rallied to Eric's defense. "Calm yourself. He's seeing to his duties as a man should."

Eric half-expected Mars to challenge her as well, but he just started unbuckling his armor. Apparently he had no intention of running in it.

"So much preparation just to lose," Mars said. "Imagine if he actually intended to win." He chuckled heartily at his own joke.

That rankled Eric a little. Okay, a lot actually. He was overwhelmed on all sides by challenges he hadn't sought out and battles he couldn't possibly win. To make matters worse, he was certainly going to die in the end. There was nothing he could do. Nothing. So he might as well go down fighting.

"How do I get down there?" Eric asked Juno.

"Olympus is actually much closer to earth than it appears," she said. "All you have to do is step and you'll find yourself on solid ground."

Eric looked down at the oil painting that was the earth. It was so far away. The trees were just grey rivulets, the field a few swipes of gold.

"That seems unlikely," Eric said.

"Many things do at first glance."

Eric squeezed Ryan's shoulder. "It'll be okay, buddy.

This will be over soon."

"I'll take care of him as though he were my own," Juno said.

Eric closed his eyes, and took a step of faith. At first he thought he'd misjudged the distance. His foot landed on solid ground without so much as a jolt. But then he opened his eyes. He was standing in an open field next to a single scraggly olive tree.

A few gods had already gathered there. Even as Eric fought to catch his bearings, Mars appeared. He was as naked as a statue, more naked, even, because most statues that Eric had seen included strategically placed fig leaves. Mars made no such concessions to modesty. Mars made no concessions at all.

Eric's face felt hot. He pulled his eyes upward. "I don't have to be naked do I?"

Mars snorted. "It hardly makes a difference."

Pax stepped forward. "I will be your starter. The challenge is a footrace, from this tree to that one."

She pointed off into the distance, where Eric could just make out a second grey smudge that might have been a tree or a house or a statue made entirely of fig leaves for all he knew.

"First to reach the tree is the winner. This is a footrace, so no flying or morphing. Minerva is at the finish to see fair play. If the human loses he will be killed and his slave will revert to Mars. If Mars loses he will grant the human a boon."

"He's not my slave," Eric said, but no one was

listening. Nobody had mentioned that Ryan would suffer if he lost. He took a deep breath, and then another when the first one got scared and tried to camp out in his throat.

"Are the challengers ready?"

"The sooner we start the sooner I can finish beating Minerva in Latrunculi," Mars said.

Eric just nodded.

"Runners, take your marks."

Mars settled into the perfect runner's stance of an Olympic athlete on the blocks, which technically, he was. Eric sank into a far less graceful ready stance, as though he were preparing to start a sack race at a family reunion.

"Set."

Eric squinted, trying to gauge the distance to the second olive tree. It was a long way. He was used to running in short bursts, from the breakroom to the bus, or from the bus to the front door of a house. He wasn't a marathon runner; he wasn't even much of a sprinter if it came to that. But he didn't have any gear to carry. It was just him. Him against a god.

"Go."

They ran. Eric knew that running flat out was probably a bad idea. He couldn't sustain that pace very long, and the racetrack seemed very long indeed. It was a bad idea, but that was a hard thing to remember with Mars quickly widening the gap between them. It was possible Mars would tire out, but it was more likely that gods didn't get tired, and if they did, they probably didn't do it as quickly as humans. Eric put on a burst of speed.

He tried to imagine a kid, bleeding under that tree, a kid who needed his help. It was always kids who needed the most help. They got into trouble they couldn't get themselves out of because they were curious and energetic and had no fear of Death.

Eric wished that Death hadn't gone away. It was some kind of Stockholm syndrome probably, but Eric felt better knowing that Death was there. Whatever else happened, Death had seemed like a stable point he could rely on. But then he'd left and Eric was alone. Alone except for the kid who depended on him, the kid he still hadn't succeeded in saving.

Eric's lungs were beginning to burn. His legs, too, had started to protest. The olive tree was still so far away. He doubted he'd even make it there. Collapsing seemed the more likely outcome. The only outcome. Eric was gasping, and Mars was only increasing his lead.

Nobody believed in him. Not Death, not Morpheus, not his squad or his mother or his friends. Even Ryan only stayed with him because he had no other choice. Eric was going to lose and Mars would kill him and the gods only knew what would happen to Ryan. His soul was forfeit if Eric failed.

Mars chose this moment to turn in mid-stride and begin jogging backward toward the goal. It infuriated Eric. God or not, Mars deserved to be beaten. He'd slapped a child. He'd picked a fight with someone weaker than him, someone less powerful who didn't know the rules. He didn't deserve to win. He deserved to be pounded into the ground like a stake. If only Eric were taller, and stronger, and less human.

Hot, wild anger crashed through his veins. He forgot everything. He forgot his gasping lungs. He forgot his aching legs. He ran and it was as though his feet had suddenly sprouted wings. The wind seemed to shove him forward, and the earth itself pushed back with every step, forcing him to cover more ground with each stride.

Bound by bound he closed the gap between himself and Mars. Mars noticed. With some satisfaction, Eric saw the look of surprise and then anger on Mars' face before Mars turned around and began running in earnest again.

By then it was too late. Eric had caught up to him, was running past him. Would have run past him, that is, except that Mars threw himself sideways, slamming into Eric with the full weight of his muscular form. Mars was a foot taller and a good fifty pounds heavier at least. Getting hit by him was like getting hit by a linebacker in full attack mode.

Eric, running faster than he'd ever run before, became a tangle of legs and feet. He hit the ground with enough momentum to sheer the skin from his forearms and nearly dislocate his shoulder. His teeth snapped together, sending shock waves down his spine. These collided with the ones coming up from his knees causing instant nausea in the pit of his stomach. Eric thought he might pass out.

Meanwhile, Mars barely lost his footing. He stumbled for a moment, but quickly regained his equilibrium and continued on toward the goal. He reached it at an easy lope, confident that Eric was no longer a threat.

Eric managed to roll onto his back and lie there gasping. Clouds drifted by overhead. They were light, wispy clouds, too weak to hold a kingdom. Olympus seemed to have vanished. Maybe it had never existed. Maybe it was all a hallucination. Wouldn't that be nice?

If Eric could only catch his breath it would be peaceful to just lie here, staring up at those clouds. He could lie here forever, maybe, and never see another bleeding kid or overdose victim or dying cop ever again. Yes, that would be heaven.

Eric had only just concocted this fantasy when the clouds were eclipsed by a head topped with a crown of flowers. Pax.

"Are you all right?" she asked.

"He. Cheated," Eric gasped.

"Yeah," Pax said. "He does that. Mars hates to lose. How did you run so fast? That was inhuman."

"Don't. Know."

Pax looked incredulous but stuck out her hand to help him up anyway. Eric took it and let himself be pulled to a sitting position. He couldn't go any higher than that. His lungs were still about thirty yards behind him and refusing to catch up. It wasn't until he stopped gasping that he noticed the commotion going on near the finish line, or tree, or whatever. Mars and Minerva were shouting at each other.

"You cheated," Minerva said. "How pathetic are you that you have to cheat to beat a human? I'm embarrassed to call you brother."

"Half-brother."

"Well I'm more than half-embarrassed."

"He cheated first. Did you see him run? No human runs like that."

"He's a human. Why did you even challenge him? You should have been thanking him. His brother stopped you from certain defeat in Latrunculi."

"You're delusional. I was winning that game."

"Nobody wins when you play. You're such a child."

Eric slumped on the sparse grass, his hands loose between his knees. He still didn't feel capable of standing. Pax hovered nearby.

"Oh, I wish they wouldn't fight," she said. "I don't know why siblings have to fight so. Isn't it much nicer when everybody gets along?"

"Yes," Eric said. "That would be nice."

"I just don't see why they have to fight. I'm going to go talk to them."

Eric watched her go, wondering if he was going to be killed. He'd lost, technically. But even more technically, he hadn't. Mars had cheated, so he should have to forfeit and grant Eric a, what did they call it, a boon? Eric watched Mars shove his sister. A reward was not likely, he decided.

Juno approached with Ryan in tow as Eric climbed to his feet. When she was close enough, she reached out and caught him by the jaw. Her fingers were long and her grip like a vice. The choice was turn his head to face her, or learn to enjoy eating through a straw. He turned his head.

Juno looked deep into Eric's eyes. She reminded him of his mother trying to tell if he'd lied to her about where he'd been the night before. That stare had worked on him for years, but eventually he'd developed an immunity to it. Juno's was stronger.

"What did you do?" she demanded.

"I don't know. I just ran and then I fell."

She held his stare. She probably expected more from him. He had nothing to add. Finally, Juno let go.

"Where has Death got to?" she asked. "He has some questions to answer."

"I think he's coming back. I hope so anyway."

Juno strode away. Eric waited until it was clear she wasn't returning before he attempted to massage feeling back into his face. Ryan spun in her wake. Eric reached out his hand to the soul, forgetting for a moment that he wouldn't even notice. Eric wished Death and Morpheus would come back.

CHAPTER TWENTY-TWO

Memento Mori

Deep under the sea, Death hesitated. He didn't want to go back to the council and tell them that he'd failed. For one, he didn't think that they'd accept such a non-answer. For two, his pride would not allow it. Admitting defeat in front of the council was something he simply couldn't stomach.

Of course, he was older and wiser than all of them combined, but letting them see him as weak would upset the order of things even more, and this balance was in place for a reason. It was a good reason too. During the black plague, thousands of souls had been lost in the void. Things like that couldn't be allowed to happen in the modern world. Death just wished there was something he could do to stop it.

"Are you listening?" Mercury asked.

Death shook his head. "You could have gotten out of this, you can get out of anything."

"I probably could, you're right. But I didn't. And if I was going to pick a fight it wouldn't be with you or the council. I like to have a bit of fun, but I'm not an idiot."

Morpheus had stopped making dream bombs and was now just muttering to himself. He'd drawn closer.

"Could have fooled me," he said.

Mercury rolled his eyes. "I'm wounded. Really. Look, we all know I'm a thief and a trickster and you have no reason to believe me. Go talk to Neptune. He'll tell you I've been here the whole time."

Death turned his back and lowered his voice. "We could just go find more proof," he said to Morpheus.

"You know, I'm getting really tired of this," Morpheus said. "While I'm gone the Oneiroi are just recycling old dreams. That can't go on for too long."

"Think how I feel," Death said. "Human souls are imprisoned in dying bodies while I'm away." He lowered his voice even more. "And between you and me, you're going a bit native."

Morpheus sighed and dragged one hand across his eyes. "You don't know what it's like, Death. You are you, and you will never be anything but you. Whether they see you as a shadow or a saint, a man in black or a woman in gray you are, and always will be, Death. No more. No less.

"I, on the other hand…" He looked down at his twelve fingers splayed out before him. "I can be anything. I can be anyone. You don't understand the pressure that puts on me. When I'm around Olympians for too long, I start acting like an Olympian. When I'm around humans for too long, I start acting like a human."

Mercury was eavesdropping. It wouldn't have been hard. In his distress, Morpheus had raised his voice.

"I actually kind of like humans," Mercury said.

"You are not helping your case," Death snapped. He gave Morpheus a reassuring pat on the arm. "Don't worry. It will all be over soon."

Morpheus didn't seem convinced, but he nodded anyway. Death left him and went back to Mercury's rock.

"You are coming with us."

He swung his scythe and chopped through the chain that held Mercury's left wrist. Snick. It might as well have been spider silk for all the resistance it put up. Chain links drifted toward the ocean floor. *So much for the forges of Vulcan*, Death thought.

"Neptune isn't going to like this," Mercury said.

He actually seemed worried. Death swung the scythe again. Snick. Mercury's other arm dropped to his side, trailing a chain. Death gathered up the severed chains in one hand. They would be helpful in keeping their suspect from escaping.

"Don't worry. We'll either return you or punish you to such an extent that Pluto himself will pity you. I'm sure Neptune will have no objection either way."

Snick-snick went the scythe near Mercury's ankles, and he was free from the rock. Death jerked on the chains. Mercury stumbled forward, dragging his shackles behind.

The water around them seemed to be getting warmer.

Strangely, it also seemed to be getting darker, as though a huge form were bending over the face of the water. A school of fish darted by. Mercury cast his eyes around.

"I wouldn't be so certain of that. My uncle has few powers of understanding."

"Morpheus will stay and explain it to him," he said.

Before Morpheus could object, Death stepped sideways pulling Mercury with him.

~

Olympus was far quieter than it had been when they left it. Death was surprised. He had expected some sort of celebration over Eric's defeat by Mars. Instead, Olympus looked like a bar after all the regulars had gone home.

A few gods were still lounging about, and the ubiquitous lyre music was still playing with no perceptible musician in attendance, but the general bustle was gone. Death grabbed a random demigod.

"Where is everyone?"

"They've gone down to watch the challenge."

"Down where?"

The demigod pointed at the hole in the clouds.

Death stepped.

~

Eric jumped when Death appeared next to him. He would never get used to a skeletal man in a black coat popping up without warning.

"What happened?" Death asked.

"Mars cheated."

"So you were winning? How?"

"I don't know. I was running…wait. How did you know I was winning?"

"Mars has his honor, after a fashion. He wouldn't stoop so low as to cheat unless he thought he might be at risk for losing."

Eric snorted. "He's practically a saint."

Death shrugged. "He's an Olympian. But you were winning, weren't you? How?"

"I have no idea. I thought there was no way I could win. I mean, I was most definitely losing. But then I got mad and all of a sudden it was like my feet had wings, they just flew. But then Mars tripped me and I fell."

Eric held up his scraped arms as proof.

"That's all in your head you know," Mercury said. "Just stop believing you got hurt."

"That's stupid."

"Oh excuse me. Here I thought I was a god and you were just a puny human with a boo-boo."

"Who is this?" Eric asked Death. He tried to imagine that he didn't have abrasions all over his arms. It didn't work. It was hard to imagine something didn't exist when it was causing a throbbing ache.

"This is Mercury," Death said. "God of messengers,

thieves, merchants, and tricksters. He's the one who's been meddling in your dreams."

"Have not," Mercury said.

Eric cocked his head and looked at Mercury. He looked familiar: the hair, the beard, the wings. All the elements were there. Yet something wasn't quite right. It reminded him of the dream version of his childhood home. Almost perfect but somehow slightly off. Eric couldn't put his finger on exactly what it was.

Mercury noticed him staring and struck as much of a godlike pose as he could with his arms chained. "Make a statue," he said. "It'll last longer."

Death jerked at his chain. Mercury stumbled and gave Death a dirty look.

"Come along, Eric," Death said. "It's time to settle this."

"Did Morpheus give up on us?" Eric asked.

"He is…indisposed," Death said.

"He's in trouble, just like you're about to be, human," Mercury said. "Better start running again."

He was looking over Death's shoulder. Death and Eric turned to see what had drawn Mercury's attention. It was, in fact, trouble. The red-faced god of war was striding toward them. He looked belligerent. Eric shifted so he was standing between Mars and Ryan.

"Your pet human cheated, Death."

"As did you."

"He cheated first."

"I have bigger problems to deal with than your

wounded pride, Mars. Call it a draw and be done with it."

Mars settled his feet as though he expected a fistfight to break out. It would have been more threatening if he wasn't still naked. Apparently Romans, or at least Roman gods, were comfortable with challenging people to fisticuffs in the buff.

"I will not be talked down to. Defend yourself or be defeated."

At first it seemed like a trick of the light. Death advanced on Mars and with each step he darkened. His darkness stained the world around him, as though he were a flame that cast shadow instead of light.

Mars held his ground at first, but as Death drew ever nearer, the god of war began to collapse in on himself. His hands dropped, his chest deflated. The glow fled from his skin and hair. He looked older somehow, and much, much smaller.

"You forget who you are speaking to, Roman." Death's voice was a sibilant murmur and somehow that was more terrifying than if he had shouted. "I am the remover of suffering. I am the bringer of sorrow. I am the first breath of darkness in the heart of the world. I have been here since the beginning of time, and when you perish, you, tiny, insignificant personification of human folly, it will be I who carries you forth into the next world."

During this speech, Mars slumped closer and closer to the ground. It was as though he were trying to be invisible, as though Death would forget him if only he could make himself small enough. But Death never forgot anyone. He leaned even closer. Wings of darkness folded around Mars, who whimpered.

"Think carefully now," Death said. "Do you dare to challenge me?"

"No, Lord Death."

"No. What?"

"No, I do not dare to challenge you."

Light came back to the world. In the space between one blink and the next, Death returned to his humanoid form. He rolled his shoulders inside his black leather trench coat.

"Good. Time to go."

Mercury, who'd been dragged on his chain behind Death while all of this was going on, and so had a front-row seat to the terror, was still whimpering softly when Death stepped sideways, drawing them all away from Olympus.

Death didn't bother with formality but appeared inside the council chamber, bypassing Cecil entirely, a move that would most certainly offend the little man's sense of decency when he learned about it. All the more so because Death brought along the whole mad menagerie: a Roman god in chains, a clueless human, and an unmoored soul.

CHAPTER TWENTY-THREE

Judgement Day

The council chamber looked completely different from the last time Eric had seen it. The dark room and torches were gone. Instead, the gods sat around a long conference table under a sky overcome with stars.

From what Eric had learned about gods thus far, he guessed that each of them probably believed their land and their sky was more important than any other, and so the stars displayed in the council chamber were like the star charts for every nation printed on clear film and then stacked all together. Every star that was and ever had been in the sky twinkled and shimmered above the council table, but there was no moon to be seen.

He only noticed the sky at all because he'd acquired a kind of sympathetic habit of looking up, like Ryan did. People so rarely looked up. It was amazing what you could notice if you just looked.

When he finally did look down at the gods, he wished

he hadn't. They weren't cloaked or hooded anymore. Each wore his or her most comfortable form.

On Olympus the gods had been larger than life, but they'd at least appeared human. Here the gods appeared however they wished. Only two seemed mostly human. Two arms, two legs, a head each. One was naked and winged, another ghost pale and draped in white with black hair and eyes. The god at the head of the table was green, but at least he wasn't a giant feathered snake. Eric had to look away from them.

That's when he spotted the scribe, if that's what he was, standing off to the side behind his podium. He was the only one still wearing a cloak and hood. Eric wondered about that, but then Death spoke.

"Here is the answer to all our troubles," Death said.

Shoved forward from behind and still shackled, Mercury stumbled and nearly fell. The scribe twitched. The other gods did not.

"You intrude on us unannounced," Osiris said.

"You sent me to solve the problem," Death said. "I have solved it. Here is your culprit, now reinstate my power."

"And what proof do you have?" the record keeper said from behind his podium.

Eric twitched. The record keeper had never spoken before. No, he had. He'd been the one who read the bylaws when they'd taken Death's power away. Was that why his voice seemed so familiar?

Eric looked more closely at him. It was hard to tell

with the hooded robe, but he did seem to be humanoid. Eric couldn't see his face. He thought he saw a beard, but couldn't be sure, because it was black on black. One of his hands clutched the podium, the other, the left, held a pen.

Osiris gave the record keeper a sharp look, as though he'd done something rude. Maybe he had. Maybe he wasn't supposed to speak without an invitation.

"Yes, Lord Death," Osiris said, composing himself. "Tell us how you came to this conclusion. I must say this type of ruse seems far beyond Mercury's usual mischief."

"We entered the dreams of the human and found the places where Mercury had been. He left a trace of himself behind, which we found."

"I never—" Mercury began, but Death silenced him with a look and a shake of the chain. Eric noticed that the record keeper took a step away from his podium, his own chain tinkling.

"And then he helped the human cheat in a challenge against Mars."

"That windbag," Yama said. "I hope you walloped him, human."

"Not exactly," Eric said. He tugged at Death's robe.

"What is it?" Death said, his voice low and sharp. He clearly didn't want to be interrupted at the moment.

"Who is that keeping the record?"

"Hermes," Death said.

"I really didn't—" Mercury began again, but this time Osiris interrupted him. "Have you any proof of your innocence, or only feeble excuses?"

Mercury had no proof, but he did have a quick tongue, which he attempted to use to his advantage. It would have worked on a human. It might have worked on most gods. Osiris did not seem impressed.

While Mercury was still talking, Eric whispered to Death, "Yes, but who is Hermes?"

Death rounded on Eric, his eyes flashing emptiness. "He is the Greek messenger god. He has been charged with keeping the record. Would you like to further delay the rebalancing of the universe while we present you with a puppet show detailing his life story?"

"Is he also a god of thieves and tricksters?"

Death became very still then. He looked like a wax figure. Not breathing—not that he ever had—not moving, not blinking, just standing still and silent.

Mercury was still talking, but his voice seemed far away. It wasn't the right voice. That Eric knew for certain. That's what had been bothering him.

"Why do you ask?" Death said. He said it carefully, as though he already knew the answer but felt compelled to ask the question.

"The Greek gods and the Roman gods were basically the same with different names, right? Earlier Morpheus said they were like siblings. I thought I recognized his voice before. I couldn't remember why."

Death stepped sideways across the council hall. Eric had never seen him do that before. It was like a magic trick. One moment his face was inches from Eric's, the next he was holding a sword to Hermes' neck.

Silence descended. All eyes turned to Death, or more accurately, to the edge of the sword he was holding, and more accurately still, to the place where that sword met the throat of the Greek messenger god. Death's voice boomed into a world devoid of sound, and Eric could have sworn that the stars themselves trembled.

"You upset the balance of the worlds. You crept like a thief into the human's dreams. You taught him what humans should not know. You fed him the food of the gods. You gave him power he should not possess. You, a member of this council. The council charged with safeguarding the order of worlds. You did this. Now, tell me why I should not slice your soul from your body."

Another silence like the one that comes just after the priceless and completely irreplaceable vase tilts off the shelf and just before it hits the ground and smashes into ten thousand completely worthless pieces.

"You're going to need to pull that blade back a bit if you want him to be able to talk," Morpheus said. Eric looked around, surprised. He hadn't noticed Morpheus come in, or appear, or whatever it was he had done.

"Move and I will cast you into the void myself," Death said. He lessened the pressure ever so slightly. "Now speak."

Hermes spoke.

"Yes, I gave the human power. It was a means to an end. Can't you see that the council has hobbled you? It's made you cautious and deferential. Surely you can see that something must be done, and I was the only one with the courage to do it."

"And you." Hermes couldn't turn, not without losing his head, but his eyes rolled toward Osiris and the council.

"You're so—so smug, so self-righteous. You were gods once, worshiped, feared, adored. Now what are you? Bureaucrats. Sitting around your table, making your rules, keeping records. You're so enslaved to them you can't imagine things being any other way. Have you forgotten what it was like when every god was his own master?"

"It was chaos," Freyja said evenly.

"It was glorious. We were gods. True gods. Not fodder for fairy tales and fantasy stories. And now you sit there, enslaved, mocking my Roman brothers and sisters as though you were somehow better than them. You can't even see what I was trying to do for you. I was trying to free you, to free all of us."

His wild eyes rolled in Death's direction.

"You should have just handed over your scythe like they asked. Nothing could have stopped me if I had the scythe."

Death let his sword fall and disappear into the otherness that he had pulled it from. Hermes didn't try to flee. He should have, but he was lost in his own ravings. He didn't even flinch when the hand of Death fell on his shoulder.

It was not a comforting hand. It was the hand of a parent on the shoulder of a willful child being marched to the time-out chair. Held in the grip of Death, the messenger god, who could slip in and out of worlds with ease, was trapped. Hermes didn't even try to struggle as Death pulled him before the council table.

"You are a disgrace," Osiris said. "There is only one punishment fit for you. You must go to the river Styx and take the staff from the ferryman."

The collective gasp was as loud as a shout.

Mercury did shout. "You can't be serious."

Clearly this was a major punishment. Eric had no idea what it meant, but the gods themselves were shocked by it.

Osiris ignored Mercury's outburst. Proven innocent, he was no longer relevant to the discussion at hand, and therefore did not exist in Osiris' universe. Eric suspected that the gods hadn't learned anything from Hermes' rebellion. To them, he was just a revolutionary to be put down.

"You've meddled in the affairs of gods and men," Osiris said. "You've trespassed where you do not belong. You've put the very balance of the worlds in danger. And for what? For pride?"

"I did it for you. For all of us."

"Go," Osiris said. "Death will escort you. He knows the way."

Eric held the soul close as Freyja and Yama approached, carrying golden chains. They shackled Hermes hands and feet.

"I am the messenger of the gods. Will you not hear my message?"

One of the council put an end to his raving by stuffing a golden ball into his mouth. He tried to talk around it, but the result was angry gargling.

Mercury, who seemed to have realized that there was still something to be gained from this situation, tried to take advantage of the chaos. He had raised his foot to step when a heavy hand landed on his shoulder. Not the hand of Death, but the six fingers of the Dream Lord.

"Not so fast, Roman," Morpheus said. "You may not be guilty of this crime, but I promised your uncle I'd return you to the punishment you have earned, and that I intend to do."

They both disappeared. Eric could only assume that Morpheus had taken Mercury back to wherever they'd found him.

Quiet settled over the council chamber.

"We'll need a new record keeper," Izanami said.

"Perhaps it would be better to find a human for the job," Yama said. "These things wouldn't happen with a human taking notes."

"A new record keeper is a secondary concern," Yan Wang said. "What we need is new procedures to prevent these sorts of incidents in the future."

Osiris rapped his flail against the table until the council members fell silent again.

"We will deal with new business when the season is right," Osiris said. "But first, let us complete the work before us. Lord Death, would you see to it that Hermes reaches his destination?"

"And my authority?"

"Restored, of course. The council thanks you for your patience during these troubling times."

Osiris stood, crossed crook and flail over his chest, and bowed stiffly in Death's direction. The other gods nodded sheepishly or ruffled their feathers, generally showing through uneasy motion and lack of eye contact that they were embarrassed not to have caught the wolf in their midst.

Death inclined his head ever so slightly. He was pleased, Eric could tell.

"Come Eric," he said. "We have a delivery to make."

~

They stepped sideways into a desert bisected by a deep but languid river with water as black as ink. Eric gripped Ryan's hand.

"Where are we now?" he asked.

"This is a glimpse of the afterlife. If you're lucky, one day you will make it here."

Hermes was struggling in Death's grip, but Death could not be shaken. He waited patiently as a faded old boat approached them across the water.

"Say nothing and touch nothing," Death told Eric.

By now Eric had learned to listen. He gripped Ryan's hand tightly and pulled him a little away from the spot where the boat nosed to shore. The ferry captain looked at the four of them, taking in the sight of Death, a human, a soul, and a bound and gagged messenger of the gods standing together on a riverbank.

"I only ask two pennies for payment," he said. "You didn't have to bring all that."

Death pushed Hermes aboard the little skiff. "You must be tired of steering captain. Give him your pole."

Hunger flared in the captain's eyes. "He'll take it, then?"

"He will," Death said.

The captain thrust the pole roughly at Hermes. Hermes tried to back away, but his feet tangled in a rope that had been neatly coiled on the deck. He fell backward. The captain pressed his advantage and thrust again. This time Hermes' hand closed around the pole.

When that simple stick changed hands, it changed the scene as well. The captain seemed to grow and brighten until his face was like the sun. It almost hurt to look at him. At the same time, Hermes seemed to shrink, but maybe it was the sudden slouch that convulsed his frame.

The former captain looked down at Hermes, who was just regaining his feet.

"Hermes?" the former captain said.

"He meddled, as you did," Death said. "Now he'll pay his debt."

"As I did," the god said. He had to be a god, Eric thought. What else could he be?

"Yes," Death said. "Have you learned anything, Samyaza?"

"They won't burn me then?" Samyaza asked. He moved his shoulders up and down, like a man getting used to a new coat.

"I make you no promises, but for now, your debt is paid."

"Better you than me," Samyaza said to Hermes, who now stood in the boat, his hand wrapped protectively around the staff. Hermes didn't seem to hear him.

Samyaza stepped off the boat onto the shore. Somehow Eric was unsurprised when the feathered cloak he'd been wearing turned out to be a pair of wings, folded close along his back.

They unfurled now. Spread to their full length they were longer than Samyaza was tall. Glittering white gold, they caught and refracted the tiniest light so that they almost seemed to twinkle.

He flapped them once, twice. Tiny dust storms rose and died in their wake. Eric squinted against the combination of white light and swirling sand.

Suddenly, Samyaza crouched and leapt upward. He jumped much too high, higher than would have been possible for even the most athletic human. Then his wings began to beat and the tiny dust storms became a whirling dervish.

Eric turned his face away. When the wind had settled and it was safe to look up, Samyaza was out of sight. Tilting his head back, all that Eric could see was a bright point of light, like the morning star high overhead.

"I'll take you across for two pennies," Hermes said,

from behind them.

For a moment Eric had forgotten Hermes was there, but now he turned to face the god who had caused him all this trouble. His shoulders curved inward and his vacant eyes suggested he understood little of what was going on around him. Despite all he'd done, Eric could almost pity him. Not quite, but almost.

Looking from Eric to Ryan and back again, Hermes said, "Two for one since the boy is so small."

"Not at this time," Death said. "We have other matters to attend to."

The ferryman shrugged, and began to punt his skiff out toward the middle of the river. Inky water swirled below the boat. Eric backed away from the ripples of water that touched the shoreline, but after he'd done so, he wasn't sure why he felt the need to do it.

"It's like he doesn't remember us," Eric said.

"He doesn't," Death said. "He doesn't remember anything. Such is the curse of the ferryman. He knows only the boat and the river. As long as he holds the staff he is bound to them both."

"Can't he just put it down?" Eric said.

"No. There must always be a ferryman. It is the order of the worlds. And for the staff to pass from hand to hand it must be freely taken."

"Hermes didn't take it freely. You forced him to."

"He had a choice. There is always a choice. He could have fought me and lost and been destroyed, or he could have thrown himself into the river Styx and forgotten not just who he was but even that there was a him to remember.”

“That’s not much of a choice.”

“I never said they were good options.”

“No, I guess you didn’t,” Eric said. He watched the little boat bob across the water and said, “I didn’t know gods could go insane.”

“They can’t, not really, but sometimes when you look like a human, and you talk like a human, it’s hard to remember that you’re not, in fact, human.” Death sighed and this time he didn’t even try to hide it. “We become what we pretend to be.”

CHAPTER TWENTY-FOUR

Death Lies

Death stepped them sideways out of the afterlife and back to the soul's hospital room. Eric looked around for specters and noticed how crowded the room had become. Beds were pushed up close together. A few patients were even lying on blankets on the floor. Some cried out in pain, others simply lay there, staring at the ceiling.

"Are we safe here?"

"Safe enough," Death said. "It will take the specters some time to track the loose soul here. Besides," he plucked his scythe from the air, "I am with you."

A nurse plodded into the room. Eric froze.

"Don't worry," Death said. "She cannot see us."

To demonstrate his point, he waved the scythe in front of her face. She didn't even blink. Watching her cross the room, Eric thought she was about fourteen hours into a twelve-hour shift. Wild strands of hair escaped from her bun. Dark smudges under her eyes told of too little sleep.

The layers of stains on her scrubs indicated she hadn't had time to change.

When she bent to comfort a patient, Eric couldn't hear what she said. But he heard the patient just fine. "It hurts. Can't you make it stop hurting?"

"I'm sorry. I wish I could. Is there anything I can do for you? Are you thirsty?"

The man started to sob. The nurse just stayed there with him, holding his hand. Eric had known many nurses in his short career. Most were strong, dedicated people who radiated competence. It was built into them on a fundamental level. When something was amiss, they fixed it. When you asked a question, they answered it. When patients fell apart, they put them back together.

Sometimes just sitting with a patient was the right thing to do, but this man clearly needed something stronger than a sympathetic touch, possibly a morphine drip.

"This isn't right," Eric said. "What's happening here?"

"This is what happens when you remove me from the world," Death said.

"But it's over now," Eric said. "You can go back to work and I can go back to my life and everything is back to normal."

"Not exactly," Death said. "There's still the matter of your companion."

Eric looked down at Ryan. He had wandered over to stand beside his body and stare vacant-eyed at the child he once was.

"He doesn't have to die," Eric said. "We could just put him back in his body."

"He is already dead. He just doesn't know it yet."

Eric sat down at the foot of the bed and stared at Ryan's face. He looked peaceful now, as peaceful as a corpse.

"I keep trying to save them and they keep dying anyway," Eric said. "All I want is to be useful. You know? To be there when someone needs me. To matter for just one second. But all I do is mess everything up. The whole world, suffering, because of me."

If Eric had been hoping for some consolation, if he had expected Death to tell him it was all out of his control or it wasn't as bad as he thought, he would have been disappointed.

"Yes," Death said.

Eric sat, just staring at a random spot on a random square of linoleum. Death was nothing if not honest. You couldn't bullshit him, and he returned the favor by never bullshitting you. Death didn't worry about hurting feelings or making you feel better about yourself. He just came along when it was your time.

And suppose Death had lied to him? Suppose he'd fed Eric a bunch of fluff about how it wasn't his fault and he hadn't really meant to do it and he couldn't possibly be expected to understand the consequences of his actions? Would that have changed anything? Would it have made people suffer any less? Would it have freed the soul from this empty half-life it was experiencing? Would it actually have made Eric feel any better? No.

Eric blinked a few times. He looked up, ready to ask Death what would happen next. Before he could say a word, something morphed through the wall, arms outstretched, a grimace contorting its mouth.

Eric almost collapsed in fear before he recognized the apparition. Morpheus drifted toward the floor, laughing.

"Why would you do that?" Eric shouted.

"You should have seen your face," Morpheus said. Suddenly Eric was looking at his own face, screwed up in terror.

"Ha!" said Death. From his mouth, the syllable sounded like the closing of a tomb.

Eric closed his eyes. Staring at your own face on someone else's body, especially when it looked like it had just seen a soul-sucking monster, was not a pleasant experience.

"Seriously, what's wrong with you?" Eric said.

"The human raises a good point. Why are you here, brother?"

"That was hilarious and you know it," Morpheus said. He was wearing his own face again, the mismatched eyes wrinkled in amusement. "I wanted to see how all of this would turn out. What are you going to do with the human?"

"I? Nothing. The question is, what will he do now?"

Morpheus shot Death a knowing look. Eric didn't even try to guess what it meant. He had no idea what Death was up to. All he knew was that he needed to protect

Ryan. He put his arm around Ryan's soul. "Tell me what I have to do to make this right."

"Are you sure that's what you want? The price may be high."

"This was my mistake. It's my responsibility to fix it if I can."

Death and Morpheus shared another look that Eric couldn't read.

"Will you protect this child's soul on its journey to the afterlife?"

"I'll do my best."

"Oh no," Death said. "You'll have to do much better than that."

He dropped a hand on Eric's shoulder. In the instant before they stepped, Eric felt Morpheus grab his arm.

~

"Well, this is pleasant," Morpheus said when they arrived. Until that moment, Eric hadn't realized that gods could be sarcastic.

Tendrils of mist floated in the low light, limiting visibility to just a few feet in any direction. They were standing near a single barren tree, and in the gloom, Eric could almost believe it was a man, hands and fingers spread to the sky, begging for guidance or release.

The scenery was enough to chill Eric's blood, but the feel of the place was worse. He couldn't shake the sense that someone, maybe several someones, was watching them from the fogbank. The damp cold crept into his muscles and curled up in his bones. Feeling watched made him want to stay on high alert, but the cold and the fog were inside his head, slowing his thoughts, blunting his reflexes.

"Where do we go?" Eric asked.

"The soul will know. All you have to do is keep it safe."

Death was right. Ryan, while no more alert than he had ever been, was trying to pull Eric forward.

"Safe from what?"

"There are specters here and lost souls that haven't yet become specters. Beware the crevasses. They're bottomless."

Morpheus chimed in. "And if you see something that's part crocodile, part lion, and part hippopotamus run like the gods themselves are after you." He grinned. "Because they are."

Death shot him a disapproving look.

"What is he talking about?"

"Nothing for you to worry about, I'm sure," Death said. "I haven't seen Ammit in over a century."

"Who is Ammit?"

"She is, she was, the devourer of the dead," Death said, "an Egyptian deity tasked with eating the hearts of those found unworthy of the afterlife."

"But she's gone native," Morpheus added with the glee of a camper telling a scary story around the fire.

"Last I heard she was roaming the void, hunting lost souls. Tearing out their hearts and swallowing them whole."

That did not make Eric feel great about this adventure. Death, ever practical, attempted to bring a measure of sanity back to the conversation.

"As I said, I haven't seen her in many years. You're unlikely to cross her path."

He lifted his foot as if to step sideways out of the void.

"Wait!" Eric said. "You can't just leave us here."

"I can and I will. Your little adventure has left me with a most impressive backlog. While I can technically be everywhere, here is one less place I have to be. You'll probably be fine."

Eric didn't really expect any mercy from Death. Death had remained analytical and detached throughout this whole ordeal, but he protested anyway.

"I don't even have a weapon," Eric said. "What am I going to do? Challenge the specters to a thumb wrestling match? Rock, paper, scissors?"

Morpheus chuckled. Death, surprisingly, hesitated. It was hard to read his skeletal features, but he seemed to be thinking about something. After a moment, he nodded once to himself. Then he reached out with one arm and pulled a sword from the air.

Eric was past wondering how he did that or where the sword came from. He did wonder if it was the sword Death had used to threaten Hermes, or if he had more than one—swords for all occasions. Did Death have other weapons too? The dagger of Death, perhaps, or a morbid mace? That thought teetered on the edge of hysteria. Eric refused to let himself start laughing. If he started now, he might not be able to stop. Besides, Death wouldn't get the joke.

Death offered Eric the hilt of the sword. "Here, this should offer you some protection."

Eric hesitated. Even Morpheus was surprised. His eyebrows jumped toward his dark hair. "A hero's weapon," Morpheus said.

Death didn't respond. He just stood there, waiting for Eric to make a decision. After a moment, Eric took the sword and hefted it in his hand. He'd never held one before. It was lighter than he had expected. Much lighter. In fact, if he didn't look at it, he could almost forget it existed.

"Isn't this one of those giving-a-human-power-he-should-not-possess things?" Eric asked.

"Yes and no. Technically the sword can reap souls, but everyone you'll meet in this realm is already lost."

"Except us," Eric said.

"Theoretically," Death said. "Come Morpheus, Eric has his work cut out for him, and so do we."

Morpheus twiddled six fingers at Eric and grinned. "Good luck, human," he said. And they were gone. Eric and Ryan were alone in the void.

CHAPTER TWENTY-FIVE

Into the Void

Eric and Ryan were alone in the void, which really meant that Eric was alone in the void, alone in the dim mist with a kid who seemed unaware of his existence and a sword he didn't know how to use.

Ryan strained like a dog at the end of a leash, trying to pull Eric forward. Eric let him lead. Death had said Ryan would know which way to go. Each step they took sent a puff of dust up from the arid ground, so they ended up walking in a sad little dust cloud, like Pigpen from the Charlie Brown cartoons. The wind should have blown it away, but instead it just spun whirling dervishes around their knees. *We're just going for a walk,* Eric told himself—a nice, slow, leisurely walk through a nightmare landscape.

The mist was getting thicker. Something moved in the corner of Eric's eye. He spun to face it. Nothing there but mist. A trick of the light of course. Being lost made him nervous.

We're not lost though. I just don't know where we are or where we're going or how to get there. Ryan, meanwhile, was walking with purpose for the first time since his death. He led them fearlessly through the mist.

It took Eric a while to realize that the ground had a slight decline. Wherever Ryan was leading them, it was in a downward direction. Eric didn't like that. He didn't like that at all.

Again something moved, this time in front of them, and Eric realized the fog was shifting, thickening in spots to form an indistinct shape. It didn't stay indistinct for long. It didn't stay much of anything for long, but it did become a pack of wolves, and then a screaming skull, and then a snake large enough to swallow a man and then… Eric stopped watching. It was just fog playing tricks on him; it couldn't actually hurt him. At least he hoped it couldn't. Death hadn't said anything about killer weather.

Eric forced himself to ignore the shifting fog and watch the ground instead. This experience was already bad enough. Falling into a bottomless crevasse wouldn't improve it. He was focused so intently on the ground ahead that he forgot there were worse things than falling.

An unexpected noise tore through the mist. Eric looked up certain he would see a specter flying toward them, arms outstretched, ready to devour them.

But it was only Ryan. The soul was crying. Tears dribbled down his cheeks. He made another little hitching sound, the same sound Eric had heard a moment ago. Eric stared at him in disbelief.

Ryan, who hadn't so much as blinked while wandering in a war zone, being pursued by a zombie, and standing before a council of the gods, was definitely crying. He had the tears, the red face, the ragged breath, all of it.

Eric squeezed his hand. "Hey buddy, you okay?" he said.

He didn't expect an answer, it just made him feel better to treat the soul at least a little bit like a person. After all, Ryan had been a person once.

"Wh-where are we?" Ryan said.

Eric grabbed him by the shoulders. "Did you just talk?"

That probably wasn't the best response. Ryan started to sob.

Eric got down on one knee so they were at eye level. He stared at the red-faced kid. Even through the tears he could see more animation, more intelligence, than had ever been there before. Clearly something had changed. Until now, Eric had been toting around a soul. It hadn't really seemed human. Now it did. He was face-to-face with a very young and very frightened human.

"What do you remember?" Eric asked.

Ryan couldn't seem to stop crying. He was trying, but the tears just kept coming.

"I don't know," he said.

He collapsed toward Eric and Eric caught him, pulling him close and holding him there while he cried. "It's okay, buddy," Eric murmured. "You're okay. I'm here."

Ryan rubbed his eyes. "Who are you?"

Eric's heart crumbled in his chest. He tried to tell himself that it was better if Ryan didn't know who he was. It meant he probably also didn't remember all of the weirdness Eric had dragged him through. Which was obviously a good thing.

"My name is Eric. I'm a first responder. Do you know what that is?"

Ryan shook his head. The crying had stopped now, except for the occasional hiccup. He was waiting, waiting on the grown-up to make the world make sense again.

"A first responder is someone who comes to help you when you're hurt or in trouble. We come to make you safe again."

"Like a police officer or a fireman?"

"A lot like that, yes. Sometimes I work with police officers and firemen, but today it's just you and me."

"Who's that?" Ryan asked pointing past Eric's shoulder.

Eric spun with the sword raised in front of him. A specter was coming up fast. In another instant it would be able to grab him. Eric couldn't tell if it was male or female. He couldn't tell if it had ever worn clothes or if that was its tattered skin whipping in the wind.

From behind him, Ryan gasped. He'd clearly realized that the thing coming out of the mist was most definitely a what, not a who.

In fact, it looked inhuman enough that Eric didn't

hesitate to attack. He had a sword and there was a monster. He knew exactly what to do. He swiped the sword from left to right. It passed through the creature's belly with only the slightest resistance. The specter hung in midair. Then it made a sound like a balloon being slowly deflated. Eric couldn't tell if the noise came from its mouth or the slash in its stomach. Either way, the specter disappeared.

Eric scanned the mist, looking for more, but there were no more to see. He turned to Ryan, who was clutching Eric's right hand like his soul depended on it, his eyes shut tight.

"It's okay, buddy. It's gone."

Ryan opened one eye just a slit. When nothing jumped out at him he allowed both eyes to roam the mist.

"Did you kill it?"

"I, uh, sent it away, I guess," Eric said. Honestly he wasn't really sure what he had done. Maybe he should have asked Death a few more questions.

"I have a question," Ryan said.

Eric mentally prepared himself to explain the concept of a specter that eats human souls to an eight-year-old kid who was a human soul, but Ryan surprised him.

"Do first responders usually carry swords?" he asked.

Eric almost laughed out loud. He held it back though, because the kid looked so serious and asked the question so earnestly. Eric didn't want to upset him.

"No, not usually. Hardly ever."

"I didn't think so."

Eric actually allowed himself to smile. He was feeling a little more confident. The specters were slow and they didn't seem all that smart. Really, once you got past the terrifying body issues, they were hardly scary at all. He'd gotten rid of that one easily. If that was the worst the void could throw at him, this would be a walk in the park. A very dark, very dreary park.

CHAPTER TWENTY-SIX

The Last Great Adventure

Eric was so confident in his ability to defend them, that he almost didn't spot the next specter until it was too late. It moved faster than the last one he'd seen, darting out of the mist straight toward Ryan. Ryan screamed and dove to the left. The sudden motion was enough to pull Eric off balance.

In the instant it took him to recover, the thing got one hand on Ryan's arm. Ryan's face instantly went slack. The color drained out of it.

Terror clawed Eric's heart. He slashed Death's sword at the specter's face. The creature popped out of existence with a sad balloon wail.

Eric glanced wildly around, almost eager for more targets. Reassured that he and Ryan were alone, he fell to his knees in front of the kid. Dust plumed up around him and was whipped away by the wind.

"You okay, buddy? You okay?" Eric asked, already

knowing the answer. He pressed his hands to Ryan's temples, his cheeks, his shoulders.

Ryan didn't respond. He'd withdrawn into himself again. The expression on his face was that of an empty soul, just allowing itself to be towed along.

For the second time, Eric wished he'd asked more questions of Death. Was this temporary? Was Ryan just startled? Would he snap out of it? If he never spoke again, would it be Eric's fault? Eric had no idea.

He wanted to scream but swallowed the sound. It might attract more specters. Instead he sat back on his heels and clutched the sword hilt until his hand ached.

Eventually, Ryan tugged at him. Hope bloomed in Eric's heart, but withered when he looked up into Ryan's blank face. The kid was acting on instinct again. Eric stood up. They should keep moving. He didn't want to stay in this place any longer than they had to.

Although Ryan seemed once again unaware of the void, he did appear to know where he was going. He drifted in a purposeful direction. Once, Eric tried an experiment. He pulled Ryan off to the right of the invisible path. As soon as he stopped pulling, Ryan reoriented back the way he wanted to go. The kid was like a compass needle, and about as talkative.

The wail of the wind was getting on Eric's nerves. He kept thinking he heard voices in it, crying, shouting. *Probably another illusion*, he thought, *like the shapes in the mist.* Twice he'd slashed at something that looked like a specter, only to watch the fog split and curl away.

Eric wondered how far they had to walk and how long it would take, and after a while, wondered why he wasn't hungry or thirsty or needing to go to the bathroom. All of this was like a dream, a really shitty dream.

Although, honestly, if Morpheus had been involved, there would probably be more gore. The specters would ooze green pus and scream in agony instead of deflating like balloons. Morpheus was a jerk that way.

When the next specter materialized out of the mist, Eric picked Ryan right up and held him on his hip. He was light enough that it hardly mattered. Eric swiped at the specter until he heard the hiss. Just as he was about to put Ryan down, he caught a movement out of the corner of his eye.

Shit, another one. Eric spun, slicing the thing across the throat. It disappeared as well. Eric looked around carefully before he put Ryan down. He'd never seen more than one at a time before. Was this downward path leading them to some kind of specter nest?

"You sure you know where we're going kid?"

Still no answer. Ryan's face was as blank as an uncarved pumpkin.

~

Morpheus found Death in the dream of a hiker succumbing to hypothermia on the side of Mt. Everest. The man was dreaming of a nude beach he'd once visited in Columbia.

Inexplicably, he was the only male present. Female forms lounged on beach towels and played overly flirtatious games of tag along the beach. Morpheus grinned at his handiwork. He'd really outdone himself with this one, and he wasn't too modest to admit it. Each and every woman was magazine perfect.

The only mar on the whole experience was the presence of Death. He wore a one piece Victorian bathing costume and skulked along the shoreline, waiting for his cue.

Morpheus strolled over to him. "What are you wearing?"

Death barely glanced in his direction. Most of the reaper's attention was focused on the dying man. "I did not expect to see you so soon, brother."

"Seriously, read the room," Morpheus said.

"This is a beach," Death said, watching the man whisper in the ear of a gorgeous dark-eyed woman.

Morpheus could have been offended by his inattention, but he understood Death's caution. After all that had happened, it would be silly to botch a simple pickup like this.

"You have a very literal mind, brother," Morpheus said. "I've been looking for you."

Death managed to spare him a glance. "Has something else gone wrong?"

"No, but I realized something." Morpheus paused for dramatic effect. "You lied to him."

Death ruined it by answering, "To whom?"

"Eric. You lied. There's no reason you couldn't have escorted them both."

"Yes."

"Why?"

"It's a hero's task. Unforgivable as his actions were, Hermes was right about one thing. We've become too complacent. We didn't even see the viper in our midst. It's time the council remembers who is the true master of the realm."

"That would be you, right?"

Death glared at his little brother.

"Yes. And they will see that whatever happens under my eye will be turned to my advantage. Who knows, a demigod may come in handy."

Morpheus tilted his head to one side. "I think you might have gone a bit native yourself, brother."

Death shrugged. "Excuse me."

He stepped past Morpheus and swung his scythe at the dying man, severing body from soul and effectively putting him out of his misery.

Morpheus chuckled. "Next time the humans give you trouble, look me up again. All this traveling is good for the creativity."

Death made no answer. He just grabbed the soul and stepped.

~

Eventually Eric started to talk. Ryan might not be listening, but at least it would help Eric cling to the fraying edges of his sanity.

"When I was a kid about your age, my little sister and I got lost in the woods behind my grandparents' house. Well, really Amelia got lost. I didn't know exactly where we were but I was pretty sure I knew which direction was home. I'd spent a lot of time in those woods. Mom and Dad used to send me and Amelia to visit Grammy and Grampy for weeks at a time during the summer.

"Anyway, I used to just take off after lunch and nobody minded where I was as long as I was home by dinnertime. I built a fort and I named all the landmarks. There was Eric Rock and Three Trees and…it was my little world. Amelia almost never came along because even as a six-year-old she'd rather stay inside and read or draw one of her weird picture stories.

"Well one day, Amelia wanted to come with me and I said okay as long as she promised not to cry. So we go out in the woods and we were actually having a pretty good time. We stayed out there longer than we should have, and Amelia starts complaining that she's hungry and wants to go back.

"And I say, okay, and then I realize we're in a part of the forest I've never seen before. I'm pretty sure back is that way but I'm not certain. I head off in that direction.

"Amelia's fine at first, but then she starts freaking out. How much farther? I'm hungry. Is this the right way? I'm sure it is, pretty sure, mostly.

"This is not the answer she wants to hear. She says, 'I'm going to scream.'

"I told her not to. We were almost home. The trees will open up in just a minute, you'll see. But they didn't.

"'I'm going to scream,' she says again. And by this time I'm a little nervous too, so I say, 'Sure, go for it.' She opens her mouth and I cover my ears and she screams.

"Have you ever heard a little girl scream? It's like someone is trying to shove an ice pick in your ear.

"She stops when she runs out of breath and everything, absolutely everything, is silent. All the birds and animals and everything must have just stopped wondering what the fu-heck is that?

"Amelia's face is all red and I can't tell if it's because of the scream or because she's freaked out. We walk about five more steps and she says, 'I'm going to scream again.'

"And I say, 'Please don't,' but she does.

"Ten seconds later Grampy comes running through the woods like he's being chased by a bear. He'd heard Amelia screaming and thought she'd been shot or something."

"My brother shot me," Ryan said.

Eric froze. His joy at Ryan reentering the conversation warred with his regret that he'd brought up such a painful memory. He groped for the right response, one that wouldn't freak Ryan out like last time.

"I don't think he did it on purpose," Eric said.

"We were playing." Ryan rubbed his chest with the heel of his hand. "Dad told us to stay out of his room, but Kevin didn't listen. We were playing GI Joe and Kevin said we needed a gun to fight Cobra. He got it from the bedside table.

"Dad's going to be really mad at him," Ryan added.

Eric just squeezed his hand and tried not to burst into tears in front of an eight-year-old. Looking around for something to distract them, Eric thought they were deeper now. The ground had a definite downward slant. The path was only about twelve feet wide. To their left, a crumbly cliff face rose out of the mist. To their right, it dropped off completely. Was it one of those chasms Death had mentioned? Eric didn't want to find out. He stayed well back from the edge and made sure Ryan did too.

He wondered if Ryan was still sure where they were going, but he didn't want to ask. Following the invisible path through the void was like carrying an overfull glass of water through a crowded room. It was fine as long as you didn't look at the glass. As soon as you did, you were cleaning up a mess. Anyway, it hardly mattered now. They'd come from upslope, so the only way left was down.

"Um, Eric?" Ryan said and pointed.

Eric saw two specters materializing out of the mist. They were on the downslope ahead of Eric and Ryan, evenly spaced to cover as much of the path as possible. They weren't drifting forward. They were just hanging there, like sentries.

With a sinking feeling, Eric looked over his shoulder. Two more specters were approaching from behind. He hadn't expected this. Maybe they weren't as dumb as he'd thought. Maybe they'd herded him into a trap.

He hesitated for a moment. Should he turn and face the ones behind him, or take care of the ones in front first? Another glance over his shoulder told him that the specters in the rear were approaching quickly. The ones in front still hadn't moved.

Eric squeezed Ryan's hand. "Stay close to me."

Ryan didn't need to be told. He was already pressed close enough to Eric that it made walking difficult. Eric's heart pounded as he shuffled them toward the cliff face. He'd feel better with stone at his back. At least then nothing could sneak up behind him.

In the movies, the bad guys always approached one or two at a time, giving the hero plenty of space to show off his fighting skills. These specters clearly weren't movie buffs. They all closed in at the same time. Eric swiped the sword in a wide arc as a kind of warning. It didn't seem to bother them. Either they were confident in their superior numbers, or their hunger for souls was greater than their self-preservation instincts.

Eric was just calculating whether he should let them get close enough that he could take them all out with one swing of the sword, when two more rose out of the abyss in front of him. Great. Apparently they could fly up as well as side to side, and now there were six.

He decided to take the fight to them. Just a touch of the sword seemed to be enough to destroy them. He could hit all six before anyone got close enough to touch Ryan.

"Ryan, I want you to stay here," he said.

Ryan whimpered.

"Just keep your back against the wall and you'll be okay. I'm going to take care of these guys before they get near you," Eric said without looking down. He was trying to keep his eye on all six specters at once.

Rushing toward the closest pair of specters, Eric swung the sword. The specters hissed and disappeared. He turned to the second pair, the uphill ones. Before he could swing he heard a scream. It was Ryan. Something, something that looked like a deformed hippopotamus, had grabbed him and was running downhill with him. The downhill specters actually cowered away from the thing as it ran past. That was the first time Eric had seen them show any kind of emotion.

He had no mental space to spare for surprise over the reaction of the specters. He was already running after Ryan. Eric swiped wildly at one as he went by. He heard the hiss of its death just as the hand of the second specter brushed his shoulder.

Its touch was like mainlining despair. Suddenly Eric was fourteen years old again, standing in the garage next to his father who was talking him through cleaning the carburetor he'd pulled out of their ancient lawn mower. Eric was so intent on the work that he hadn't noticed how pale his father had gotten, or the sweat soaking his shirt.

In Eric's memory, he watched again as his father slumped sideways off the stool. The smell of sweat and motor oil filled his nostrils. Pain stabbed his knees as he fell to the floor next to his dad. His mouth tasted like bile.

"Dad!" he said. "Dad!" Again he felt the spiraling powerlessness. The fear. The despair. The desperate delusional hope that none of this was happening.

Then Eric swung the sword around and chopped off the specter's head. The vision faded. Eric was alone in the void, well and truly alone this time. Ryan was nowhere to be seen.

CHAPTER TWENTY-SEVEN

Oblivion

As soon as he walked through the door, Andy took his shoes off and lined them up with boot-camp precision next to Amelia's. Being in Mrs. Silva's condo made him feel like he was sixteen years old again, with all of the accompanying angst and uncertainty. He felt too big, too loud, and too dirty, even when he wasn't touching anything.

Mrs. Silva insisted on serving them an improvised dinner of leftovers that somehow still included two forks and cloth napkins, plus a dinner guest. Hector had been around years ago, when Mrs. Silva first moved into the condo. Andy had thought for sure that she would have gotten rid of him by now. But no. There he sat at the head of the table like he owned the place.

Andy tried not to glare at him. The man had always been a mooch, but it grated on Andy's nerves now more than ever. Eric was in the hospital and Hector still thought it was reasonable to beg a free meal.

Andy would have liked to pick a fight with the man, but Amelia would never forgive him if he caused a scene. They ate their dinner in silence.

Finally, dinner was done. Mrs. Silva followed Amelia into the kitchen to bicker over who would do the dishes, leaving Andy and Hector alone at the table. Andy couldn't take it anymore.

"You really think it's okay to make that woman cook you dinner when her son is lying in a hospital bed?" he whispered sharply.

Hector sighed like he was putting down a heavy pack. When he spoke, his voice was low enough that it wouldn't carry to the kitchen.

"It may not seem this way to you, son, but Debra was a young woman when her husband died, a young woman on her own with two children to support and no one to confide in. If making me dinner soothes her pride enough to allow me to buy her groceries and make sure her car gets serviced, well it seems like an even trade to me."

Andy opened his mouth, but Hector interrupted him before Andy could figure out what he wanted to say.

"No, listen to me. I should have said this to Eric a long time ago, and I hope one day I'll get the chance. He's never liked me being around. And I'm sorry for that, but I know for a fact that my presence gives Debra some comfort, particularly when life is unpredictable. My own Cynthia, may she rest in peace, passed on fourteen years ago, and I think both Debra and I deserve to find what comfort we can in the companionship of someone who understands."

Andy blinked rapidly while the world reordered itself into a new shape around Hector as a steady man with a good heart. Finally he said, "You're right. You should say that to Eric."

Hector nodded. "As soon as he wakes up, I will."

While Hector stood up and went into the kitchen, Andy stayed in his seat, staring at the crumbs on the table and feeling more clumsy and awkward than ever.

~

Eric slashed the last of the specters into oblivion. It didn't quell the rage rising inside him. He wanted something solid to punch. How could he have let Ryan be taken? Hot tears welled in his eyes. He screamed in frustration, almost hoping the sound would lure more of the creatures. At least then he'd have something to fight.

Overcome, he threw the only thing he had on hand, the sword. It landed on the ground with a soft whump, splashing up a cloud of dust. That did nothing to dispel his rage. Why did the void have to be so empty? He gasped a few deep breaths, his heart pounding in his chest.

What next? What was he supposed to do next? Somehow, he had to find Ryan again. He couldn't let the kid become a specter. It was his fault Ryan was here, his fault he was in danger. Another scream built in his throat but he swallowed it back. He couldn't panic now. He had to keep cool. Normally, he was good at that.

"First things first," his dad had told him so many times that they all melded together into one ultra-memory. And that reminded Eric of what he had seen when the specter touched him. His worst memory in blinding technicolor. No wonder Ryan had stopped talking before. Eric didn't have to imagine what the kid might be experiencing now; he was pretty sure he knew. Your brother shooting you in the chest would be pretty high on any eight-year-old's list of worst memories.

Eric bent to pick up the sword. And noticed the footprints. He felt stupid for not thinking to look for them in the first place. The thing that had taken Ryan wasn't a specter. It hadn't been floating. It had run across the ground, and things that ran left footprints.

Eric felt his heart beat faster. Maybe he could still catch them. He snatched up the sword and followed the footprints. The ground sloped downward even more steeply than before.

The trail traveled away in a double line, as though a four-footed creature had run through here. Eric certainly had thought he saw something with four legs. Yet the tracks looked like they came from two different types of animals. One set was as long as Eric's foot and about two-and-a-half times as wide with four splayed toes overlapping the pad. The other set was slightly smaller and looked more like the prints of a housecat if a housecat could be the size of a motorcycle. Eric remembered Morpheus warning him about the crazy Egyptian goddess. What was her name? Amulet, Amit, something like that.

"Run like the gods themselves are after you," Morpheus had said. Eric ran.

CHAPTER TWENTY-EIGHT

Death Speaks Truth

Normally, something like one hundred and eight humans made the acquaintance of Death each minute. His absence from the world for just one hour left 6,480 humans awaiting his ministrations. After a single day, the number reached 155,520. Death had been dealing with the Eric problem for days now. The backlog was staggering.

Though he was proverbially known for being slow, Death could address his duties with alacrity when called upon. The ability to be in many places at once was an asset in that regard. It did irk him though. He found himself rushing with souls that might have benefited from a gentler approach. Still, he had managed to catch up with no souls lost. That was something to be proud of.

When it was all over, he went to make his report to the council. Once again he bypassed Cecil's reception hall. He did not need an appointment to demand an audience. It was they who served him after all, not the other way around. By the end of this meeting they would understand that.

Death appeared in the council chamber into the midst of an argument over who was going to take Hermes' place.

"…little page turner makes my skin crawl," Yama was saying. "Mark my words. You let him in here and he'll have us all out of a job before you know it."

"He's just a human, you coward," Xolotl said.

Osiris noticed that they had a visitor and pounded his flail against the table until the room fell silent. "It would seem Lord Death has something to tell us."

"I do, thank you," Death said. He'd taken the form of a shaven-headed man in a black suit. It was important to remind the gods that while they stayed here bickering in their council chamber, he was keeping up to date with the changing world.

"The issue has been dealt with," Death said. "All souls have been reaped and delivered, and Hermes is serving his punishment even as we speak. There is nothing left to do."

"Well done, Lord Death, but there is in fact one issue still unresolved."

"And that is?" Death knew what it was. This was going to be about Eric. Well that was fine. Now the council would learn who its master was. He'd left them to their own devices long enough, and their shortsightedness had nearly destroyed everything. It was time he took the council in hand.

"There is still the matter of the human. Does he retain the powers granted to him by Hermes?"

"I believe so. I don't see any way of taking them from him. Hermes set him on the path to becoming a demigod, and he is even now undergoing his hero's journey."

Lady Freyja leaned forward. "I wonder, Lord Death, who set the human on his journey?" Her penetrating look said she already knew the answer.

"You must reap him early then," Osiris said.

"It is not prudent to allow a human such power," Izanami said.

"Soon they'll all be demanding it," Xolotl said. "They're hard enough to manage as it is."

Death resented being ordered about, and he was not in the business of handing out punishments to humans. They lived and they died on their own time. He was merely there to see that the final transition went smoothly. That Osiris should not just ask, but demand, that he reap a soul before its time was inexcusable. That any of the gods should question his motives was insolent. Yet, Death strove to be reasonable. There had been enough discord here.

"He has served the council well. He saw what none of us could see. He has done all we asked of him and more. This is how you would repay him? With the thing that humans fear most above all things?"

"It's unfortunate, of course," Osiris said. "But in the grand scheme of the worlds it hardly matters. There are so many humans, and their lives are so very short. No one will notice if you make one a bit shorter."

Death drew himself up to his full height and stared with the haughtiness of a king. The time for reason was passed.

"Eric will notice," Death said. "His family will notice. His community will notice. The entire ecosystem of the human world will be that much poorer for his loss, even if it never knows his name.

"Hermes was right about one thing, though he chose a poor method of proving it. You have lost your vision," Death said.

"We are not here to observe, we are here to protect the order of the worlds," Osiris said.

"No. You are here because humanity made you. You are here because they looked into the chaos and they saw you. You are here because they drew you forth and gave you form."

He looked around the council table as he spoke, taking care to meet every eye. "Even when they forget your names, even when they no longer worship, they need you. You are not here for the order of worlds. You are here for them. Keeping order is just the mechanism. It is a tool, nothing more."

"Lord Death, you must—" Osiris began, but Death interrupted him. His anger had reached a cold clarity. He was weary of all of this, weary of the council and the gods and their games. He simply wanted to do his job, to do what he was made to do. When he spoke, his voice was low and even. It was a voice confident of being heard because it would allow for no alternative.

"No. There is nothing that I must. I am the Lord of Death, and I and I alone have been granted the ultimate power over human life. I will not reap this human before his natural time. There will be no more discussion."

The council all began to speak at once. Death waited, patient, immobile. Finally the noise settled to a grumbling murmur and faded out. Osiris alone had remained quiet, his eyes locked on Death. Death, for his part, had not moved. He was as silent as the grave.

Osiris inclined his head. "Very well, Lord Death. But you are charged with watching over him until such time as his reaping becomes necessary."

"I will watch over him to his last breath, as I have watched over every human on the earth since time out of mind. And my eye will follow this council as well, you may depend on it."

The uneasy looks that passed between the gods told Death that they were taking him seriously. What he would not admit, at least not today, was that he was as much to blame as they were for this debacle. If he had not given away so much of his power, none of this would have happened.

Not wanting to upset the council any further, Death actually took the door this time instead of stepping right there in front of them. Cecil was at his desk in the lobby.

"Shall I assume that that the matter at hand has been resolved then?" Cecil asked.

"Yes, Cecil. It's over, more or less. The natural order

has been restored. If we're both lucky it will be at least a decade or two before you see me again. Farewell." Death stepped.

Cecil, alone in the reception hall, shook his head over his ledgers. He'd never understand these gods and psychopomps. They were so dramatic.

CHAPTER TWENTY-NINE

Devourer of Souls

Jogging alone through the mist gave Eric's imagination plenty of time to work. What if Ammit had already eaten Ryan's heart? What if she hadn't but Eric couldn't defeat her? She was a god after all, not a disembodied soul. He was just a guy with a sword he didn't really know how to use and a bubbling anger that he was trying desperately to control.

As Eric ran downhill holding a sword powerful enough to slice a soul from its body, a tiny hysterical corner of his brain remembered his mother telling him not to run with scissors. She should see him now. If he got out of this he could never, ever tell her about it.

He was almost relieved when he spotted a red glow up ahead. At first it just added a slight pink tinge to the mist, and he wasn't even sure he saw it. But soon the mist was clearly red and getting warmer. Eric slowed. It felt like walking through a cloud of blood. He fought the urge to gag.

A few steps more and the mist began to clear. He saw the source of both the red light and the heat. It was a lava pit. The surface of the lava bubbled just a few feet below. The tracks went right up alongside it.

No way he was falling into a lava pit in the void between worlds. It would be just too cliché. He gave the pool a wide berth. As wide as he could at least. The cliff face had edged closer, narrowing the path.

It forced him to slow down, which was good, because that gave him the time to notice the voice up ahead before he came across its owner. It sounded like a woman who had smoked two packs a day for her entire life and was now trying to talk around a retainer.

"Put the soul on the scales," the voice said. There was a slight echo, as though she were in a bare room, or a cave maybe?

Eric slowed even more. Now he was creeping along, head swiveling and eyes scanning, trying to spot where the voice had come from. There, a darker shadow in the cliff face. Just a few steps brought him to the mouth of a cave.

Pressing his body against the cliff wall, Eric peeked into the cave. In the red glow of dripping lava that spilled from the ceiling and slithered across the floor, Eric saw a scene that froze him to the wall. He didn't know what to make of it exactly, but he knew it wasn't good.

At least two dozen specters filled the cave. Eric had never seen so many at once before. The sight surprised him. From what Death had told him, he'd expected that any group of specters would quickly become one as they all tried to consume each other. These were eerily still, their attention on the back of the cave where two more of them were holding Ryan up off the ground.

Ryan hung like a rag doll, his face completely blank. That might be something to be grateful for. Maybe it meant he had no idea what was going on, just like before. Then again, it might mean he was reliving his own shooting, which wasn't much of an improvement.

The specters were setting him on one side of something that looked like a teeter-totter made by a deranged woodsman with a dull axe. It looked like it had been assembled from the corpses of the scrawny trees Eric had seen when they first arrived in the void. The surface of the wood was barely wide enough for Ryan to stand on.

When the specters set him down and drifted away from him, he just settled on the splintered wood, complacent.

If that had been all there was to see, Eric would have rushed right in to rescue Ryan. As long as he kept the sword swinging the specters posed no real challenge. He could mow them all down and get the hell out of there before they knew what hit them.

But something else was standing to the left of the weird teeter-totter. Eric saw a reptilian jaw full of teeth, vicious claws, rubbery skin encasing enormous haunches. He froze. This had to be Ammit. Morpheus' description of a crocodile fused with a lion fused with a hippo hadn't prepared him for the reality of such a hybrid beast. It looked like something stitched together by an Egyptian Dr. Frankenstein.

Somehow he didn't think she would pop out of existence with a single swing of his sword. Eric looked for a weakness and couldn't find one. She was all predator. In fact, she was all the predators of Egypt merged into one terrifying creature.

"Bring in the feather," Ammit said.

A specter drifted toward the opposite end of the teeter-totter with something clutched in its hand. The feather, if that's what it was, fluttered toward the rough wooden surface.

Ammit stared. The specters drifted closer to the scene. Eric took advantage of their focus to inch closer. He wouldn't get a better chance than this.

He slashed through the first couple of specters before anyone noticed he was in the cave. Then his luck ran out, their hissing death-cries gave him away. In the next second he was mobbed on all sides.

Just keep the sword moving, he thought. Hissing filled his ears.

One of them must have gotten behind him, because he was suddenly in the garage watching his father's face fade from red to strangled blue. It wasn't real. He swung the sword. More hissing. Someone was shouting. Ammit. And someone was crying. Eric.

Then, his father toppled from the stool. Eric spun in a circle, the sword outstretched. Hisses echoed over each other in a sibilant chorus. Eric was on his knees, holding his father's hand as the life drained from his eyes. His heart was breaking. He was helpless, useless, cowering in the shadow of Death, but no. He surged to his feet, the sword in blazing orbit around his body.

Suddenly his vision cleared and he saw the cave was empty of specters. Any he hadn't killed must have run away in the chaos. Ryan, still insensible, hadn't moved during the battle. Ammit, on the other hand, had. She was just a few paces away.

Her lizard eyes glowed golden. She opened her mouth, revealing row after row of yellowing but still razor sharp teeth. Out of her throat came a hissing sound that was as different from the sound of a specter as a kitten's meow from the roar of a lion.

Instinctively, Eric cowered back. That hiss had awakened primal instincts he hadn't known he possessed. His legs wanted to run. They stumbled back a step before his brain could overrule them. But Eric put a stop to that. He told his cowardly legs to shove it and stood his ground. Running away wasn't an option. Ryan was right there and he needed Eric more than ever.

Eric raised the sword, trying his best to look like he knew what the hell he was doing.

"If you want to eat his heart, you'll have to go through me," he said.

If he'd hoped to distract her with banter, he was disappointed. Ammit didn't say a word. She just lunged, but her body wasn't really made for lunging. A beast with the head of a crocodile and the ass of a hippo can't move quickly or gracefully.

Eric thrust the sword at her. The tip of it disappeared into her shoulder. Surprised to feel the resistance of actual skin and flesh after only fighting ghosts, Eric yanked the sword out again. Liquid gold dribbled from the wound. *Of course a god wouldn't have red blood,* said a corner of Eric's brain. *That would be ridiculous.*

The flesh wound only enraged her further. She snapped at Eric, who dove sideways out of the way. The motion brought them both closer to Ryan, which was the exact opposite of what he wanted. What would happen if the sword accidentally touched the soul of the boy? Eric didn't want to find out.

He rolled away awkwardly, trying not to impale himself in the process. Ammit lunged again, and this time it didn't matter that she was graceless, because Eric was on his side and the sword was partially pinned under him.

A lion's paw smashed into the side of his head, pressing his cheek into the stone floor. Eric felt his bones creaking. Another second and his skull would pop like a grape.

He squirmed, trying to free the sword. Black lights flashed in his vision. He felt the sword jump free and slashed blindly. It whipped Ammit across the flank. She reared back on her hippo hind legs and bellowed.

Eric rolled. With a scream of rage and fury and terror he thrust the sword upward just as Ammit dropped. The weight of her body drove the sword deep into her heart, deeper than Eric could have managed on his own. The crocodile mouth snapped inches from his face but her awkward neck couldn't bend enough to reach him. He smelled her hot breath, like stale blood and lost souls.

With the strength of blind panic, Eric thrust the sword deeper. Gold rained down his arms, burning wherever it touched. Ammit's mouth was still snapping, but her body convulsed, once, twice.

An echoing stillness descended. The god was dead. Now all Eric had to do was get out from under her stinking corpse. In the few gasping seconds he lay there, trying to figure out what to do, the body inched closer and closer, sliding down the length of the blade. Soon, there was only a sword hilt between them. Eric wriggled and rolled, eventually succeeding in overbalancing the body of the god. It crashed to the floor beside him, and he was able to pull the sword free.

Eric wanted nothing more than to lie down and sleep for a year, but he knew that if he stopped moving he wouldn't be able to convince his body to start up again. Besides, he didn't want to spend even another second in the cave. He picked Ryan up under one arm and burst out into the red light of the open air.

Death was standing on the bank of the lava pool, head tilted back like a commuter reading billboards while waiting for his bus to arrive.

"Oh, hello, Eric."

"Hello?" Eric's voice teetered on the edge of hysteria. "Hello?"

"I see you still have Ryan's soul. Well done."

Eric looked down at Ryan's blank face. He set the child carefully on the ground. "Ammit is dead."

"Yes, I saw," Death said.

"You were watching? Why didn't you help?"

"Far be it for me to meddle in the affairs of gods," Death said, his face as expressionless as a skull. "Besides, you seemed to have it well under control."

"Under control? Ryan got kidnapped and I had to track him here and the place was full of specters, and Ammit. Holy shit. I killed a god."

"You've surpassed my expectations, really," Death said.

Eric turned on him, eyes reflecting the red light of the lava flow. "You knew. You knew this would happen and you sent us into this death trap anyway."

Clutching Ryan's hand like it was his last line to sanity, Eric advanced toward Death, sword upraised. It was still dripping the golden blood of Ammit. Death faced it, unperturbed.

"I didn't know exactly this would happen, no. I'm omnipresent not omnipotent. But I trusted you to lead Ryan to the afterlife."

"We barely got out of there. She wanted to eat both our hearts."

"Yes, she was fairly single-minded in many respects. That's what happens when you have the head of a crocodile; small lizard brains don't take change well."

He was so calm. As though all of this were normal. As

through Eric hadn't just been fighting for his life. As though he hadn't killed anyone. The calm, more than anything, filled Eric with rage. He swung the sword at Death.

~

By his third night in Mrs. Silva's condo, Andy had nearly adjusted to the time change. Unfortunately, his bladder hadn't. When he snuck out to the bathroom, the glowing clock on the bedside table said it was after ten-thirty. As he darted across the hall, he noticed Amelia's door was open a crack. Light poured through. Was she still awake?

On his way back, he stopped and peeked through the opening. Amelia sat at her desk with her back to him. The desk lamp picked up the lighter highlights in her hair, which spilled loose down the quilt she wore wrapped around her shoulders.

"What are you doing up?" he asked, his voice soft so as not to startle her.

It didn't work. She twitched, turned, saw him. Her eyes widened. She made a frantic 'come here' gesture with one hand while the other pulled the blanket more tightly around her. Andy stepped into the room. Amelia stood, still without saying anything, and brushed past him to push the door shut. Again he smelled the hint of vanilla that seemed to follow her everywhere.

"You'll wake Mom," she said finally.

Andy shrugged. "If she's anything like the rest of us, she's probably too anxious to sleep."

"That's even worse. Do you want to explain why you're in my room at eleven o'clock at night?"

Andy sat down gingerly in the desk chair. "Not particularly. No."

Amelia sat at the foot of her bed and crossed her legs. Now there was a miniature wall between them in the form of her wooden footboard. It stood only about eight inches higher than the mattress, but it felt like a barrier to Andy. Maybe he should have just gone quietly back to his room. Then again, she had pulled him in here.

"Why are you here?" Amelia asked.

"I walked by and saw your light was on. I was going to tease you about studying in the middle of the night again."

Amelia sighed. "Trying to study. The words won't stick. I swear I read the same sentence three times before you came in." Her voice sounded strained.

"You're worried about Eric?"

"Yes. I mean, I've been worried about Eric ever since the first accident. Now I feel like there's an elephant on my chest and my head is full of mice all running in different directions." She clenched her hand on her knee and stared at it. "What if he never wakes up?"

"He's going to wake up."

"Dad didn't," she said and started to cry.

Andy's heart crumbled. He knew that Eric and Amelia's dad had died of a heart attack. Eric had been there when it happened. He'd said it felt like he'd watched his father die. In reality, Mr. Silva had drifted in a coma for almost three days before a second heart attack had killed him. From Amelia's perspective, this probably didn't look much different.

He looked at her, curled in on herself with the blanket clutched tight around her shoulders that shook with sobs. Then he stood up and sat down on the bed beside her. He put one arm around her shoulders and she collapsed against him, her cheek on his chest.

CHAPTER THIRTY

Death Match

Death struck like lightning, catching the blade of the sword between his thumb and forefinger. It stopped moving so abruptly that Eric stumbled. Death chuckled.

"I don't blame you for being frustrated, Eric, but let's be civil about this. Besides..." He yanked the sword out of Eric's hand as though it were nothing more than a stick. "...The sword can't harm me. I have no soul and no body to sever it from."

He plunged his fist into the empty air and the sword disappeared. "There, now we can talk reasonably."

Eric wanted to strangle Death with his bare hands, but before he could make a move he would most certainly regret, a small voice claimed all of his attention. Ryan said his name.

Eric dropped to one knee so he could look the boy in the eye. "Hey buddy, you okay?"

"I want to go home."

Eric hugged Ryan fiercely. "Me too, buddy, me too."

"You're almost to the end of your journey," Death said.

Still on one knee, Eric looked up into the face of Death. "We are?"

"Yes." He addressed Ryan with the same stiff formality he'd used on the council. "Young man, would you lead the way please?"

"You're Death," the little boy said.

"Indeed. Thank you for noticing."

"I'm not afraid of you."

"Nor should you be," Death answered.

Ryan tugged at Eric's hand. "This way," he said.

They walked together, the three of them, into the mist. In no time at all they came to a door. It was just a door, no frame, no wall, just a door. For some reason the thing that bothered Eric most about it was its gleaming modernity. It wasn't a cracked wooden door. It didn't have a great iron knocker or an ornate bronze doorknob. Somehow that would have seemed right despite the utter wrongness of a freestanding door in the mist. Instead, this door was tinted glass with a metal handle that invited you to push it. It was the kind of door you might see on the front of a bank, or a doctor's office.

"What is that?" Eric asked.

"It is a door," Death answered.

"I can see that," Eric said. "What is it doing here?"

"Waiting to be opened."

Eric sighed. Apparently, Death was determined to be

obtuse. "I mean, does it lead somewhere?"

"Of course. That's what doors do," Death said.

Ryan touched the door with his fingertips. It swung open slowly with a sound like tinkling bells. As it opened, it spilled white light into the fog. The light refracted and echoed until Eric was nearly blinded by it. He blinked and looked away.

"Go on then," Death said.

Ryan looked up at Eric. Eric did his best to meet Ryan's gaze, but he was still blinking sunspots from his vision. They stepped forward together. The scythe dropped, blocking their path.

"No," Death said. "Your time has not yet come."

"But—"

"No. You have already seen far more than should be allowed to any living human. You've done your duty by the child, now let him go."

Eric opened his hand. Ryan clung just a moment longer. "I don't want to go," he said.

Crying was not an option here, Eric decided. He got down on one knee and grasped Ryan's shoulders. "I know. You've been very brave. Just be brave this one more time."

Ryan's lips pressed together. He looked up at Death. "What's in there?"

"I can't tell you. You have to find out for yourself."

"Is it scary?"

Death cocked his head to one side, thinking. "New things are always scary. But you do them anyway."

"Okay." Ryan turned and squared his shoulders. Then he looked back at Eric. "Thank you for helping me."

Eric felt tears standing in his eyes. He blinked hard, forcing them back. Ryan would not see him cry, not now.

"That's what I'm here for," Eric said, his voice only cracking a little.

Ryan stepped into the light and through the door. The door swung shut. He was gone.

Eric, still down on one knee, sagged like a loose-stringed marionette. His shoulders dropped, his head listed forward. "Now what?" he asked.

Death shifted his grip on his scythe. "Well there were some on the council who thought I should kill you," he said.

"They're welcome," Eric said. It was the closest he could come to biting sarcasm in his current state. He suddenly felt almost too tired to move. Standing up was an act of pure will, but he managed.

"You've done a hero's work today, Eric."

Eric snorted. "Hero? I was terrified."

Death nodded. "Yes, that's why. And so, I'm bringing you home."

"Really home?" The thought awakened an ache deep in Eric's heart. He hadn't known he could feel so acutely homesick, and for such an odd constellation of things. He missed his mother's nagging phone calls, and the light on his blinds, and the white expanse of his bed, and the expectant hush that filled the station house on the long night stretches before a call came in. He missed feeling his lungs strain as he ran up a flight of stairs. He missed the satisfaction of stretching a kink from a tired muscle.

"Back to your body," Death said, and no sweeter words were ever spoken.

"Will I remember any of this?"

"Most definitely. This isn't one of your human movies. You won't wake up and think you've had some ridiculous dream. I would advise you not to talk about it much, however. In my experience, humans get testy when their concept of reality is questioned. Most likely they'll believe you to be insane."

"I'm not totally convinced I'm not."

Death dropped his hand on Eric's shoulder. "Humans so rarely are," he said.

And then he stepped, so Eric had no chance to ask him if he meant that humans rarely believe themselves to be sane, or that humans rarely are sane. In the long run it hardly mattered.

CHAPTER THIRTY-ONE

Afterdeath

The beeping machines, institutional décor, and privacy curtain made it very clear that Death had brought Eric to a hospital room. The curtain was half drawn, hiding the second bed. Eric's body was lying in the one closest to them. Andy was asleep in a chair by the window, his head tipped back and his mouth wide open. He wasn't snoring so much as gargling. Amelia was asleep in the chair next to him, the book she'd been reading open on her lap, her head pillowed against Andy's shoulder.

"Tempe!" Eric tried to nudge his friend's boot with his toe, but his foot went right through Andy's. Eric drew back.

"Tell me that's not going to keep happening."

"No."

Without warning, Death reached into Eric's chest and closed his hand around Eric's heart. Eric felt himself instantly immobilized. The world collapsed around him until there was nothing left but the eyes of Death looking into his.

Eric had seen before that Death's eyes were empty, but they were more than that, they were emptiness itself. They were the void before the void. They were the first and last darkness. Looking into them, Eric saw that he was nothing and that he was everything and they were one and the same. And then Death picked him up by his heart and slammed him down onto the body lying in the bed.

Eric went deaf and blind. He couldn't move, couldn't feel anything. Death must have lied to him. Eric was dead and that was it.

Then out of the nothing came a sound. Eric recognized it as the steady *ba-dum ba-dum* of a heartbeat. Quickly afterward came the rush of breath through nostrils, his nostrils. These sounds were loud enough to fill the world. The smell of hospital disinfectant was like a firework exploding inside his nose.

He felt his lungs fill with air and then deflate. The muscles of his chest stretched to make room for the fullness of his lungs. His skin stretched too, ever so slightly, and as it did so, he felt the brush of fabric.

He twitched his fingers, excited to notice that he had fingers to twitch. Under them he felt the rough weave of hospital sheets. He twitched his toes as well, and felt fabric there too. He was back in the world. Back in the real world.

With some effort, he managed to force his eyelids open. Not only were they sleep encrusted, but his body was struggling to understand everything he was asking of it. When they finally did open, all he saw was white. The light was so bright it hurt, like the light through the door where Ryan had gone. The thought of Ryan brought a stab of pain at his absence, softened by a sense of pride that he had brought the kid safely through.

Eric's eyes adjusted to the light. Soon he could make out the familiar pits and tiles of a drop ceiling and the rings of the curtain half pulled along the runner to shield his bed. He let his eyes loll sideways until they fell on Andy and Amelia asleep in their chairs. They would be so surprised to see that Eric had come back.

Eric tried to call out, to startle them awake, but his mouth and throat were dry. All he could do at first was croak.

Waking up in the hospital for the first time all those months ago, his body had felt the same as it did now, but his brain had been a mess. He'd been confused and scared.

Now he felt alert and alive in a way he hadn't before. Maybe that was a bit of Hermes still clinging to him. Maybe it was a common side effect of returning from the void. He'd probably never know.

Eric tried again to say something, but his mouth was so dry. His body seemed to have forgotten how to make saliva. There must be water nearby somewhere, or at least a call button. He just had to sit up and find it.

He thought his body could probably manage sitting up if he took it slowly. He clenched the muscles in his stomach. Normally, that was how you went from lying to sitting, except not this time. This time his muscles protested as though he'd just done three hundred crunches and was demanding one more.

By trial and error, he managed to roll onto his side. From his new position, he could see the call button taped to the rail of his bed. With a great act of will, he lifted his hand to the side rail and lowered his fingers onto the button. It resisted slightly and then depressed. He didn't hear anything, but the nurses probably had.

While he waited he watched Andy and Amelia sleep. He noticed that their fingers were intertwined on Andy's lap. A week ago, that would have annoyed Eric. He would have worried what Andy was up to, whether Amelia knew what she was doing. Now he was just happy, happy that his sister and his friend had found each other. They were both alive, and here, and so was he. Wasn't that amazing?

The nurse started talking before she rounded the curtain, "Is everything okay…" but she stopped when she saw Eric on his side. At least, he assumed that's why she stopped. He had his back to her, so he couldn't know for certain. Her rubber-soled shoes squeaked on the linoleum and then green scrubs appeared in his line of vision.

"Eric, you're awake," she said.

He lifted his eyes to her face. It was a simple face, full in the cheeks and slightly square in the jaw. A handful of freckles formed constellations on it. Above the blue eyes a thickness of red-brown hair had been pulled up into a bun in a way that suggested convenience rather than fashion.

He smiled. "Could you wake up my sister, please, I have to tease her about her new boyfriend," he said, or tried to say. It came out in a raspy whisper.

The nurse gawped at him. Then she turned and patted Andy's shoulder insistently. He tried to wriggle away from her, but couldn't go far because he was trapped between the arms of the chair. All at once his eyes snapped open and he sat up straight.

"What is it? Am I late for watch?"

"Your friend is awake, Andrew."

"No shit?" He leaned to peek under her elbow at Eric.

"Don't try to talk yet Eric," the nurse said. "Let's get the doctor in here to take a look at you first."

She squeaked out of the room.

"Hey there, Doc," Andy said when they were alone. "Nice to see you've rejoined the living."

Eric managed a smile, which Andy returned with interest. Then Andy nudged Amelia, who twitched. Her hand shot out just in time to save her book from slipping off her lap. Eric smiled again. An army of gods and specters could invade the world and Amelia would still be Amelia.

"What's wrong?" she said before her eyes were even fully open.

"Nothing, Lia. Everything's great. Look at your brother."

Amelia looked at Eric who looked back at her. They tried to out-smile one another. "You're awake," Amelia said.

It all seemed so familiar. Maybe Eric was just now waking up from a dream. Maybe the last few months had happened only in his mind. But no. That was wishful thinking. It had been real. If he needed proof, he only had to look at Death, who was still hovering at the foot of his bed like a ghost in a cheap horror movie. He'd been there the whole time, but Eric had subconsciously avoided noticing him.

Eric looked at him now, met his eyes squarely and unflinchingly for perhaps the first time in their entire association. Eric blinked once. In response, Death lifted his scythe in a kind of salute and disappeared. Eric was certain they'd see each other again soon.

The room felt lighter with his going, but also emptier. Amelia reclaimed Eric's attention by poking his arm and saying, "This better not become a habit with you. I'm missing school, you know."

Eric pulled a mock sad face. He reached out his hand. Amelia took it.

"Don't let her fool you, Doc. You had her worried sick," Andy said.

Eric wanted to tell Amelia that it was over, that he'd fixed everything and life could go back to normal now, but talking still made him feel like he was gargling diamonds.

Just then, the nurse came back with the doctor in tow. Amelia let go of Eric's hand and sat back.

"Nice to see you awake and alert, Eric. I'm Dr. Sagan.

How are you feeling?"

Eric gave Dr. Sagan his brightest smile. "Good," he said, or tried to say. It came out as more of a croak.

"Ms. Evans, could you get Eric some ice chips please?" He gave Eric's arm an encouraging pat. "I know you're probably parched, but I don't want you to have liquids until we've got a better handle on what's going on with you. You gave your family quite a scare, you know."

"I should go call Mom," Amelia said.

She started to stand up, but Andy pressed her back into her seat. "Let me do it. I want to see if getting good news from me will make her head actually explode."

Amelia rolled her eyes but stayed where she was. Dr. Sagan sat down in the chair Andy had vacated. This put him closer to Eric's eye level and Eric could see that he'd missed a spot shaving, a nearly circular spot in the hollow of an otherwise smooth cheek.

"Do you know why you're here?"

"Passed out?" Eric said. His voice sounded like it belonged to someone else.

"You did, yes. You were out for quite a while. Once the nurse comes back with those ice chips I want to ask you a few questions, if that's okay."

Eric shrugged. The hyperaware feeling he'd had when he first woke up had mostly faded, but he still felt like everything was too bright and too sharp. Everything seemed so incredibly real. He wondered why he felt this way. Had Death given this to him, this feeling that life was so precious he had to drink in every moment while he had it?

While they waited for the nurse to come back, Dr. Sagan ran some basic physical tests. When the nurse came back in and handed him a cup of ice, Eric grinned and thanked her too profusely. It seemed like the greatest gift anyone had ever given him, water frozen and fetched and carried just for him. She actually blushed a little at his gratitude.

As Eric brought the cup to his lip, he smelled the waxy paper and the crisp sharpness of the ice. He tilted the cup so that a single chip of ice passed between his lips. It was frigid, and then merely cold as it almost instantly began to melt. Eric closed his eyes and let the completeness of his focus settle on his tongue, where the ice chip was dissolving into liquid water.

"Now that you've got some hydration, I want to ask you a few questions." Dr. Sagan's voice broke into Eric's experience of water. Eric dragged his focus back to the room.

"What's the last thing you remember?" Dr. Sagan asked.

"We brought in a boy, a gunshot victim. He was bad. I didn't think he'd make it to the hospital, but kids are usually tougher than you think." Tears came to his eyes as he remembered Ryan, pale and barely breathing, his soul hovering over his still body.

"After my shift was over I went up to the ICU to check on him. He was still there. I checked his chart. It wasn't good. And then…"

And then Death called me and I talked to a council of gods and stepped inside my own mind and remembered dreams I hope I never have again and found a golden feather which led us to Olympus and we discovered a god but he wasn't the right god and then we found the right god but it wasn't over, and then I walked the void and relived my father's death and killed a goddess and then I opened my eyes and my family was here and I knew that it had all been real and that there's so much more to life than I ever saw before.

"…I don't remember," Eric finished.

"Do you remember anything from the time you were unconscious. Did you hear anyone speak to you? See any lights or images?"

"No," Eric lied. "Nothing at all."

The doctor seemed disappointed. Eric almost felt bad that he didn't have one of those near-death experience stories to tell, or rather, that he had one he wouldn't dare tell to anyone. He could have made something up, something safe about a white light and the faces of his dearly departed relatives smiling at him, but he didn't. It just seemed like so much effort for nothing.

Eventually Andy came back and the doctor wrapped up his questions. He left Eric and Amelia and Andy alone together. There was an awkward silence. At least, it should have been awkward. Eric was surprised to find that it wasn't anything really. It was just silence, to be filled or not filled as they saw fit. Eventually he filled it.

"So are you guys like, dating now?"

Andy and Amelia looked at each other. Watching them, Eric couldn't help but laugh. They looked so uncertain, so comical and so wonderfully human.

~

Death left Eric to the rest of his life. This situation was very nearly resolved. He had only one last task to complete.

When Death stepped sideways into the records room, Bunny spotted him immediately. Fury flashed in her eyes and she advanced on him like the wrath of gods. He held the file out as an offering of peace.

"I have come to return your file."

"It never should have left here in the first place."

"It is in good order. I haven't spilled coffee on it or folded any of the pages." These were the types of things keepers of paper worried about, Death knew.

She snatched the folder from his hand and bent her head over it, presumably to discover whether Death was a liar as well as a thief. He took advantage of her distraction and stepped away, back into the void.

~

Death walked through the void with a new spring in his step. He was certain again, and the memory of a time when he was uncertain was quickly fading from human consciousness. It had been a fluke, one of those one-in-a-million coincidences that surely must happen in a world governed by random chance and logic. Humanity would deal with it as it always dealt with such things—by forgetting what it could and ignoring what it couldn't.

The balance of worlds was also well on its way to recovery. Death had cleaned up the last of the mess caused by Hermes. The backlog of souls had been processed. Now it was up to them to get the rest of the way on their own.

He'd even managed to make a demigod for himself. Which meant he'd have an ally the next time the order of the worlds was disrupted. It was bound to happen sooner or later. The universe always had tended toward chaos.

In the meantime, the council was talking about adding some new procedures. They claimed that some sort of process should be put in place to prevent the accidental binding of a soul without its consent. Death feared this might result in paperwork, a chore he'd so far managed to avoid.

For some reason the council loved paperwork. This fact boggled the mind. All of them had risen and then fallen out of favor in civilizations that had never seen a filing cabinet, but there was something about the group consciousness of a council table that demanded paperwork at every turn. Or maybe Cecil had more pull on the council than Death had ever thought.

That seemed like something to look in to. Someday.

When he had time. For now, he had a job to do, and he would go on doing it, one soul at a time as he had always done.

Death grinned and stepped sideways into the world.

Nothing's Ever Lost

The prequel to *Assembling Ella*

Jack and Anna are supposed to be BFF's, but can their friendship survive an adventure through the afterlife?

Assembling Ella

Companion to *On the Bank of Oblivion*

A long-ago loss is keeping Ella stuck in the past. Can a mythical friend help set her free, or will he just make things worse?

On the Bank of Oblivion

Companion to *Assembling Ella*

Owen just wants to escape his mysterious illness, but a deal with a goddess may be more than he bargained for.

Please leave a review wherever you buy books; they help other readers find stories they'll love.

Read on for a Sneak Peek at

Nothing's Ever Lost

available now wherever books are sold

CHAPTER ONE

Start

Anna couldn't find her phone. It wasn't in her room anywhere, which meant it had to be downstairs. The question was, where? And, more importantly, could she find it before Jack got there to pick her up? She did not want to be the one who delayed their first beach trip of the summer.

She rushed down the stairs so fast, she almost tripped halfway down, but she managed to catch the banister just in time. At the bottom, she slid to a stop in front of her mom's office door. It was open, which meant it was safe to interrupt her. Well, safe-ish.

"Mom, have you seen my cell phone?"

"I have not," her mother said in a clipped voice, not looking up from her work. "Do you need me to call it?"

"No, I can handle it myself, thanks."

Anna started to leave.

"Tell your brother TV time is over."

"He's going to whine about it."

Anna's mother waved her hand, as if to say, *Thank you for pointing out the obvious, run along now.*

Anna ran along. On the walk to the living room, she tried to remember where she had last seen her phone. It wasn't in her room, she was certain of that. It wasn't in the bathroom, she knew because she had checked. It had to be in the living room somewhere. She'd been texting last-minute plans with Jack before bed last night.

In the living room, she found her brother sitting on the floor about five feet from the television, a juice box on his knee. Cartoon colors danced across his face.

"Nathan, Mom says no more TV."

"Five more minutes." As predicted he was whining.

"It's a commercial. By the end of the five minutes you'll be watching another show and won't want to shut it off."

Anna grabbed the remote and clicked the TV off. Nathan heaved the world's biggest, most pathetic sigh. He dragged himself upright and stormed off in the direction of the kitchen.

Anna rolled her eyes at his back and began searching for her phone. It wasn't on the side table next to Dad's chair. It wasn't on the coffee table. It wasn't on the charger. There was only one place left to look: the couch.

She held her breath and stuck her fingers between the couch cushions. You never knew what you might find in the space between. It was where gross things went to die. Once, Nathan had dropped a grape down there and it had turned into a little puff of mold that squished between

Anna's fingers. She'd squealed, and Nathan had practically fallen on the floor laughing while their older brother, Michael, sighed and told her not to be so dramatic.

Today she was lucky. She found seventy-five cents in change, which probably belonged to Michael. On the rare occasions when he wasn't at work or driving around in his very own car, which he had paid for himself and refused to let anyone else drive, he was always sitting with his ankle propped on his knee, making all the change in his pockets slide out and fall between the cushions. Oh well, finders keepers. She stuffed the coins into her pocket.

Between the next set of cushions she found her phone. It was pretty much dead. She stuck it on the charger and went into the kitchen to make the sandwiches. Jack was already three minutes late, which meant she had only about twelve minutes to make their lunch before he showed up.

She got the bacon going and then pulled out the other ingredients. It took almost no time to slap peanut butter on some bread. She just had to wait for the bacon to cook. While she was working, Nathan wandered in and sat down on a stool on the other side of the kitchen.

Anna prodded the bacon with her spatula, and a drop of hot oil leapt from the pan to her wrist. She hissed through her teeth and jerked her arm away from the stove. That had hurt—a lot—but she didn't have time to whimper about it. Jack would be there any minute.

Nathan rocked the stool from side to side, making a

thumping noise each time a pair of legs hit the floor. It was annoying.

"Stop it," Anna shouted, not turning around.

"I want to come too." *Thump*-pause-*thump*.

"You're going to break that stool."

"Mom said I could rock as long as I promised to buy her a new one if it breaks."

Anna scooped the bacon from the pan and dumped it onto a paper-towel-lined plate.

"Fine, but who's going to buy you a new skull?"

Nathan ignored this.

"Besides," Anna continued, "you're ten. How exactly would you pay for it?"

Nathan snorted. "I get an allowance," he said with all the haughtiness of the know-it-all teenager he would someday be. Then he ruined it by whining, "Why can't I come?"

Anna flapped her hand at the bacon to make it cool faster. "This is a trip for grown-ups."

"You are not a grown-up."

"Okay, it's a trip for teenagers then." She poked at the bacon. It was cool enough to pick up, but only just.

"I'll be good," Nathan whined.

Anna snatched pieces of bacon from the plate and dropped them onto slices of peanut-butter-covered bread. "Why can't you go bother Michael?"

"He's working."

"Of course. Well, go play Mario then."

Nathan slumped across the breakfast bar. "Can't. Dad

took it away. He said I wasn't allowed to waste another beautiful summer day staring at a tiny screen."

Anna felt a breath of sympathy. She'd heard that line from Dad before, usually in relation to her phone. Nathan must have sensed his advantage, because he started begging again.

"Please?"

"No."

"Please?"

"No."

"Pleeeeze?"

Their mother appeared in the doorway, a handful of papers in one hand. Their argument had apparently been loud enough to reach her office.

"Nathan, you're too young to go to the ocean without an adult," she said.

Then she turned on Anna. "And how many scholarship forms did you fill out this week?"

"Anna's an adult," Nathan said.

"Mom, it's summer," Anna said.

"No she isn't, but when she is, she'll have a mound of debt because she didn't want to put in a little effort." Their mother shook the handful of papers as though they were past-due notices on Anna's future bills. Anna knew Mom was right in theory. But when she had a job, a real job as an architect at some big firm in Austin or Chicago, she'd make plenty of money to pay back student loans. The odds of actually winning a scholarship seemed too small to waste her summer on.

Sunlight glanced through the room, reflecting off the windshield of a car pulling into the driveway. Anna stuffed the sandwiches into a zip-top bag and dumped them into her lunchbox.

"Jack's here. I've got to go." She kissed her mother on the cheek. "I'll do it tomorrow, I promise."

"That's what you said yesterday."

"No matter what. I promise."

Her mother looked skeptical—her signature look. "Be careful."

That sounded like permission to leave. Anna ran for the door. "I'm always careful," she said. She grabbed her backpack on the way out, and nearly crashed into Jack, who was halfway across the mudroom. Anna pushed him back toward the front door.

"Let's get out of here before my mom thinks up something else for me to do. I brought peanut butter and bacon."

"You're awesome."

"I know. You have the sour gummy worms?"

He raised two cellophane packages for her inspection.

"Sweet." Anna thrust the lunchbox at him and swiped the candy out of his hands.

Anna's mother called her name from somewhere on the other side of the house. "Quick, out, out." She practically shoved Jack through the door.

When they were safely in the car, Anna said, "I am going to be so dead later."

"As long as it's after we get back from the beach."

Jack backed the car out of the driveway. "What did you do?"

"I don't know, but I don't want to stick around and find out." Anna ripped open the first bag of gummy worms.

"Well, sorry I'm late," Jack said. "I spent at least twenty minutes convincing Ella that she couldn't come with me."

He dropped one hand off the wheel to dig through the cargo pocket on his shorts. He came up with a small red toy, which he stuck on the dash. Anna squinted at it. It was a plastic octopus, about the size of a golf ball. The expression on its face suggested that there should be little cartoon birds flapping circles around its head.

"What is that?" Anna asked.

"Ella gave it to me. She said that if she couldn't come with me, I had to take Octavius so he could tell her all about it later."

"Couldn't you tell her about it later?"

"She says he's better at telling stories than I am, because I always make things up."

Anna didn't know what to make of him. Half the time, Jack acted like his sister was the most annoying child on the planet, and the other half he might as well be six years old too. Anna couldn't tell which half this was, so she said, "All right, let's get this octopus to the ocean."

Jack flipped on his blinker and turned left onto the main road. It would take them through the center of town, with its single stoplight, and onto the interstate.

As they drove past the coffee shop, Jack said, "Do you want to stop and say hi to Michael?"

"No, he'll just say he's too busy to talk."

"He takes his work really seriously for a guy who smells like burned coffee fifty percent of the time."

"Yeah, no kidding. You want a gummy worm?"

"Sure."

By the time they'd gotten off the interstate and onto Route 1A, Anna had opened the second bag of sour gummy worms. She lounged in the passenger seat of Jack's car with the bag in her hand and her feet on the dashboard.

Jack glanced at her. "What are you grinning about?" He almost had to shout to be heard over the wind and the radio.

"I'm just happy, that's all."

Anna selected a red-and-yellow gummy worm from the bag and bit it neatly in half. She looked at the yellow half worm between her fingers. Somewhere she had heard, or maybe read, that an earthworm could survive if you cut it in half. They had two hearts or something, so if one died, the other could go on beating. It didn't seem likely. No matter how many hearts you had, being cut in half seemed like a ticket to a cozy bed six feet under, which probably wouldn't be so bad if you were a worm.

She was about to ask Jack if he had heard the heart thing too, when the first words of "Mexican Wine" came through the speakers. She hadn't heard that song in ages. Anna handed Jack the yellow half of the worm and leaned forward to turn up the radio.

He glanced at the half worm in his hand, then shrugged and popped it into his mouth. His foot rested heavier on the gas pedal. The speedometer needle slipped past ninety.

They were flying around one of the sharper curves when Anna offered him the blue half of a blue-and-orange gummy worm. He lifted one hand off the wheel to take it from her.

Anna saw it first, the eighteen-wheeler overturned across both lanes of the road. She screamed. Jack was swearing, slamming on the brakes. Too late.

The hood snapped when it crumpled against the undercarriage of the eighteen-wheeler. The tires squealed. The brakes locked. The airbag inflated, filling the car with fine powder. It smelled of fireworks and talcum powder.

A metal shaft shattered the windshield and tore through the airbag toward Jack's face. Anna turned her head. Her knees slammed into her chest, emptying her lungs. She watched her leg break. A splinter of bone erupted through the skin. The pain split her world in half.

ABOUT THE AUTHOR

Emma G. Rose intended to become a kick-ass girl reporter like Nellie Bly, until the Christmas Eve she stood on a riverbank waiting for rescue divers to pull a body from the water. That's when she stopped waiting and wandered off to explore the world instead.

Follow Her Adventures

Facebook – YouTube - Instagram
@ImperativePress
www.emmagauthor.com

Email her at emmagauthor@gmail.com

Acknowledgements

Writing the acknowledgements doesn't get any easier the second time around. Here we go:

My mother, Sue Potvin, who instigated this book by asking "What was up with that EMT guy anyway?" This book literally would not exist without you, and neither would I.

Lanette Pottle, my coach in both life and business, who keeps giving me new opportunities to become a better business woman and author.

Madeline Clark Frank, my constant supporter, friend, writing buddy, and adventuring companion. Someday our names will be next to each other on the cover of a book.

The writers of The Hourlings and the Michael Rodenkirk Writer's Group. You both helped shape and reshape this book in too many ways to mention.

Matt, my partner and go-to car consultant.

Special thanks to my beta readers: Jessica Tubbs, Lauren Platt, Liz Hayes, Mitchell Kohls, Roger Hammons, and Sarah Taylor.

Thank you. All of you.